I0664500

FRONTIER CIRCUIT

A STORY OF
THE CREEK WAR

JACK CUNNINGHAM

Frontier Circuit: A Story of the Creek War
Ashland Park Books
Mobile, Alabama
ISBN: 978-1-7322488-5-4
Cover Design: Teddi Black
Interior Format: Megan McCullough
Contact Information: ashlandparkbooks@gmail.com
Website: www.theauthorscove.com

Copyright 2025 by John "Jack" M. Cunningham Jr.

All Rights Reserved. Except for brief excerpts used in reviews, no portion of this book may be reproduced in any manner or by any means without the author's permission, including electronic and mechanical, photocopying or recording and information storage and retrieval systems, nor may it be reproduced by any means invented or in the future.

This is a work of fiction. Any resemblance to any person living or dead, or to the plot, is purely coincidental.

This book is dedicated to all preachers of the Gospel
and their predecessors who carried it to America's frontiers.

Books by John M. Cunninham, Jr.

Southern Sons-Dixie Daughters Book 1:
Vengeance & Betrayal

Southern Sons-Dixie Daughters Book 2:
River Ruckus, Bloody Bay

Turfmen and the Prodigal, A Story of Old Mobile

Squire. A Mascot's Tale

Books by Jack Cunningham

Reflections of a Southern Boy, Devotions from the Deep South

Frontier Circuit, A Story of the Creek War

.

MAIN CHARACTERS

CIRCUIT RIDERS

Phineas Steward: Preacher in Charge
Thomas Murcher: Preacher in Training

CHOCTAWS

John Wolf (Nashoba nowa, aka Wolf Walking)
Kana Wolf: John's wife
Gray Eagle: Kana's uncle, village of Foha's war chief
Brave Fox: Foha's village chief
Red Panther: Kana's cousin and nephew of Gray Eagle
Chilita: Kana's cousin and nephew of Gray Eagle

SETTLEMENT OF KING'S BROOK

THE RUFFIANS

Richard King: planter, store owner, boss of The Ruffians
Sehoy King: Richard King's Creek wife
Clay King: Richard and Sehoy King's youngest adult son
Barnaby Hatch: planter, blacksmith, second-in-command of Ruffians
Gopher Harkins

OTHER CHARACTERS

Annabelle Lawson: parents owned the Ox Yoke Tavern
Maggie: Annabelle's slave
Zander Oglesby: leatherworker and small farmer
Constance Oglesby: Zander's wife
Frank Oglesby: Zander and Constance Oglesby's son
Hiram Vance: farmer
Laurice Vance: Hiram's wife
Mary Vance: Hiram and Laurice Vance's daughter
Lemuel Cooper: manages a livery stable owned by Richard King
Dempsey King: Richard and Sehoy King's oldest adult son
Crazy Wildcat: Sehoy's brother

HISTORICAL CHARACTERS

William "Yellow Billy" Weatherford: leader of the Red Sticks
Supalamy Weatherford: Willliam Weatherford's wife
Charles Weatherford: William Weatherford's son
Polly Weatherford: William Weatherford's daughter
William McIntosh: chief of the Lower Creeks and leader of the Law Menders
Samuel Mims: wealthy resident of the Tensaw region
Doctor Thomas Holmes: surgeon
Hester: slave
General Ferdinand Claiborne: commander of territorial militia
Josiah Francis: Creek prophet

NOTES TO THE READER

This novel is set against the backdrop of the Creek War (1813-1814), fought on Alabama's frontier when it was part of the Mississippi Territory. Although there were many reasons for this conflict, it began as a civil war between those Creeks who wanted to keep their traditional ways of life and those who'd adopted the White man's ways.

The Creeks were divided into two nations: the Upper Creeks who lived in central Alabama and the Lower Creeks, who lived in southwestern Georgia. During the War of 1812 the radical Creeks allied themselves with Great Britain and Spain. Spain occupied West Florida with Pensacola as its capital. Inevitably, the White settlers got drawn into this conflict. The radical Creeks were not called Red Sticks till after the events in my story. However, I used that term here to distinguish them from those Creeks who supported the settlers.

A quick note about the word "Indian." According to Gregory A. Waselkov's book, *A Conquering Spirit*, the Southeastern tribes today have not adopted the label "Native American." He writes in his book's Introduction that most of these tribal members "refer to themselves officially and familiarly as Indians."

The Creek and Choctaw societies are matrilineal. In other words, an inheritance is passed down through mothers, not fathers. This explains why I refer to a setting as Kana Wolf's Farm instead of her husband's.

Regarding the events of the Creek War, I only covered the early engagements to keep the story focused on its Red Stick leader William Weatherford.

Also featured are the circuit riders, preachers who braved numerous trials to bring the Gospel to the Southeastern Frontier. Many were Methodist preachers. Lorenzo Dow passed through the Tombigbee region in 1803, preaching the Gospel, but he was a controversial figure. One historian, Anson West, said his preaching was "accidental, irregular, and occasional" whereas John G. Jones, in his *History of Methodism in Mississippi*, praised Dow's commitment to follow God's leading.

The first official Methodist circuit rider in Alabama was Matthew P. Sturdevant, appointed to the Tombigbee settlements by Bishop Francis Asbury in 1807. In 1808-1809, Michael Burdge labored in the Tombigbee region. In 1810-1811, John W. Kennon rode the circuit with Burdge.[1] In my story, I used fictional circuit riders for the sake of its central message and the literary freedom I needed to place them where they were needed in the plot.

Although I haven't found any records of Christian Choctaws in this era, I engaged in some historical license. Perhaps Lorenzo Dow led them to faith? Perhaps.

A note about the Methodist denomination's structure. The church is divided into regional conferences, which are further divided into districts. Over each conference is a bishop who presides over all the conference's districts and appoints ministers to the places where they're to serve. The presiding elder, also appointed by the bishop of the conference, supervises the ministers in his/her district. Nowadays, the presiding elder's title is district superintendent.

---

1   Lucille Griffith. *Alabama: A Documentary History to 1900.* University, Alabama: The University of Alabama Press, 1968.

CHAPTER ONE

Monday, August 15, 1808
Alabama country, Mississippi Territory

Astride his brown horse, Thomas Murcher followed a packhorse path through red oaks and longleaf pines, his Kentucky long rifle clutched on his lap, the sun's rays lancing the heavy forest. Perspiration coated his gun's maple stock and pasted his hunting shirt to his wiry frame. On his left, a woodpecker hammered a hole in an oak. Fallen leaves rustled beneath strutting doves' feet. The Alabama country sweltered this time of year just as it did back home in Mississippi. He frowned as he studied the ground. *Ah.* He found them again. Black bear tracks in the clay earth.

His best friend and neighbor, Aaron Underwood ... dead. Killed by a big black bear, if the paw scratches belonged to that beast. His swallow lodged in his throat. During a visit, the attack happened. He and Aaron's poor wife, Maude, witnessed the tragic event. He'd grabbed his musket to shoot the bear, but by the time he loaded his gun the bear up and fled. Though black bear attacks were rare, as they usually ran off at the sight of a human, this evil beast was predaceous.

His bloodhound, Perro, squatted low and sniffed the tracks, then forged ahead. Did he pick up the bear's scent? A good dog, Perro. Thomas found him a year ago wandering a beach in Spanish West

Florida on the Gulf of Mexico's coast. Perro took right to him and followed him back into the Mississippi Territory and home.

Swearing, his saddle creaking, he urged his horse onward. He eyeballed everything that moved— birds, a raccoon, squirrels. An armadillo's armored shell scurried and waddled beneath brush.

He and his older brother, Noble, buried Aaron, and Noble's wife comforted Maude. Because Thomas promised Maude he'd hunt down the bear and exact retribution for its foul deed, he'd tracked the animal from Aaron's home west of the Tombigbee Valley into the Mississippi Territory's Alabama country over the past days. "Hope these paw prints lead us to it, boy."

Perro stopped, lowered his big head. Again, his wide nose sniffed earth. His jowls drooled. His floppy ears wiggled. He growled.

Thomas, his lips tight, reined in his horse a few yards shy of him. "Easy, big boy."

Focused on the scents, his quivering nose sniffing the ground, the dog trotted ahead. His head snapped up. He stared straight at a rustling noise, the crunching of dead leaves beneath feet.

"You hear it? Smell it, do you?"

A large shadow passed through the timber.

Perro crouched, growled.

The bear! Thomas dismounted and quietly hitched his horse to a stout shrub. He darted behind a red oak, Perro at his heels. He glanced up. His heart thundered. He smelled his sweat. Likely, the bear did too. Bears had good noses on them, as good as a dog's.

The bear slipped out of a stand of pines into a half-acre clearing. Thomas squinted through the sunbeams. The beast was huge. Its powerful limbs moved with a lumbering gait and carried it through some tall grass. Its hindquarters swaggered. "A sizeable bear, ain't he, Perro?" Thomas whispered.

Perro snarled.

Thomas pulled a paper cartridge from the leather pouch belted round his waist, bit off part of it, and emptied some of its powder into its flash pan. He shot another glance at the bear, swaggering back into the woods. Within half a minute he finished loading his gun, powder poured into his gun's barrel, followed by his ramrod driving paper and a lead ball down it.

The bear burst into the clearing, halted, and rose on its hind legs.

Thomas's eyes flew wide. The beast stood about six feet high. He cocked back the hammer.

Perro crouched, his growl menacing.

If it was the murderous predatory bear that killed Aaron, the beast must die. Thomas lifted his rifle.

The bear dropped to all fours and charged.

A ball cracked from Thomas's gun. *Missed.* He cursed.

Perro lunged for the bear.

The bear stopped and swatted Perro's head. Perro yelped and flew backward. The bear thundered forward.

Gun tossed aside and his knife whipped from its sheath, Thomas stood ready. Tears flooding, he screamed. "Kill my dog, will you. And my best friend." He sprinted toward it. "I'll kill you!" He and the bear clashed head-on. A paw swatted his head. Thomas stumbled to the ground. The bear attacked his neck. His world— dark.

A few minutes later, as Thomas's eyes eased open, he stared into three grave, tattooed faces. Another man knelt beside him applying something on his wounds. "A p-poultice?" The words forced themselves from his mouth.

"Good for toothache." The man raised Thomas's head. Reaching into the deerskin satchel slung over his shoulder, he withdrew a cotton cloth.

"I ain't got a dang toothache." Thomas touched his painful injuries. The bear? Perro? He stretched out his palm and saw ... *Blood.*

"It comes from the prickly ash tree," another man said.

The man tending Thomas wrapped the bandage around Thomas's wounds. "My people use it for many things. My woman made this medicine. I bring it with me on hunts." His long black hair draped his powerful chest filling out his brown hunting shirt. His leggings were buckskin. Slung over his shoulder, besides the satchel, was a powder horn. Dangling from his neck, an otter skin shot bag.

Since he was in the Choctaw Nation, Thomas asked, "You're Choctaw?"

"I am Chahta. I'm with my hunting party. My name is Nashoba nowa, Wolf Walking. My warrior name is Nashoba nowabi. White people call me John Wolf. It was Providence I saw you when I did. I saw the bear go for your neck."

"Providence? The Great Spirit or something?"

"I am a Christian. I follow the Great One, the One you call Almighty God."

A Christian Choctaw. Strange. "You killed the bear?"

"I did."

"I shot at it and missed," a tall Choctaw said.

"I shoot better than you, Red Panther." John Wolf gave a small smile.

Red Panther and the other Choctaw laughed.

Thomas lowered his bloody palm to his side. Despite his aches, he sat up. "It killed my dog. And a neighbor."

After John Wolf finished wrapping the bandage around Thomas's head, he and Red Panther assisted Thomas to his feet. "I do not live far from here," John said. "Our farm is a few miles from our village."

"A plain ole dirt farmer about all I am too, John Wolf. My brother's farm. Help him and his sons work it. Grows cotton, mainly. And some corn. A few acres. Ain't much to it. Thomas is my name. Thomas Murcher, plain ole dirt farmer."

"Do your slaves help you farm?"

Thomas shook his head.

"Slavery is evil. A bad thing."

Thomas nodded.

"I saw your horse tied up."

Thomas's gaze lit upon Perro lying on the ground, his legs outstretched, and his head twisted in an awkward direction several feet from where the bear's body lay. He staggered to the dog's side and collapsed on his knees. Stroking the hound's wrinkled face, his fingers traced its bumps to Perro's jowls and picked up drool. "I'm sorry, good boy. So … so very, very sorry."

John clasped his shoulder from behind. "Follow me, my White brother. I will get my shovel and bury your dog. My woman will stitch your wounds and cook you supper. You will spend the night in our cabin. I will also take care of the bear."

"I will tell the others what happened." Red Panther strode off, through the trees.

The Choctaw Nation and the White man had always been on sociable terms, as far back as Thomas recollected, but he'd never met a Choctaw who shared their religion. That's all Christianity was, after all. Another religion.

Once he recovered his horse, he grasped his saddle's pommel and raised his foot toward a stirrup. He winced, slumped, caught his breath. Pains stabbed his head and pierced his legs. After two more efforts, he made it astride his mount. On the way to John's home, John spoke several times about Providence and the Great One. Thomas squirmed. "I'm obliged for your saving my life, John Wolf, but don't go trying to make a Christian out of me."

John's upraised palm assured him that he wouldn't. They proceeded along a dirt path in silence.

Poor Perro. Poor Aaron. Thomas touched his temple. *Poor me.*

CHAPTER TWO

Monday, August 15, 1808
King's Brook, Alabama country, Mississippi Territory

Sunrays fanned through swaying treetops as Barnaby Hatch closed his blacksmith shop in King's Brook. He locked its wooden double doors when Clay King, a young man with disheveled red hair and a close-cropped beard resembling a mat that hugged his narrow chin, spoke behind him.

"He's here again, Barnaby."

Barnaby slapped the doors' big padlock. "The horse preacher?"

"Going to have us a sure enough camp meeting tonight, he says. Father and Mother will be amused." Clay waved a handbill advertising the event.

"Be a shame to miss it. We're overdue for some entertainment in this forsaken wilderness. Let's me and you grab us a bite at the tavern first. Annabelle promised me a tasty meal tonight. Me and you'll plan us some fun once we get ourselves fed."

"Annabelle's getting powerful sweet on you."

"Ain't she, though."

They followed a stone path to the Ox Yoke, a two-story log structure identified by the large yoke above its entrance. Despite the breeze, the summer heat pounded their necks. Annabelle Lawson swelled Barnaby's thoughts. What would his late father have thought about her? Had Eleazar Rawlins not killed him ten years ago, his father might still be alive. He owed Clay's father a debt for avenging his father's murder by hanging Rawlins from the highest tree.

His mother, Addie, certainly approved of her, and the Lawsons made a respectable living, though not as well off financially as his mother and Clay's parents. The Lawsons didn't own but a handful of slaves—their tavern's cook Maggie and those who worked their one hundred sixty cotton acres behind the tavern. Also, a cabin. Mister King claimed Lawson's land belonged to him too but the land office, after a lengthy process, disagreed and granted it to Lawson.

Many of this region's earlier settlers had moved on. However, a few families stayed and tried making a life for themselves.

"Well, look at you two handsomes." Annabelle flounced around the tavern's pine bar, her willowy hips switching. She winked at Clay and fluttered her dark lashes at Barnaby.

Barnaby led her to a corner table. "Fetch us a beer, Clay."

Clay hurried behind the counter.

Annabelle fingered the brunette ringlets bouncing around her hard, pale face. "Reckon you heard about that preacher man being back here."

Clay tossed the handbill on the table after he gave Barnaby and Annabelle their beers. It advertised the circuit rider's name, Reverend Phineas Steward, in bold black letters across the top. Beneath his name, in capital letters, were the words: REVIVAL TONIGHT. COME SEE WHAT THE LORD HAS DONE.

"Your parents ain't stopping him, Clay darling?" Annabelle stretched and yawned loudly.

"Nuh uh. They're sorta bored same as us. Father wants to see how far we can throw 'em. Promised money to the one who throws 'em farthest and best." Clay swaggered to the bar for his beer.

Annabelle giggled.

Barnaby took a long sip, his lustful ogling devouring her. He set down his tankard. His lips parted. One day, they'd get hitched, if she'd quit refusing his proposals. The handsomest filly in the Tombigbee Valley, Annabelle. "Your papa around? Your mama?"

"Pa promised that preacher man he'd help him set up things for tonight, and Ma's out visiting Mrs. Oglesby. Sewing a quilt together or something. I'm taking care of this place right now."

Annabelle's parents weren't of a religious persuasion, but her father Paul did possess a streak of self-righteousness. So did her mother Grizelda. Their low opinion of him may be the reason for Annabelle's consistent "no's" regarding his "will you marry me." They hated him because he was a member of the Ruffians, the settlement's gang. Two years ago, he'd humiliated Clay's brother, Dempsey, in a brawl because Dempsey stole money from them. Dempsey tucked tail and fled with it to parts unknown, and Clay's father appointed him to replace Dempsey as the Ruffians' new leader. The only people he answered to were Clay's parents.

"Handsome"— Annabelle's fingers drummed the table— "I ain't going to go to that fool meeting."

Her words drew Barnaby out of his musings. "We'll tell you who wins the throwing contest, little darling."

"It'll be me." Clay's tankard touched his lips. "'Cause I happen to possess the strongest arms in this place." He flexed his big biceps.

Barnaby scoffed. "Not as strong as me."

"Will venison suit your fancy for supper, Handsome?" Annabelle scooted back in her chair.

"Sounds mighty tasty," Barnaby said.

"Maggie's cooking some. I'll go check on it."

"Soon as me and you are done stuffing our stomachs, Clay"— Barnaby cracked his knuckles— "round up the boys and meet me at Mama's farm. We'll make us some plans for Phineas What's-his-name. Mama may even have herself some ideas."

"Can't wait."

"You ain't the only one."

CHAPTER THREE

Thomas rubbed the rough bandage wrapped around his forehead, sat up in a cane bed, and surveyed his sparsely furnished room. John Wolf's home was a dogtrot cabin, a White man's house. A breezeway threaded its center, separating rooms. His open door and windows welcomed an early evening breeze. Chopped beautyberry plants scattered across windowsills and on the floor warded off mosquitoes. A stubby cane table holding a small, flickering candle stood in the room's center, the candle's soft glow kissing the log walls.

Slow footfalls on the breezeway brought a young Choctaw girl into his room. Kana, John's wife, who'd mended his wounds. She stood scarcely taller than five feet.

"You slept well?" Kana poured water from a pitcher into a tin basin on a table at the entrance.

"I figure I did," Thomas said.

Kana placed a bar of lye soap beside the basin.

Wincing, due to Kana's tight stitches and the ache in his back due to his lying on the hard bearskin-covered bed, Thomas swung his legs off the bed's edge.

Kana smiled, warm and cordial.

He returned the smile. *Quite lovely.* Her black, braided hair fell forward over her shoulders. Her doeskin dress touched her calves. She walked barefoot.

"Pork for you tonight?" she asked.

Thomas rubbed his growling stomach. "I'm hungry enough to eat a whole possum with all his teeth still stuck in his head."

"The soap I made this morning." Kana pointed at it. "Wash yourself first."

Thomas studied the dried blood on his fingers. At the basin, he reached for the soap when John poked his head through the doorway.

"You are better, my brother?" John cocked a brow.

Thomas nodded as he dipped his fingers into the bowl.

"A friend visits us in a few days."

Thomas scrubbed his hands with the soap.

"You will meet him," Kana said.

"Please accept my regrets, but I figure I won't. I'm leaving here tomorrow for Mississippi country. Figure I owe y'all for your kind hospitality first, though."

Kana squinted at his forehead, rose on tiptoes, and touched his bandage. "You will not leave until your welts heal, and I can remove your stitches."

"Let your brother and his sons work their farm." John offered him a towel.

"Why ain't you living in your village?" Thomas asked, receiving John's offer.

"I was," John said. "It is called Foha, a half-day's ride from here. A small village. Our ancient custom, for the man to move from his village and live in his woman's village when they are married. When we became believers in Jesus the Christ, after one of my woman's aunts died, she left Kana this farm—her inheritance. Her aunt married a White man, who died of a fever. They had no children. She died a few months after his death."

"Didn't Kana's mother leave her anything too?"

"A house and some farmland on the other side of the creek, but this is where we prefer to live."

"Interesting." Thomas dried his hands, then gave the towel back to John. They made a good point about his wounds needing mending. Couldn't Brother Noble remove the stitches? Or Martha, Noble's wife? "My sister-in-law'll take out my stitches when it's time."

"No." Kana stepped in front of him. Her thin brows knit. "Do not leave this farm till I say so."

John grinned at Kana. "Be a wise man, my brother. Listen to my woman. We will sleep in the other room till you are gone. You will help Kana and her friends in the fields at sunup. You said you owe us for our hospitality. You will repay us that way. You will teach Kana and her friends how to use the plow. I and the men of my village are going on a hunt before the sun rises."

"You telling me you own a plow?"

"Teach her and her friends. Tomorrow." John rested his palm on Thomas's shoulder. "In two days, you will help me work my cattle. Seven days you will stay."

"Then you can go," Kana said.

Defeated, Thomas slumped. He hoped those two didn't jabber about religion during his stay here. He imagined his cousin Reuben over in Georgia doing it. He and his wife Agnes converted to Methodism a year before he left Georgia to help Noble work his farm, some six years ago. Or was it seven years? He wasn't certain on that particular.

John gestured for him to move ahead. Thomas crossed the cabin's breezeway, over scattered clippings of beautyberry and into the room opposite his bedroom. Not much to the room. Just a cane table about four feet high, covered with deerskins. Also, a Bible sat in the middle of it. When he spotted scuppernongs in a wooden bowl beside the sacred Scriptures, he licked his lips. Scuppernongs, his favorite fruit.

But scuppernong grapes or no scuppernong grapes—Thomas clenched his teeth— no way would he become a religious fanatic. If John Wolf tried converting him, he'd give him a taste of his justice.

CHAPTER FOUR

Monday, August 15, 1808
King's Brook, Alabama country, Mississippi Territory

Barnaby, standing behind King's Brook's settlers seated on the ground listening to the preaching, reached into his bulging coat pocket and gripped one.

Reverend Phineas Abel Steward, pausing periodically with an enthusiastic gesture for his small congregation to join in, worked his bow across his violin's strings while he sang a hymn. Two raccoons trotted past him. From somewhere in the woods, coyotes gave blood-curdling howls.

The settlers coughed and pretended to listen to the lanky preacher, the tension tauter than a circus performer's tightrope.

Off to the left, Clay stood beside his parents. His Creek mother, Sehoy, wore a pale blue gown with a low bodice that exposed her tattooed shoulders. Her black hair, also, resembled a White lady's—ringlets spilling from a straw bonnet—instead of the Creek woman's traditional topknot fashion. Ruby earrings, which she'd purchased in nearby Spanish-held Mobile, dangled from her ears. She yawned. Clay's White father, Richard King, eyed Barnaby shrewdly, a black-and-tan bloodhound puppy named Lucky cradled in his arms. He scratched his dog behind his floppy ears.

Barnaby wiggled his forefinger at the circuit rider and nodded. "When we doin' it?"

This question from Gopher Harkins, a stocky Ruffian who limped, interrupted his thoughts. Always hankering after mischief on Mister and Mrs. King's behalf, Gopher reminded him of a small dog nipping at people's heels. He clapped Gopher's back. "At the time we're told. Don't you worry none."

"When Clay gives us the signal from Mister King," another Ruffian said.

"Y'all keep y'alls eyeballs on jabbering preacher man," Barnaby said. "I'll tell y'all when."

Barnaby, too, feigned interest in Phineas's preaching but scoffed silently at the circuit rider as he paced behind a small table, waving his fist, thumping his Bible, talking about sin and salvation and repentance. *Crazy man.* He'd do his repenting when it snowed on the Tombigbee.

The hollow-cheeked preacher appeared emaciated. His energy and swift moves, however, spoke a different tale. Preacher Man wasn't starving. He was living off other folks' charity.

Barnaby reached into his pocket and closed his thick fingers around two this time. He shifted his attention to his five fellow Ruffians. Clay and himself brought their number to seven.

Old man Jasper— a trapper, hunter, and carpenter when sober— staggered and zigzagged in front of them, drooling and muttering nonsense. He reeked of whiskey. An oversized knife belted round his ample waist was a matter of pride for him. He made it himself and often showed it to folks.

An hour passed. Phineas gave the invitation traveling preachers or their exhorters always gave.

Barnaby shouted a sarcastic, "Hallelujah."

"Please. Friends." Phineas waved his Bible. "Today is the day of salvation. Please, please come. Trust Christ as your Savior. You ain't knowing what tomorrow may bring."

A few men guffawed. Others spat tobacco. The women tugged on their dress sleeves and bonnets and dipped snuff.

Barnaby caught Clay mouthing the word, "Now."

He and his friends rushed upon Phineas and hurled their missiles. Eggs splattered Phineas's cheeks, lips, and black coat. Spluttering, he spit out eggs and shells and whipped out a handkerchief.

Raucous laughter rocked the woods amidst the little congregation's applause. A fistful at a time, the people dispersed.

Richard King hurried to drape his arm around Barnaby's shoulders. "Fine work, my man. I regret your father wasn't alive to witness it. It'd make him proud."

Clay punched Barnaby's shoulder.

Barnaby punched him back. "Next time, I'll let Clay do it, and I'll give the signal."

Their attention drifted to Annabelle's parents who escorted Phineas, wiping his mouth with a handkerchief, up the main path.

"Paul and Grizzie going to help him clean off his eggs." King spat in disgust. "They better not get religion else they'll build a meetinghouse here. Too nice a folk for my taste in company."

"I despise them." Sehoy wound her beaded necklace around her forefinger. Glancing up at Barnaby, she added, "It is Annabelle's parents I despise. Not her. They should let her marry you. If they do not, marry Annabelle anyway if I were you. I married my husband against the wishes of my village."

"I despise them too," Barnaby said. "It's only Annabelle I love."

Sehoy gripped King's arm. "Take me home, Husband. I am tired."

King steered her toward his wagon parked beneath a crepe myrtle.

Barnaby watched them leave. Mrs. King despised religion, even her own people's superstitions, and she spoke the truth about marrying Mister King despite the disapproval of her relatives and the leaders of her village. By leaving her people to live with him, she'd violated Creek custom. Creek custom required men to leave their villages to live in their wives' towns.

Barnaby gathered his friends together to discuss his next plan when his mother approached. She probably wanted a report on their endeavor to get rid of the preacher. Oh, they'd get shed of him, sure enough, next time he set foot in this settlement. They'd make Preacher Man leave permanent the same way they did Dempsey, once they finished with him.

CHAPTER FIVE

WEDNESDAY, AUGUST 17, 1808
KANA WOLF'S FARM, ALABAMA COUNTRY, MISSISSIPPI TERRITORY

Seated on a tall stool with his arms folded on Kana Wolf's table, Thomas glared at the Reverend Phineas Steward. The Choctaw couple tricked him. What did they take him for? A dang nincompoop? During this week of farming, neither John nor Kana mentioned religion—likely figured he'd catch an earful when their preacher friend visited. That's why they wanted him to stay, *not* because of his stupid stitches or helping Kana and her female friends learn how to use a plow. They already knew how to use one and did use them on their farms. They'd pretended they didn't.

John gasped. "They threw eggs at you, my brother?"

Phineas whipped a handkerchief from his coat pocket, mopped his forehead, and slapped the table. His booming laughter ricocheted off walls.

Thomas, scowling, covered his ears.

"When those young Ruffian lads came into the Lawsons' tavern aching after"—Phineas's shoulders bounced— "aching after me to turn wrathful, I told 'em to throw tomatoes next time. Those lads, they didn't know what to make of me. I prayed hard for 'em on my way here. Always an honor to get persecuted for your faith. The Good Book says it's a blessing."

Kana gestured at her scuppernongs for Thomas to take one, but at this moment in time he hankered after nothing except getting shed of this place. What was so dang funny about getting pelted with eggs? Anyone who pelted him would be tasting his fists. He and one of King's Ruffians brawled last year when he passed through that settlement. The Lawsons' daughter, Annabelle. He'd never forget her, a girl who might be pretty except for her "high and mighty" attitude.

Seriousness dampened Phineas's amusement. "They stormed out of the tavern after telling me my preaching was against the law in their settlement. Worse things have happened to me. Ain't no sense in getting mad." His light brown eyes danced between the Choctaw couple and Thomas. "Don't let on my sense of humor to no other preacher. Us traveling preachers are always s'pposed to be serious and sober. Can't help it, though. The Great One's given me my humor." He arched his tawny eyebrows at Kana. "Now, my dear Lady Grace, do you happen to have a bit of delightful fare for my poor hungry stomach?"

"I do." Kana stepped into the breezeway.

"Grace?" Thomas finally grabbed a scuppernong.

"Kana is Chahta for grace," Kana said. "So that is Reverend Steward's name he's given me. The Great One shed His grace on me." Her footsteps faded as she headed outside to her kitchen.

"Your next stop, Bassetts Creek?" John asked.

"Right sociable folk there. God-fearers, lots of its people are. I'll also be calling on Maryvale, a new settlement."

Thomas had never been to the Bassetts Creek settlement, though he knew it lay somewhere near the creek's junction with the Tombigbee. Weary of this religious talk, he popped his scuppernong into his mouth. He moved to leave, but the preacher's piercing gaze pinned him in place.

Thomas squirmed, again moved to rise, but failed in the effort. *Preacher's dang peepers.* He stared out a window, at the kitchen's brick chimney. Smoke no longer wafted from its fireplace. At the time of his growing up in Georgia, his mother often talked about Hell's eternal oven, forever ablaze with lost souls. She owned a faith deeper than folks could shake and passed away a few years after his father was killed at the Battle of Cowpens in the revolt against Britain. His Cousin Reuben's father, Uncle Henry, adopted and raised him and Noble. Uncle Henry's wife, Aunt Jenny, did most of the educating of them.

"Are you a God-fearing man, my dear Thomas Murcher?" Phineas asked.

The question yanked Thomas out of his musings. "Cousin Reuben's a practicing Methodist."

"I'll be a cat's kitten. Where so?"

"Georgia."

Phineas slapped the table. "I'll be."

"Figure I'm going on home in the morning. Mississippi country." Thomas hastened across the breezeway into his bedroom. *Dang preacher, sleeping in this same dang room.*

As he flopped onto his bed, religious conversation wafted in from the breezeway. He folded his arms on his saddlebags behind his head. All he'd hear tonight—religion and Bible-quoting. He'd done enough repayment of the Wolfs' kindnesses. He tumbled into a fitful sleep.

Hours later, he awoke in darkness. After fumbling around for several seconds, his feet touched the floor. He grabbed his hunting shirt off it, slipped it on, cocked his head at the silence as loud as Phineas's snores, which no longer shook the walls.

Adjusted now to the moonlight streaming through a window, he didn't see him. Where in tarnation did that horse preacher go? He found his hunting knife beneath his bed and belted it around his waist, followed by his large leather pouch that held his balls and flints and cartridges. He slung the saddlebags he used for pillows over his shoulder. He grabbed his rifle leaning in a corner. Also, his boots.

In his stocking feet so his footfalls kept silent, Thomas sat on the edge of the porch where he pulled on his boots. His horse was in the small log barn up ahead, past a fetid hog pen. He'd better fetch his mount before someone spotted him. He tiptoed over a thick blanket of pine straw.

Hogs stirred. A few waddled to the pen's rail and grunted.

He threw his finger to his lips. "Hush, varmints, less you wanna be bacon."

At the barn door, he glanced left and right. A cool breeze stirred longleaf pines in the shadows against the brilliant, star-spangled night. An owl hooted. No crazy preacher, no John, no Kana. The barn door creaked on its hinges as he slipped inside the building.

"Good early morning to you, Mister Murcher."

Thomas groaned. The preacher's pleasant voice rang out from the rear of the stables. "Uh … hi." He reached for his horse's stall door, hesitated.

Phineas, seated on a bale of hay, a lap desk and Bible beside him, held his flickering lantern high and patted a bale. "Glad you came to join me in my devotions. Please, sir. Do take a seat."

"Ain't got time. I'm going on home."

"Of course." Phineas chuckled. "But we've just met. Please do me the kindness of talking with me a short spell."

"About religion?"

"About yourself. I enjoy making new friends."

"Don't care about that none." Thomas reached for his horse's bridle draped over its stall.

Phineas came to him and gripped his sleeve. "I do s'ppose we do ought to talk. For a little spell."

Thomas whipped his knife from its sheath. "I *don't* figure so, Preacher. Leave me be, else …" He pressed the blade's point against Phineas's stomach.

Shoulders bouncing, Phineas chuckled. "Go ahead. Kill me."

CHAPTER SIX

Thomas doubled over, gasped, and gagged in the inferno's stinging smoke. Flames' fiery tongues licked sulphureous air. Thunder reverberated. Thrashing arms. Kicking legs. Wails.

A skull hovered out of the oppressive blaze. It opened its ragged mouth. "Thomas! Help me!" Beneath a scorching tidal wave of fire it melted, disappeared.

Thomas's throat ached. He gulped. Trapped. In this horror.

The conflagration devoured the shrieking throngs compassing him. "Why didn't we listen? Can't we go back?"

"Too late," a diabolical voice echoed from an invisible somewhere, above fiendish cackles. "You're mine. Mine."

His legs jellified. Thomas's eyes darted left and right. *There.* A light. A gap. He jumped through it. He examined his limbs. *Ain't burned. Yet.*

A powerful figure strode before him. Clothed in majestic brilliance, He gestured at the perishing, then fixed His compassionate countenance upon him. "I need you, Thomas Murcher, my child. Do not let others such as these perish. I need you to preach my salvation to the lost."

Thomas bolted upright in bed, soaked in sour sweat, puddles of it on his sheets. Souls lost? Hell? This was his third such dream in three nights. The figure who'd addressed him was Jesus, something made clear from his two previous dreams. Was God calling him to become a preacher? He wasn't a speechifier, nor a sermonizer, nor a believer for too long a time. Standing up in front of people, speechifying and sermonizing, folks focused on him, hanging on his every word. *No.* He couldn't do it.

He rolled out of bed, threw on his clothes, and flew out of his room so fast he left his suspenders on his dressing table. Sprinting down Cousin Reuben's outside stairs, pounding them loud enough to waken the cemetery nearby, he staggered back into his cousin's house puffing and heaving to regain his wind. He grasped the dining room's counter and leaned over it.

"You got that strange look again, Cousin." Reuben busied himself slicing a loaf of bread. "Another one of those 'Gone to Hell' dreams?"

Thomas plopped into a chair at the dining table, his bones atremble. Sighing, he tilted back his head. "It wasn't a pretty sight. A nightmare."

"What was it like this time?" Zachry, Reuben's eldest son, a strapping man of twenty-five years, sipped tea. Several drops spilled on his unkempt pumpkin-colored beard.

"Misery, flames, same as other nights. You don't wanna get there, Zachry."

"Jesus coming to you again?" This eager question from Reuben's son, Hank, a year younger than Zachry. Hank, as did his brother and his sister Kate, shared their parents' devoutness.

Thomas's fingers clenched so tightly into the heels of his palms, they hurt.

"Agnes'll be interested in learning you had it again." Reuben placed the sliced bread on their table.

"What'd you figure it means?" Thomas asked. "I ain't a preacher."

"Preaching?" Agnes brought an aromatic plate of sizzling bacon into the dining room. Kate, a pretty little brunette, followed carrying a plateful of scrambled eggs.

"Agnes darling," Reuben said, "Cousin Thomas had another one of those 'Gone to Hell' dreams of his."

Thomas, Reuben, and Reuben's sons stood for the ladies while they set breakfast on the table. Thomas battled seeping tears. Crying, especially in public, embarrassed him. His gratitude to the Lord for forgiving the errors of his ways, and for Phineas, too, who'd shown him the right path, those grateful tears always sneaked up on him.

Because he desired to be involved with a Methodist society instead of struggling alone with his faith in the Mississippi Territory, he'd gone back to Georgia. Brother Noble owned the farm there anyway, and his four grown sons helped him work his crops.

Reuben pulled out a chair for Agnes, and Zachry did the same for Kate. Once the ladies sat, Thomas and the other men joined them at the table. At their request, Thomas described his dream.

"Why, Cousin Thomas, it may be the Lord is calling you into His service." Agnes set a napkin in her lap.

"Can't do it, Cousin Agnes. Speechifying in front of folks makes me scareder'n a mouse in a nest of snakes."

"Nonsense," Agnes said. "If the Lord's calling you into preaching, He'll help you do it."

"I can't."

"Thom—"

"No, Cousin Agnes." Thomas dinged his fork on his tin plate decisively. "I ain't doing it. Y'all remember a-way back when we were children, when I stood up in your ma's church in front of all them folks and tried reciting a verse I'd memorized?"

Reuben buttered his bread. "The other children teased you 'cause you were so nervous you got the words scrambled."

"Y'all laughed too."

"We apologized later."

"That happened years ago," Agnes said.

"A long time," Thomas said, "and speechifying and Bible-quoting still scares the suspenders off me."

"One way or other, we're going to find out whether you're called," Reuben said. "You've got to do the Lord's bidding." To his sons, Reuben added, "You boys do the plowing till me and Cousin Thomas get back." Reuben set his knife beside his plate. "Soon as we're done partaking of our breakfast, Cousin Thomas, you write a letter to Elder Matthias. Try to arrange a meeting with him to discuss this matter, then we'll hie ourselves off to town and tell the other society members what's happened. Let's thank the Lord for His blessings and get to eating."

Thomas groaned. Why did Cousin Reuben always pressure him to do something he didn't want to do? Went back to their childhoods, it did. Dang it. Cousin Reuben always got his way.

He scooped up his scrambled eggs after Reuben thanked the Lord for His bounty. Maybe this *was* a chance to find out whether God was truly calling him. When he passed on to his reward, would there be a reward for obedience in this matter? Reuben, as always, was right. Agnes too. God may be calling him, and if such was the case, he must answer it no matter how yeller he was.

Two weeks later, after a service at the meetinghouse when most of its members left, Presiding Elder Matthias Cumberland, supervisor of the district's preachers, sat on the front pew and lent his ears to Thomas's story.

To settle his nerves and collect himself lest he show fear in front of Elder Matthias, Thomas paced, his fists at his sides. A few hard breaths later, he stood in place and recounted growing up with a devout mother and not-so-devout father. He told stories of his sinful ways, recounted his drinking and swearing and gambling and carousing and how he used to mock religion.

Following this, he moved on to life in the Mississippi Territory where he'd lived with his brother's family. He described the black bear story and how a Christian Choctaw saved his life.

"John and his wife talked me into staying with them for a few days," Thomas said.

Matthias stroked his flowing gray beard.

"That's where I met Reverend Steward. He's one of the Wolfs' friends."

"Reverend Steward's a good man. My friend too." Matthias flicked his wrist and patted his beard. "Please continue."

Thomas did so. "When I pulled a knife on him, sir, he laughed."

Matthias scowled. "Laughed?"

Uh-oh. He didn't want to get Phineas in trouble. Always be sober and serious, Phineas told John and Kana. "He didn't laugh longer'n a second. Serious, mostly. Said if I killed him, he'd go right on up to his heavenly home, and it'd suit him fine."

"He's a brave man, our Phineas Steward."

Thomas nodded. "I got so puzzled by him and his way of talking, me and him palavered till daybreak. I ain't got an inkling how it happened, but the Holy Spirit convicted me of my evil ways. By the time John's roosters got to crowing, I'd fallen on my knees crying out to the Almighty. It was like even the roosters were rejoicing."

Matthias questioned him further. Thomas answered the best he knew how. When his examination ended, he exhaled loudly, relieved to be finished.

"I'll get back to you on this later, Brother Thomas." Matthias stood. "Provided the Lord wills it, you'll start out as an exhorter for your cousin's society, of course." He pulled his watch out of his vest pocket and opened its lid. "It's late. Another appointment awaits me in a town up the road. You're in my prayers."

Elder Matthias jogged out the meetinghouse's double doors.

At the altar, Thomas dropped to his knees. Could he exhort others if someone asked him to do it? Could he lead more people to Christ in this town? Exhort them to repentance after a horse preacher did his sermonizing? Suppose he quoted a Bible verse wrong or got it all scrambled? Worse, suppose he forgot it? *Embarrassment.*

A shiny brass cross hanging on the wall above the pulpit caught his attention. "Dear Lord, this poor dirt farmer sure needs help. Powerful help,'cause I'm more scared'n a rabbit hopping from a hawk." His prayers stretched the hour, and his burden for souls weighed heavier on him.

CHAPTER SEVEN

Two miles south of the settlement, over dinner at Mister Richard King's frame house, Barnaby listened to Sehoy's younger brother, Crazy Wildcat, recount his trip to the Upper Creeks. He was a whale of a man. From the back of his thick neck, square red and black tattoos traveled up his face to his plump, bronzed cheeks. His fierce, beady black pupils shifted back and forth.

Barnaby suspected he visited Sehoy without his fellow Creeks' knowledge, because if his village found out he'd come here he'd find himself in serious trouble, for no family member dared call on her after she'd eloped with Mister King. Except him. A brave man, Crazy Wildcat, and not one to be trifled with.

Barnaby's mother, Addie, also listened to his and King's discussion.

"Rumor has it the government intends on building its post road down this way." King sipped champagne from a flute. "It'll help my business if they do. More settlers to fleece, those who aren't aware of the government trading house in Saint Stephens."

"All the Nations talk about the road, not just the Creek," Crazy Wildcat said. "Cherokee, Chickasaw, Choctaw. Our father in Washington wants to build it through our land all the way to New Orleans."

"What does Chief McIntosh think?" Sehoy asked. "What side is he on?"

"I went to Yellow Billy's farm," Crazy Wildcat continued, ignoring his sister.

Sehoy, impatiently twirling a golden bangle around her thin wrist, frowned at her stoic husband.

"Yellow Billy shared concerns about the new road." Crazy Wildcat scooped up his mashed potatoes in a spoon.

That name Creeks gave William Weatherford amused Barnaby. Though Yellow Billy didn't hold the position of chief, he did come from a prominent and politically powerful clan, a métis, an influential mixed-breed of the Upper Creeks. On several occasions, Barnaby had been entertained by Yellow Billy. Not one cowardly bone in his body. His nickname came from another name he possessed, Billy Larney. Yellow Billy was simply a translation of it.

"Answer my question, Brother," Sehoy snapped.

Crazy Wildcat's barrel-chest heaved. A deep sigh left his thick lips. "Chief McIntosh is on the settlers' side, my sister. We may avoid war, but we also may not. Why should you care what our chiefs think, since you no longer live in your village?"

"Your sister is asking, my brother, because she is curious."

"Your brother has answered your curiosity."

Barnaby respected Crazy Wildcat, probably the only person alive who knew how to manage Sehoy.

One of Sehoy's servants brought in a tray of warm tea in china cups.

Sehoy snatched her cup off the tray.

The slave set a cup and saucer before each person, then quickly departed.

"Many Creeks want us to keep our old ways, our ancestors' religious superstitions and customs." Sehoy stabbed her finger at the food. "Enough warrior talk. This is my house. Do what I say. Eat."

Addie aimed her fork at Barnaby. "I'll figure a way to get you and Annabelle hitched, son. I'm tired of her parents. They make me ill."

"You are a lady of material means, Addie." Sehoy's finger slowly traced the rim of her teacup. "There is no reason for her parents to forbid such a marriage."

"They been doing it for too long a time." Addie's raven-colored hair dangled past her chin while she focused on cutting her pork into manageable portions.

"Addie."

Addie glanced up at Sehoy, whose voice softened into a friendlier tone.

"I will help you get your Barnaby married to Annabelle." Sehoy pretended to shoot a bow. "Right in the Lawsons' little hearts, easy as killing a doe."

Everyone laughed.

"Eat now." Sehoy gestured impatiently. "The food is almost cold."

Barnaby nibbled his buttered corn cob. One thing certain as a flea on a dog, if he ever did marry Annabelle, he'd run his household the way a White man would and not be like King, in whose home Sehoy was in charge. He hoped Clay didn't let his wife, whenever he found one, order him around. It'd be best for him to marry a pretty White woman who'd always do his bidding. A girl like Annabelle.

On their way home in their buggy, Addie patted his knee when he lifted his team's reins. "I love you, son. Don't you ever forget it."

"Yes'm. You are my shining star."

"Oh, stop. Save such nonsense for Annabelle."

Barnaby clucked at the buggy horses. They moved into a trot. He wasn't growing any younger, nor was Annabelle. It was time to do something about her parents. The waiting time was over.

CHAPTER EIGHT

John dropped the last armful of bundled deerskins, Red Panther's bundle, into his canoe aground on some limestone rocks on Foha Creek. Red Panther, preparing for a stickball game to be played in a few days against a village from Mississippi, was not able to come on this trip.

"I am leaving, Kana." He worked his way up the steep wooden planks connecting the rocks to the brushy riverbank. His long arms encircled her tiny waist as he drew her against his body, his rapid heartbeat in rhythm with hers. Her sniffles pricked him. He withdrew and cupped her moist cheeks between his palms. "What's wrong, dear wife? You have been troubled many days."

Kana shook her head. "The Great One has not given us children. He is displeased with us. Is that why I cannot have a child?"

John tilted up her round chin. "Maybe the next preacher who visits us will bring an answer." He kissed Kana's forehead, her cheeks, her lips. "Two or three days, dear wife, your husband will return. I will be back in time for our village's stickball game." He descended the bluff's planks to his canoe. Swallowing hard, John gave her a final wave goodbye. Wind ruffled her dark hair. Her short fingers waved back. After he shoved off, John prayed for her protection. Also, for a child.

A child, a child. Had the Great One abandoned them? Like a thousand arrows, troubled thoughts assaulted John. What had he and Kana done wrong? Why was the Great One angry with them? He shared his woman's fears. To show fear, to not be strong, it was not a Choctaw man's way. *Please, Great One. Please give us a child.*

He paddled his canoe slowly, around the creek's twists and turns, careful to avoid sandbars. Hawks soared and glided over treetops. Crows cawed. He kept a lookout for alligators and prayed for his wife. By late afternoon he arrived at King's Brook, located at the confluence of a tributary flowing into the Tombigbee River. His bundled hides in hand, he traveled a dirt road to a large square structure built of corner-notched pine logs. Four windows, two to a side, flanked its whitewashed panel door. A metal sign hung above the door, its words in bold black letters: "Richard J. King, General Store."

"The White chief better not try to cheat me," John muttered in Choctaw. His people once had a White trader in their village, but the man died last year, and no trader had taken his place. Although he didn't trust Chief King, and the trading house at Saint Stephens dealt honestly with his people, he'd promised Red Panther and Kana he'd be back in time to watch their game. The contest might last several days, or it might end quickly. He took no pleasure in breaking his word to those to whom he'd given it, and if he didn't return in time Kana would be worried. He best watch Chief King with the eyes of an owl.

John entered the store and set his heavy bundles on its pine floor.

Merchandise, neatly arranged, crowded the building. On its left stood bolts of fabric on a three-tiered rack. To the right, against the wall, hogsheads stood in a rank. Other necessities—hand mirrors, toothbrushes, cups, saucers— occupied other shelves in the middle of the store. Behind the building's main counter the store kept settlers' mail in a shelf with pigeonholes.

In three quick strides, King exited his back office, his drooling bloodhound at his heels. "Where've you been hiding, John Wolf? Haven't seen you in many moons. You brought me skins to trade?"

"I did," John said.

King, his bloodhound at his feet, took John outside. "I'll trade with you this time, but deerskins aren't in much demand these days. Next time, you better bring money. Good White man's money."

A protest touched John's tongue, but he stifled it. This would be his last time to trade with this dishonest man. Perhaps other braves in his village would help him bring some of his cattle to Saint Stephens and sell them there. The Great One would show him what to do.

Behind King's store stood three stout limbs angled against each other, their tops bound by leather straps. A crossbeam, also secured with leather straps, lay along their tops. From the beam, a large hook attached to a thick rope dangled. Iron weights sat on a wooden rack.

"Weigh my cousin's bundles first." John put Red Panther's bundle on the ground.

King pointed at it. "Not there. Pick it up."

John did so.

"Father." Clay, his arms swinging fast, hastened to them from up the path. "Mister Mims is coming here."

"An old friend has arrived," King said. "We'll weigh these things later."

Scowling, John lowered Red Panther's bundle onto the ground.

King tapped Clay's shoulder. "Finished your collecting, son?"

"No sir."

"Hop to it. You want your parents in the poor house?"

"No sir." Clay hastened off.

The Ruffians collected money from many settlers in the immediate vicinity, though John had never witnessed them in the act. Only heard the talk. Protecting them from bad braves and bad White men, is what his friends who lived here told him.

"Let's go welcome our caller, Lucky." King patted his thigh.

His drooling tongue dangling, Lucky bounded ahead.

John snatched up the bundles and passed Samuel Mims, his buggy halted at the store.

Mims's shock of iron-colored hair matched his goatee and wide sideburns. People in this village often mentioned him. He'd lived in this region for many years, owned land on the Tombigbee River and on the Tensaw not far north of Mobile. Beyond that, however, John knew nothing about him.

John moved on, catching bits of their conversation, something about a dance, a party, land, and slaves. He cringed at the word *slaves*. Owning other men was wrong. Now he must stay overnight because Chief King would be talking to his friend for who knew how long.

On his walk to the Ox Yoke, John hoped the Lawsons had a room. Their daughter, Annabelle, troubled him. She hated her parents. He did not understand why. White man's business was White man's business, so he never asked. Children should obey their parents. Annabelle was an unruly child, something he'd witnessed on previous visits.

Female fury exploded when he entered the tavern. Addie Hatch and Grizzie Lawson, nose-to-nose, screamed at each other at the same time. He sat at a table. In vain, he tried to ignore them. White woman's business was White woman's business. When women did battle, he considered it wise to keep his distance lest they claw or scratch or bite, or worse.

"This is the last time I'm a-telling you, Grizzie." Addie Hatch, hands propped on her hips, breathed in Grizzie Lawson's flashing green eyes. "My son's more'n a blacksmith. He's got brains, he's got brawn, and he's got money and slaves on some mighty decent land."

"Ain't nobody owns my Paul or tells us what to do," Grizzie snapped. "We've got our own minds 'bout things."

"So does my Barnaby. He's got his mind set on marrying your Annabelle. Y'all best let him and her get hitched."

Grizzie, an inch shorter than Addie, rose on her toes and leaned into her. "Your child can own all the gold in the world. I don't give a hoot. He ain't fittin' for my daughter. Me and Paul agree on this."

John noticed Annabelle seated at a corner table beside Jasper Jones, whom the settlers often teased. Jasper sipped something from a tankard and wiped the flat side of his big knife's blade on his shirt sleeve. On more than one occasion, Jasper drank too much. Last time he came to this village the poor man was so "out of it" his legs wobbled him. Today, he appeared to be sober, and his graying black beard wasn't as ragged as usual.

Fingering her ringlets, Annabelle riveted her attention on her mother's spat. John knew little about Mrs. Hatch's son, other than his being the leader of a gang called the Ruffians who hated preachers of the Great One's holy word. If he and Annabelle did become husband and wife … John's fingers drummed the table. *White man's business.*

"Well." Addie's countenance softened to a motherly expression when her gaze shifted to Annabelle.

"Well?" Grizzie folded her arms. "Well, what?"

Addie crossed the room to stand behind Annabelle. "I reckon it don't matter you letting your daughter become a spinster. I reckon it don't matter she ain't never going to give birth to young'uns"

"She'll marry when we tell her." Paul Lawson stomped down the tavern's staircase fast as a boulder descending a steep hill. "To a decent, law-abiding gentleman."

"Pa," Annabelle cried, bolting from her chair. "Me and Barnaby fancy each other. It's been going on two years. We want to get hitched."

"No." Paul tilted his head at John and a young couple who'd entered the tavern, a silent greeting. He softened his tone. "Fancying and loving ain't the same thing."

The young couple, Zander and Constance Oglesby, waved a greeting to John. John responded to his friends in similar fashion. Zander was big-boned and owned a neatly trimmed, waist-length brown beard whereas Constance wore spectacles balanced on her narrow nose.

"Leave my tavern, Mrs. Hatch." Paul, breathing rapidly and hard, closed on Addie. "We don't allow your kind in here no more."

Huffing, Addie stormed out.

"You tell her, Mister Lawson," Jasper shouted and guffawed. "Ain't that right, John Wolf? You heered 'bout the giant gator I wrestled last week? Musta been one-thousand pounds."

John withheld a response. Jasper always told wild tales.

"Another beer." Jasper lifted his tankard. "Let me tell you about the time I killed one of Gen'l Cornwallis's majors. I was—"

Paul's steely stare silenced him.

Jasper set his intimidating blade on the table, leaned back in his chair, and ogled Annabelle, who put her face in her palms.

Mrs. Oglesby glowered at the distraught girl.

"I'll help y'all in a minute, Zander," Paul said.

"Take your time, my friend." Zander waved him off.

"Staying the night here, John Wolf?" Paul asked.

"I am," John said.

"Come." Paul pivoted toward the staircase. "I've lots of bed space for you. No other guests are staying here tonight."

Ascending the tavern's stairs, John considered asking Paul about the women's argument but rebuked himself. White man's business was White man's business. He'd listen, though, if Paul decided to make it his business, something every honorable friend did.

Upon entering the room, John tossed his bales onto the pine floor. He grasped the satchel slung across his chest, slid it off, and reached inside it for Kana's Bible. Even though its English was difficult to understand, he opened it to read. Within minutes, he stretched out on the floor and sank into a deep nap.

A ruckus startled him awake.

White man's business.

Shouts on the first floor. Louder.

White man's business. Suddenly, he scrambled to his feet. From the staircase's first landing, he watched.

Three young men crowded Paul and Grizzie. Clay, he recognized by his disheveled red hair and Gopher Harkins, by his slight limp. The third young man, however, John didn't recognize. Jasper, his head laid sideways on a table, snored up a drunken storm with his big knife beside him. Maggie, their cook, peeked out a rear door crumpling a dish rag.

Paul folded his arms and thrust out his square chin. "For the last dang time, I ain't selling my land or my business to stupid King. This is *my* place, *my* business. *I* built it. *I* own it. *I* paid for it. The land office said *I* own it *and* my land."

"My father admits you own the land fair and square," Clay said, "but he's offering you a decent price for it. He's doubled the offer from last time."

"I ain't selling."

"You can move farther west. Plenty of room in this territory for settlers."

Paul shook his fist at them. "I ain't moving. I ain't selling. I ain't starting over again. And I ain't paying no more of your so-called taxes to your gang, neither. Get off my property."

Clay smirked. "Your decision."

Grizzie propped her bronzed fists on her hips. "You heard my husband. Go."

Swaggering out with the other Ruffians, Clay winked at Annabelle. Annabelle winked back.

John hurried down the last flight of stairs to his friends.

"Annabelle, tell Maggie to clean the pantry." Grizzie swiped her apron across her brow.

Her hips switching, Annabelle sauntered past them. "Best be careful, Ma, Pa. You know how them Ruffians are. Best let Barnaby and me get ourselves hitched, else—"

"Your mother gave you an order, Annabelle," Paul growled.

Annabelle disappeared into the pantry at an even slower pace. Slamming cabinets echoed. Maggie, tidying up.

"I do not like what my ears heard." John studied his exhausted friends. "It sounds like they wish you dead."

"We'll be fine," Paul said.

"I can send word to my village. It will send warriors to protect you."

Paul grasped John's arm. "No, no. I thank you. You're a good man, but we'll be fine. I can handle King."

"Chief King is not one to be trusted."

"I'll tell you, my friend, if we need you. Your offer of protection is much appreciated."

John returned to his room. Some evil thing was happening tonight. He sensed it. He washed up in a basin of water on his dresser, grabbed a chair, and carried it into the tavern's hallway. At the rear of the hallway, a window overlooked the Lawsons' cabin. He'd keep watch all night if he must. He'd not let harm befall his friends.

In his struggle to stay awake, John blinked often. The rustle of a tree alerted him. A raccoon climbed along one of its limbs. Something moved behind him, a creak of the floor, but he didn't bother to identify who or what it was.

He leaned against the window. Paul and Grizzie were outside. Two people confronted them.

Paul raised his fist. Grizzie shouted something at them. *The Ruffians.* John bolted from his chair, upended it, and shot downstairs. He sprinted to the tavern's front door. He jiggled its knob. *Locked.*

"Please, Almighty Great One. Please let me out, let me help my friends." He reached for the door's latch, sensed someone's approach … *Ugh.* He crumpled to the floor.

CHAPTER NINE

Sunset touched the horizon. Kana trotted her gray pony up a wide path to a field where cheers, singing, and drumbeats called her attention to the contest in progress. Her whole village, turned out for the stickball game to settle a dispute with a village from Mississippi. Despite the fact that she was in no mood for a game she guided her pony to its animated spectators, dismounted, and led it by its reins.

She tethered her pony to a post next to other horses and ponies and made haste to the contest. Dust tickled her nostrils. Much dust the players caused in this game, hundreds of players constantly running. She asked the Great One to let the game end soon. She must speak with her uncle, Foha's war chief Gray Eagle. Her head twisted left and right in search of him among the animated crowd—the dancing and singing women on both sides of the field, the shamans shouting from the sidelines, the players getting tackled or else stumbling from a whack on the head with two-foot long hickory sticks.

Her cousin Chilita, wearing white warpaint, tossed a small deer hide ball with his hickory stick to another teammate, who caught it in his stick's small rawhide cup and raced toward their opponents' goal. An opposing player in red warpaint tackled him, stole the ball, maneuvered around Foha's players but when he tossed it to his teammate Red Panther snatched it in the air with a low leap. Agile as a cat, he wove and darted between numerous opponents chasing him, his ball nested in the stick's cup. He rushed the ball toward the goal, a tall sapling. He passed it to Chilita, whose stick snatched it.

Chilita raced around the mass of players in pursuit. He next tossed the ball to a teammate, who ran with it then tossed it back to Red Panther. Spectators withdrew to clear his path. His long black hair flying, he evaded three more opponents, passed the ball to Chilita who sent it flying into the sapling. A scorekeeper drove a sharp stick into the ground. Ten sticks to the opposing team's seven. Applause and cheers erupted from the sidelines.

Kana did not cheer.

Foha's village chief, Brave Fox, stepped onto the field with the opposing team's village chief. Their raised hands signaled an end to the game, their dispute having finally been resolved, the village of Foha the victor.

Her short legs pumping fast, Kana thrust herself between others till she spotted her uncle and Brave Fox engaged in conversation with the opposing team's chiefs. When her uncle spotted her, he quit his conversation.

"Where is Nashoba nowabi?" Gray Eagle asked her in Choctaw.

"Chief King's village," Kana said, puffing from her sprint. "He's been gone longer than he should be gone. I'm worried."

Red Panther and Chilita, dripping sour-smelling sweat, approached. Red Panther stroked the back of her head as she buried her face in her uncle's muscle-packed chest.

"Kana's husband has not come back from the village of King's Brook," Gray Eagle said.

"But my uncle, he promised me he'd return in time to watch," Red Panther said.

"Something has happened to him?" Chilita took one step closer.

She withdrew from her uncle. "I fear it has."

Red Panther's thumb wiped her moist eyes. "We will go there, Cousin."

Gray Eagle gestured to his nephews, his Tvshkamikushi, his "little war chiefs"—lieutenants. "Get eight of our best braves. We're going to Foha tonight. From there, we'll leave for the White village. I'll tell Brave Fox and the elders what's happened."

Chilita and Red Panther hurried off.

"I will go with you," Kana said between sniffles.

Gray Eagle's fingers lifted her chin. "This is a warrior's duty. You stay with the women. Panola will take care of you till we return." He indicated her Aunt Panola walking across the stickball field with another woman.

"I'll speak with her first. It is our decision if I go." Kana hastened to Panola to ask her to gather the village's leading women.

CHAPTER TEN

Hoofbeats. *Must be Gray Eagle.* King slid his ledger into a desk drawer. Years ago, when Spain owned the Tensaw-Tombigbee region, before the United States and Spain set the boundary line at the thirty-first parallel above Mobile, he'd killed a man in North Carolina, a Rebel who'd fought King George and the British, who'd stolen his land because he'd been a Loyalist. As a consequence, he fled to these parts and killed two squatters. Spain's authorities ignored his killings. In those days, every man fended for himself.

Gray Eagle didn't frighten him. He'd not flee from here. He'd planted his roots too deep. The main things he wanted, though, were to keep his grip on the settlers along this creek and in this vicinity and keep religion out of his settlement. If he lost his grip on the settlers, and if he didn't continue to plan his deeds carefully, he may find himself in trouble with the territorial law. As for religion, he considered it foolish. If one of his Ruffians became almighty pious the Ruffian might report him to the territorial law with evidence of the gang's crimes. Gray Eagle and a few Choctaws? He'd take care of them.

"Gray Eagle's here, Father." Clay spoke from a store window.

"I thought it was him riding in." King joined his son.

"The Choctaw are cowards." Clay glimpsed back out the window. "What'll you tell him?"

"Let's go outside, son. I'll show you."

Flanked by his nephews and eight warriors wielding bows, quivers of arrows slung over their shoulders, Gray Eagle rode to him. Musket in his lap, the chief wore a beaded cap and a necklace of metal half-moon gorgets arranged in a column over his brown hunting shirt. His sons and the other warriors, all rawboned men, wore similar adornments.

"Good day to you, Chief," King said, sociably. "What brings you here today? You have something to sell? Something to buy? Something to trade?"

Gray Eagle's sternness dug into him. "You know why I am here, Chief Richard King. Tell us what's happened to Nashoba nowabi."

"Who?"

"Wolf Walking." Red Panther spoke through gritted teeth. "My cousin's husband who you call John."

"He never showed up at your village?" King scratched his chin in a pretense of ignorance.

"You know he has not," Gray Eagle snapped. "You are chief of this village. You tell us what happened."

"My apologies, Gray Eagle. This great White chief doesn't rightly have an idea."

Jasper, his smudged forehead deeply creviced, emerged from a cluster of curious onlookers. King noted Jasper's leather sheath belted round his waist. Pitiful man's prize possession wasn't in it. The besotted buffoon said he'd lost his knife. After days of searching for it he quit his efforts.

"We'll find out, Chief Richard King." Gray Eagle lifted his musket. "If he has been harmed, if you have harmed him, we will not fight a war against the White man. Our war will be against you." He wheeled his horse around. At a trot, he led his warriors away from King's store.

King nudged Clay. "Gray Eagle's nothing. Don't let him put the scare in you, son."

"Suppose he gets the soldiers to come here?" Clay asked. "Or the sheriff or the territorial judge?"

"Let them come. No one'll talk. Get over to Barnaby. Inform him about what just transpired. You and your friends be ready in case there's a fight."

Clay snatched his cap off a peg, plopped it on his shaggy head, and departed.

WEDNESDAY, SEPTEMBER 26, 1810
KING'S BROOK, ALABAMA COUNTRY, MISSISSIPPI TERRITORY

Two days later King led Clay, Gray Eagle, Gray Eagle's nephews, and Fort Stoddert's Captain James Pemberton into the Ox Yoke. Lucky padded alongside and curled up against the bar, his head rested on his front paws. Before King joined the others at a table he tossed Lucky a biscuit the drooling dog promptly inhaled.

The captain removed his blue shako, revealing brown, receding hair. His blue coatee's standing collar enclosed a bullish neck. His soldiers patrolled the settlement. Two privates guarded the doors against intruders.

Barnaby brought Captain Pemberton a beer.

"This isn't a social visit." Pemberton waved it off. "General Gaines is extinguishing another fire you settlers ignited, and the sheriff's gone to the Flint River to serve a writ for a debt another one of your kind owes. Judge Toulmin dispatched me to investigate things here because an urgent matter required his services elsewhere. You people are driving us, me, crazy."

"My people aren't causing the trouble." King leaned back in his chair. "We're all law-abiding citizens of this territory."

"It's rumored, Mister King, that you fought the Spaniards on the border five months ago."

"The Spaniards caused the trouble, Captain. They crossed the thirty-first parallel and attacked my friends. We settlers were merely defending what's rightfully ours."

Pemberton propped his elbows on the table, lowered his head between his upright arms, his hands clasped over it. He breathed loud and hard. He then dropped his arms and, sighing, looked up. "Sir, I am, and we all are, quite exhausted by you ignorant peoples' imbecilities. I've been at this repulsive post a mere three months, and already I'm craving a transfer back east. To New York, preferably, where my wealthy and distinguished family resides." Pemberton surveyed the tavern. "First time I've been to this hovel."

All nice and pretty in his fancy uniform. King nearly spoke his sarcasm aloud but considered it best not to get on the captain's bad side. Gray Eagle's warriors had discovered John's body, Jasper's knife in his back, on a small island in the Tombigbee River. They carried his body to their piddling excuse of a village. Regarding the Lawsons, his Ruffians buried them deep in the woods where no one would find them, except maybe wild animals.

Gray Eagle produced Jasper's big knife. "Give us the man who killed Wolf Walking. The man who owns this." He slammed it on the table. "One of your men. A Ruffian. This was the weapon that killed him."

"Now hold on a dang minute." King lifted his hand palm-outward. "The Ruffians are innocent. They enforce the law."

"Your law, not ours." Gray Eagle, his determined jaw set, folded his arms over his chest.

"The territory's law."

"Let's hope so, Mister King," Pemberton said.

"Enough talk." Gray Eagle pounded the table. "Give us the man who owns this knife." He glared at King. "We will take him for Choctaw justice."

Yawning, King stretched his arms high as though unconcerned.

"Or we may kill Chief King first." Gray Eagle thinned his lips.

King shot the war chief a threatening glance. No one intimidated him, least of all, an ignorant Choctaw.

"Do you know the person who owns this, Mister King?" Pemberton picked up the knife and flipped it about in his black-gloved hand.

Yes.

"Ain't that Jasper's?" Annabelle said. "He's been hunting all over for it claiming he lost it. He's been in here drinking hisself crazy. He's always lying 'bout something."

"I'll fetch him." Barnaby left. Minutes later, he shoved Jasper into the tavern.

Soon as Jasper spotted the knife the man rushed the table and grabbed it.

"You fancy that blade?" Pemberton cocked a brow.

"Yessir." Jasper nodded quickly. "Made it myself."

Their expressions stone, Gray Eagle and his nephews stood.

"You killed one of my warriors with it," Gray Eagle said evenly.

"Me?" Jasper shook his head fast. "N-No. N-Not me. Only things I kill is bear and deer and coyotes and …" He stammered. "I ain't done it. Somebody stole it and done it."

"You lie." Gray Eagle pointed at him. "Red Panther, bind him. Choctaw justice."

"No, Chief," Jasper shrieked. "I ain't, I ain't lying."

Snarling, Red Panther twisted and jerked Jasper's arm behind his back. Jasper squealed.

After further questioning by Captain Pemberton, Gray Eagle, and King, Red Panther bound Jasper's wrists with rawhide straps. Jasper screeched his innocence. The Choctaws marched him out.

Annabelle gave Pemberton and his soldiers free beers as a friendly send-off.

"Appears we've gotten ourselves rid of the stupid Choctaw and your parents, little darling." Barnaby grasped her hands. "Reckon the Ox Yoke is yours now."

"And yours, I reckon, Mister King if you're still hankering after buying it. My father's field hands and his land too, since me and Handsome"—she glowed warmly at Barnaby— "since we're going to get hitched."

"My dear, I'll purchase them from you at an especially reasonable price." King raised his tankard. "You may keep Maggie, though."

Anabelle lifted her tankard. "Obliged."

Their tankards clinked.

Lucky barked.

CHAPTER ELEVEN

Kana stood over the large wooden mortar behind her cabin and slammed a thick pole down on its corn. Twisting and turning it, slamming the pole again, she ground the corn into meal. A warm breeze tousled her uncombed hair, uncombed because she still mourned. She swiped perspiration off her brow before she resumed grinding. A pause. She glared at the black clouds. *No husband. No child.* She smashed the corn harder. Though her husband had been dead for over a year, pain stabbed her like the thorns of a prickly ash tree, big thorns piercing her, thorns she could not pull out.

She no longer possessed the Great One's Book to help her understand. It never came back with her husband's body. She should not have let him take it to Chief King's village. It may have some answers to help her, though she did not read White men's words as well as her husband.

Her attention wandered to Cousin Red Panther, skinning a deer, something her husband sometimes did. Sometimes, too, she and other women accompanied the men on hunts to do it for them. Tomorrow, she would spend hours tanning its skin.

Her husband, a fine hunter, caught her. On her wedding day, her soul full of love for her husband-to-be, she swung open her cabin door and emerged from it, her light steps swift. She stopped short of a pole, peered behind her with eager anticipation while her smiling friends watched. Out came her husband, from behind his door. He gave chase. She slowed her run, eager for him to catch her before she reached the pole. Easily, he did so and hefted her in his powerful arms. His hand clasped hers, and he started to lead her to his cabin when her giggling friends snatched her away. They pulled her to the ground in front of the house, giggled, and showered presents upon her.

They played a grab game, each girl grabbing for the gifts. Soon after this, she and her husband were married. A year later, a wandering preacher who showed them the Way married them in the eyes of the Great One. She sniffled. Not a night passed that her husband didn't visit her in her dreams.

The deer Red Panther killed hung from a wooden bar by its hind legs, secured there by leather straps. Ever since her husband's death, Red Panther helped her. Cousin Chilita helped also. So did her Uncle Gray Eagle and Aunt Panola and other men and women from the village.

"It is true?" Kana asked.

Red Panther lowered his bloody knife. "About our war council? Tecumseh and his Shawnees?"

"Yes." Kana resumed mashing the corn.

"Tecumseh wants war. He says the White man will soon be fighting their old enemy across the ocean. He says this is the time for the tribes to unite and strike the White man, to push him off our land."

"Aunt Panola told me Pushmataha wants peace." She glanced up from her grinding.

Red Panther washed his hands in a bowl. "Chief Pushmataha followed Tecumseh and his warriors to every village Tecumseh went to. Pushmataha's speech—powerful. I, Father, and our chiefs warned Tecumseh and told him to leave our nation, or else we would kill him. He and his warriors have gone."

Kana scooped up some ground corn and emptied it into a sifter atop a basket. Pushmataha was a great warrior among their people, chief of the Okla Hannali District in Mississippi country, but he fought other tribes, never the White man.

"Brave Fox says for you to come to the village. It's no longer safe here." Red Panther sat on a bench opposite her. "The women, that is their decision too, Kana. You must leave this farm. Brave Fox sent me to bring you there."

"No." Kana shook the sifter. "I will not go."

"The women, your Aunt Panola—"

"Tell Aunt Panola I love her." Kana's expression softened. "This time, I cannot obey her, nor the decision of Brave Fox and the village council."

Red Panther stood. "Why not?"

Because if I must die in this war, if war comes, I must die. "Tell her I will go back to our village if war begins." She lifted the sifter off the basket, where the finely ground corn fell.

"I will tell her. You are a grown woman. They will not force you. But you are making a mistake." Red Panther bent forward and kissed her forehead. "We love you, Kana. The whole village. We hope you change your mind."

Red Panther resumed skinning his deer and Kana to mashing her corn.

She dumped the sifter's remaining corn back into the mortar for further grinding. If she didn't get an answer soon, why someone killed her husband, she'd no longer believe in the Great One and just as soon die.

CHAPTER TWELVE

Thomas trotted his horse up alongside Phineas's. Several weeks ago they left Milledgeville, Georgia to travel this new section of the Federal Road on their way to Alabama country. In creaking wagons, on clip-clopping horses, and afoot, a constant stream of settlers and livestock driven by slaves passed them. Various odors and nature's fragrances mingled in the stifling humidity. A young man, his legs dangling from a wagon bed, played a nonsensical tune on a flute. Another boy strummed a banjo. Most folks offered them a quick greeting, a tip of the hat, a howdy, or a wave.

"The preaching we'll be doing ain't going to be all butterflies and buttercups," Phineas said the day they left. "Keep notes on what you learn. It'll come in handy in your preaching. Write the answers to your prayers. It'll be a Barnabas to you, encourage your faith."

"Yes sir. I'm keeping a journal, same as you."

"We'll be heading up the Tombigbee and Alabama Rivers," Phineas told him. "Settlers live on the Bigbee's west side. Not many live on the Alabama River, don't s'ppose. We'll do the Lord's bidding in the Tensaw region too. Won't be easy."

"You made mention of a settlement on the Chickasawhay River?"

Phineas nodded.

A Methodist society had formed there, Thomas recalled, two years after he left Mississippi country. Noble and his family were members of it. He should've stayed there a little longer instead of hightailing it to Georgia after he came to trust Christ. "Looking forward to visiting Noble again."

"A glorious family reunion, it will be."

"Do you figure I can make it? Pass this two-year test the conference put me on?"

"Abide by my counsel, Thomas, you'll do fine as a duck in water." Phineas winked at a little girl in a wagon, seated in her mother's lap.

Thomas let his horse's reins drop onto his lap as he rocked in his saddle and his horse bobbed its head. Fine. Would he do fine? The first time he spoke before a congregation, to exhort others to repentance, his nerves got ahold of him so bad it lasted all of five minutes. He'd expected that to be the end of his calling but no, it wasn't. Folks congratulated him, slapped him on the back, and offered encouragement. Each time he exhorted, speaking came easier. However, doubts tarried. At the recommendation of his local society in Georgia, the conference gave him a preaching license and placed him under Phineas's guidance and instruction.

Thank goodness, Phineas served as his "Preacher in Charge." Because Phineas had led him to Christ, he respected Phineas immensely. He also appreciated his mentor's sense of humor and enjoyed the music he played on his violin most every night. Would he stay true to his calling or lose his faith like others he'd heard about lost theirs? Thomas hoped and prayed he'd pass this test of his faith.

The journey through Georgia proved relatively easy. Though several towns ran them out, revival broke out in another town due to Phineas's sermonizing, not his. Phineas's preaching always sparked revivals, his preaching and the Holy Spirit moving in marvelous ways among the people. The times he'd sermonized, folks scarcely uttered "amen." For three weeks they preached in another town, passed out religious tracts, and sent a report to their presiding elder before they continued along this road. Phineas opened each meeting with prayer and led their congregation in hymn-singing while he played his violin.

Thomas and Phineas always awakened before the roosters crowed and, for about two hours, they prayed and engaged in devotions. Sometimes, settlers accompanying them on the road fed them. Others, already settled, provided them with lodging, or else they slept out in the woods or inside an inn. Once, during a storm, they swam their horses across a rain-swollen creek to reach the next settlement.

In fellow travelers' camps they happened upon, or at settlers' homes along rivers and creeks, they'd hold divine services and perform marriage ceremonies.

"I now pronounce you husband and wife." Phineas's words at the end of every wedding rang in Thomas's ears. He'd never get married. Such an ambition he'd abandoned years ago. Every girl he'd taken a fancy to spurned him. Mainly on account of his physical appearance— the ugly birthmark on his forehead, he figured.

On another occasion, when a thunderstorm exploded while they slept among the timber, lightning leveled two pines that crashed to earth missing Phineas's head by inches. After Thomas roused him, Phineas saw the trees. "Hello," he'd said. "Y'all missed me." Then he curled back on the soaked grass beneath his blanket and snored himself into oblivion. The storm sent a fright through Thomas's bones. He wished he shared his teacher's fearlessness, that he possessed Phineas's godly and fearless reputation.

As part of his education Phineas gave him material to study— *The Arminian Magazine,* religious tracts, and books. The Bible, however, took first place in his lessons. Phineas's brain contained so much Bible knowledge, had his head been a lemon nothing but scripture could be squeezed out of it. He taught Thomas doctrine and aptly answered Thomas's questions. Thomas also studied Phineas's preaching style. He sure as sand wished he preached as good as his mentor.

Thomas shook his head. Should he mention his concerns about their financial inadequacies? They barely carried enough money to pay for their basic necessities. "Phineas, about our—" He clamped his mouth.

"About what?"

"Nothing." Best not to show his weak faith regarding God's provision.

Ten Conestoga wagons and six riders jerked Thomas from his thoughts. A post rider galloped past them from another direction. How many of these travelers planned to settle in the Tombigbee Valley? How many in the Tensaw? How many in Mississippi country? Times sure were a-changing in this wilderness.

"We got lots of places in our circuit?" Thomas asked.

"Settlements, most of 'em are, I s'ppose," Phineas said. "Any native villages we happen upon are ripe for the harvest too."

"Our first stop?"

"Bassetts Creek is our mission's headquarters. A society's already formed there, what Reverend Ford reported to Elder Matthias after he passed through there on his preaching journey. Lots of upstanding Methodists and Baptists live there. Very respectful of God's holy word. We'll be staying with a godly, hospitable fellow. Mister John Dean."

"What circuit was Reverend Ford assigned to next?"

Phineas shrugged. "Don't have an inkling of an idea. Be careful, though. We're going to King's Brook too, but it ain't easy to evangelize."

"I recollect that's where you got egged a few years ago."

"True." Phineas's horse snorted. A cloud settled over him. "If ever a settlement was in the devil's clutches, it's that one."

"I've been there before, remember. And I agree. King's Brook is in sore need. The Lawsons and I are acquainted. When we first met they told me they moved here from somewhere near Savannah back around the nineties, trying to start a new life."

"Yes. I quite forgot."

"Even though I've only met her a couple times, Annabelle Lawson's a hard girl to forget, what with that big ole attitude of hers she carries." Thomas guided his horse behind Phineas's to make room for more wagons. "It ain't far from John and Kana's place. Maybe me and you can pay them a little social drop by."

"A splendid idea, I'd say. More and more of us coming onto this land. This new road we're traveling is the reason, I s'ppose. S'ppose to take folks clear down to New Orleans one day."

"It's Creek Nation territory."

"The Lower Creeks. I s'ppose we'll do fine and dandy. Most of 'em down this way are on the downright sociable side of things."

When the wagons ahead rounded a sharp bend, Thomas and Phineas found themselves riding alone. For several minutes, silence prevailed. Two arrows whistled from nearby trees.

Thomas and Phineas urged their horses into gallops. Whooping, two painted warriors on horseback burst out of the timber.

One overtook Thomas, leaped from his mount, toppled him to earth, and straddled him.

On his back, Thomas spat in the warrior's face. The warrior swept his red war club toward him. Thomas seized the man's wrist, wrestled with the weapon, shoved it clear. Down it came again. Up flew Thomas's hand. Again, he snatched the man's wrist right before the club struck.

A shot rang out.

The warrior sprang off Thomas, swung astride his horse, and galloped off, followed by his companion.

Thomas's eyes met those of a young man, his dark brown beard and mustache so heavy only his lips showed beneath a broad nose. The man's blue three-cornered hat tilted low over his tanned brows, and dust coated his battered lobster-colored British army officer's coat. His fierceness softened to a gentle glow. Though the man looked familiar, his name escaped Thomas. The man slipped his arm through his musket's sling and pulled it over his broad shoulder. Then he knelt beside Phineas, flat on his back on the side of the road. Thomas gained his feet. "Much obliged. Is my friend all right?"

"I'm not sure." The man frowned.

Thomas, staggering on legs aching from the fight, joined the stranger.

The man stroked Phineas's sandy-colored hair. He put his ear to Phineas's chest. "Your friend's unconscious, but he'll live. I scared off the other warrior too, before he struck your friend."

Thomas breathed a sigh of relief.

"Your friend's horse threw him. I saw it happen." The man disappeared into the woods and, within seconds, brought a canteen and poured water on Phineas's face.

Thomas's mentor spluttered, sat up, mumbled. "Thou shalt not be afraid for the terror by night; *nor* for the arrow that flieth by day."

"*Nor* for the pestilence *that* walketh in darkness; *nor* for the destruction *that* wasteth at noon day," the man said.

"Psalm Ninety-one, verses five and six." Thomas studied the man. "You're a Christian?"

"Yes, I'm a Christian," the man said. "Also, a métis."

"Métis?" A French word. Thomas tried to recollect its meaning. He'd been away from the Mississippi Territory for too long. French settlers in this region gave the name to … *Oh.* "You're a mixed-race."

"My mother's Creek," the man said.

Thomas tugged his wide chin. "Uh, you look sorta, uh … I can't rightly place you at this moment in time."

A slow grin emerged through the man's thick beard. A flash of recognition sparked. He blinked. "Thomas? Thomas Murcher?"

The man's identity hit him. "Ain't this something! Dempsey King, of the Ruffians." Thomas slapped Dempsey's broad shoulder. "It's been years."

"Indeed. And you, a Christian same as me." Dempsey pulled in his grin. "I'm no longer in that gang. I'll explain later. Listen. I was up at Tuckabatchee late September where Tecumseh and his Shawnees were spouting off foolish war talk. Most of the chiefs and elders didn't buy into his speeches but let me warn you. There's a band of them who did, and they're the ones who'll cause trouble, such as those two who attacked you."

Brows arched, Thomas and Phineas swapped glances while Thomas pulled Phineas to his feet. A war in Alabama? "Dear Lord, protect us all."

"Amen," Phineas and Dempsey said.

"We're on our way to Bassetts Creek," Thomas said.

"We'll be moving off this road up ahead." Phineas collected his hat off the nearby grass. "Care to join us, Dempsey King?"

"Be back directly. I'd enjoy some friendly company." Dempsey ducked into the trees.

Phineas surveyed the ground. "Where's my violin?" Slumped, he kicked a clod of dirt when he spotted the instrument's shattered remains. He threw up his arms, clutched his head, and loosed a painful roar. "Oh! My music! A horse stomped it to kindling."

CHAPTER THIRTEEN

"Get lost, Frank," Barnaby snapped at the slender youth in Lemuel Cooper's livery, Zander and Constance Oglesby's ten-year-old son.

"I ain't finished my work yet." Frank, carrying a water bucket, stomped past him into a roan horse's stall. The animal hung its head and lapped the water greedily.

"Don't smart-mouth me, boy." He thumped Frank's head. "Do what I tell you."

His dimpled chin held high, Frank eyed his boss, Lemuel Cooper, standing beneath the hay loft rubbing his thighs and scratching his brawny arms. Lemuel shot him a quick, nervous nod.

Frank, expelling a breath, concentrated on working a loose suspender back onto his trouser button. He then marched out.

With a jerk of his thumb, Barnaby signaled Lemuel to close the livery's double doors. They stood toe-to-toe. Although Barnaby matched Lemuel's build—broad-shouldered and muscle-packed— Lemuel was clean-shaven and square-jawed whereas Barnaby's massive black beard stretched down to his great girth. Lemuel also stood two inches shy of Barnaby's six-foot height.

"The rent's past due, Lem." Barnaby sniffed. A pitiful thing, Lem having a big yellow stripe in him. A man his size might've been somebody important in this place. "Six dollars, due today."

"Six?" Lemuel clamped his mouth shut.

"Me and my men might tell a certain somebody about a certain li'l señorita?"

"Señorita Valentina and me are friends. No more'n that."

"Friends with the dirty Spaniards down Mobile-way?" Barnaby cracked his knuckles. "Traitor." He scratched his nose and clutched the pistol that poked out of his trouser waist. "This is a small place. Word spreads out about you in this region, your little filly'll be the first person to learn of your, uh, doings down yonder."

"W-Wait. Valentina and me ain't been loving on each other."

"You've been calling on her a lot."

"Ain't true." Lemuel eyed Barnaby's pistol.

"It ain't?" Easy as spreading melted butter on bread, frightening this man.

Like a dog tortured by ants and fleas, Lemuel scratched his arms faster.

"We got us witnesses saying you're mighty sweet on her." Palm up, he extended his left hand. "The money or the rumor."

"Mabel's been asking why I go there so much?"

"I'd say so." He was a master liar. Lemuel's wife made no mention of it at all. "Pay, else we'll tell her your li'l secret."

"I ain't seen nobody special in Mobile. I just enjoy going there."

"Sure." Barnaby winked at him. "Eh, amigo?"

"If Mabel finds out, our marriage'll be—"

"Ruined."

Lemuel swallowed twice, his prominent Adam's apple bobbing. "Mister King and I made an agreement when I sold him this place. Four dollars a month. Every dang year, he raises it. Please, Barnaby."

Barnaby whipped out his pistol and shoved its muzzle against Lemuel's stomach.

"P-Please. It ain't right, it ain't right, him raising it another dang time."

"You ain't gonna pay it today? I can't promise you protection." Barnaby's forefinger jabbed Lemuel's ribs. "I'll tell your filly of your affair with Señorita Valentina Consuelo Margarita Rosalinda Hidalgo. And if you try moving outta this town, me and my men'll track you down and tell her. Then we'll kill you."

"All right. All right. All right. Let me go into my office and get the money. I'll pay it."

"Gracias." Barnaby snickered. *Coward.*

Once he and other Ruffians delivered the settlers' payments to Mister King, Barnaby rode home. Lem was a fool. The man met Señorita Hidalgo two years ago when she and her father passed through the settlement after visiting friends who lived close to the fort at Saint Stephens. Because it was dusk they'd spent the night at the Ox Yoke. Mister King, in the stables at the time, saw the señorita give Lem a kiss and a hug— a "thank you" for something Lem did for them. Later, Lem made the mistake of going to Mobile more often than usual. What he did there, no one knew. Whatever the reason, the fool's trips played into Mister King's scheme. By threatening to spread a rumor of an affair, Mister King convinced him to sell King the livery.

Barnaby stabled his horse before he entered his single-story, whitewashed frame house. Two servants set out supper. Annabelle threw her arms around him. "Umm. I love you so much."

"My good-looking woman." He wrapped her in his beefy arms. Sweeping aside her dark tendrils, he smiled into her sparkling hazel orbs. For a full minute, their lips pressed tight. No rapid throbbing of his pulse. No thrill coursing his veins. *You happy I kissed you, you dog of a woman? Your lips taste like sand.*

CHAPTER FOURTEEN

Tuesday, December 24, 1811
Bassetts Creek, Alabama country, Mississippi Territory

On Christmas Eve Thomas, freezing and stiff as a block of ice, bounced on his toes and hugged his body in front of a small crowd gathered in a field a mile from Bassetts Creek. A devout Methodist gentleman owned it. Oh, how he hated winter. He'd be miserable this season of the year if the bishop ever assigned him to a circuit up North.

Although sizable for a frontier settlement, Bassetts Creek remained small. Its structures consisted of six scattered log buildings, including a Baptist church and a Methodist meetinghouse. A general store provided the settlers with their necessities and mail. Why weren't they celebrating the holiday in one of its churches? He wasn't no snowman. He'd rather melt.

"A Christmas tradition, us meeting outdoors," a settler told him earlier in the day.

Doggone it. Sometimes folks broke traditions, and this was one of those blame times. *Brrr.* He hugged himself tighter. His lips, numb.

Joyful carols, accompanied by a guitarist, rang out from the torch-lit field. Phineas's sad face fastened on the musician. Figuring the sense of loss surely whirling in his mentor's soul, Thomas hoped

Phineas found another violin to replace the one he'd lost. His mentor's display of temper when he flung his shattered instrument into the woods and shouted his despair— Thomas had never witnessed it before. Thankfully, Phineas's disgust quieted when Dempsey joined them on the Federal Road.

Phineas averted his pained gaze away from the guitarist. His baritone voice blended in perfect harmony with the others. Perhaps this worship service eased his loss.

Since Thomas sang about as beautiful as a rooster with a hiccup, he barely sang so as not to draw attention to himself. Phineas, Dempsey, and the local Baptist pastor stood beside him. People's countenances shone.

Phineas made it a practice not to debate those whose doctrines he disagreed with. In his thinking, Christians ought to be sociable with each other. It didn't matter whether a person was a Baptist Calvinist or a Methodist Arminian so long as they loved and followed their Savior.

Once the music fell silent, Phineas advanced two steps. "When we rode in earlier, we shared with y'all how we got attacked, and our friend Mister Dempsey King saved us. America is going to fight the British again if the newspapers I read in Georgia speak the truth."

Gasps rippled through the congregation.

"Best get your souls ready. Life's fleeting. Tomorrow ain't promised to no man." He gestured at Dempsey. "Listen to Mister Dempsey King. He's got an important message for each one of us."

Phineas took two steps back.

Dempsey, clearing his throat, stepped forward, opened his mouth to speak, but stuttered.

Thomas lowered his brows. *It'll be all right, Dempsey. Tell them the same things you told us.*

"Ladies and gentlemen, f-friends," Dempsey began. "I am a métis. My mother is a Creek of the Lower Creek Nation, my father a White man who lives in a settlement bearing his name."

Steadier, Dempsey recounted his early years as tiny puffs of cold emanated from his mouth. His father, Richard King, once served with the British. "After he lost his property in North Carolina, he —"

"Happened to lots of us," an elderly gentleman off to the left said.

The Baptist preacher's finger touched his lips for silence.

Dempsey continued. "My father settled these parts in the 1790s, recovered his wealth raising cattle and cotton and other crops and conducting business with the Spaniards in West Florida. A few more settlers moved into the area. Debates in territorial court over land and grants. Y'all know how it is. Some folks who lost land grants to my father moved on. Problem was, I tell you, the ones who stayed got into fights and all sorts of trouble. So, my father took advantage of the situation. He founded a gang of young men such as myself. He called us the Ruffians and put me in charge. We kept things reasonably peaceable, for a price."

Dempsey paused to gaze across the attentive congregation. "The day came, around a year later, I stole money from my father, money he used to pay us for protecting everybody. A man who was my friend and right-hand man, we brawled over it when he discovered what I did. Fisticuffs. He beat me so bad, I tell you, I felt like mashed up taters."

Scattered chuckles from the crowd.

Musta enjoyed the part about mashed up taters. Thomas grinned.

The Baptist minister raised a finger waist-high for the little congregation to hush.

Dempsey cleared his throat. "I fled up to Natchez. A year ago, a wandering preacher showed me the Way." Shoulders quivering, he stammered out his next words. "Have no idea whether he was Methodist or Baptist or Presbyterian. Doesn't matter. I'm a changed man." Dempsey's countenance lifted toward the star-spangled sky. "Thank you, Lord God, for sending us Jesus and changing this heart of stone into a heart of flesh."

Joyful hallelujahs followed. The guitarist played a Christmas hymn, and Bassetts Creek's God-fearing citizens sang merrily, their voices lifted high.

Thomas swelled, his singing suddenly louder than the others. Curious stares warned him to lower his voice, but his hiccup singing kept slipping into high notes.

A boy in the congregation's front row clutched a bullfrog between his gloved hands and, each time Thomas got loud, he held it chin-high and screwed up his mischievous face. After the service the boy hastened to him. "My frog sings better'n you, Mister." He thrust his pet at Thomas.

Thomas and others burst into laughter.

"And what's that brown mark on your head? Coffee stuck to it?" The boy disappeared into the crowd.

Thomas, touching his forehead, nearly yelled at him. A raven-haired girl loomed out of his subconscious— Sadie Maddox, who'd spurned him when they were youths after he'd declared a desire to court her. She'd teased him so cruelly, called him ugly and stupid, she'd branded her words and actions in his brain. He was fourteen at the time.

He bit his lip. Not a righteous example, yelling at the boy. Not proper to do it anyhow, but his birthmark was a tender spot. Sadie wasn't the only girl who'd teased him mercilessly, and not always about that. Boys bullied and teased him too. Lots of fights he'd been in back in those days. Thanks to Noble teaching him how, he'd won a few bouts. As far back as his memory served, he'd been teased. Even after those times he'd shared his past with Phineas, and despite Phineas's attempts to help him, the cruel memories still hurt.

CHAPTER FIFTEEN

In October past, King's and Barnaby's slaves finished building a theater. Constructed with corner-notched pine logs and twelve-hundred square feet, it dominated the settlement amidst the Ox Yoke, Lemuel's livery, Zander's leatherworking shop, and a loom house King owned. Sunlight spilled through its six windows, three windows to a side. Eight sconces flickered their candles.

On this theater's small stage, Annabelle often performed. Each time she did her popularity grew. Her magical soprano voice lured admirers from miles around. Folks even paid to listen to her, and King always split the profits with her, which she then split with Barnaby. Although Barnaby and the Ruffians likewise entertained in this theater, they offered their performances for free. Of limited or no talent, they did skits and plays they'd written. It provided a diversion for the region's settlers, and it distracted them long enough for other Ruffians to engage in certain illegalities, such as robbing travelers.

On this Christmas holiday Barnaby strode back and forth on the theater's stage, his heavy boots pounding its floor while he wildly waved a thick black book, doing his best imitation of Reverend Phineas

Steward's preaching. From backstage, Annabelle flounced to him and dropped to her knees. "Mercy," she sarcastically pleaded.

Scattered laughter from the audience.

Barnaby stared beyond them, at Maggie in her white mobcap and battered blue dress standing beneath a sconce. Her eyes squeezed tight as though absorbed in prayer. He pointed at her. "Ah. A sinner over yonder. A slave. Take a look at her, y'all. She's praying. Pray, Sister. Pray."

Heads turned toward her. Maggie's lips moved silently.

"Laugh at her." Annabelle scrambled to her feet. "Laugh at that sinner, praying her life away. Ain't she funny?"

Scattered, spiritless chuckles responded.

"Louder," Annabelle screamed. "Laugh louder, people. And Maggie, you better pray hard less you aching for a whipping."

King arose from the front row. "Do what the lady says. Laugh till your stomachs hurt. Laugh, I say."

The congregation obeyed, their enthusiasm forced.

Maggie prayed.

Barnaby cut to the second row where the Oglesbys sat beside old lady Patience Morgan, her wrinkled face scowling at him. He opened his mouth to scold her when the theater's front door slammed.

A hush dropped like a ship's anchor when a fancy-dressed man, clad in a wide-brimmed black hat, green ankle-length topcoat, and dusty boots made an entrance. He marched to the stage. "What is happening here?" The man pivoted to the audience. "I and my family were traveling through and heard your noise outside. I assumed it was a Christmas celebration, but what do I behold when I enter these premises? Mockers of religion. It's disgraceful."

Annabelle spat on the stage. "What right you got telling us what we can and can't do, Mister? You ain't living here."

"That's telling 'em," a Ruffian shouted from the third row.

"What rock you crawl out of?" Gopher snarled.

"Enough of this ungodly mockery," King snapped. "We ought to all be ashamed."

Barnaby feigned regret. "Sorry, Mister King. We ain't gonna do it again."

King harumphed. "Let's hope not." He approached the man. "Sir, forgive us. You are a stranger here. May we have the pleasure of learning your name so we can give you a proper welcome?" He winked at Barnaby and Annabelle.

The man glowered. "I am Adolphus Gregory Fitzpatrick, Attorney at Law, that's who I am. My wife and child are outside on my wagon. Rode in a few minutes ago. We are searching for a place to settle. But in this godless place? Never. We'll continue our journey into Mississippi country."

Barnaby concentrated on Fitzpatrick and Mister King's exchange. If Mister King persuaded the lawyer to stay here and get him on their side, he'd give the Ruffians an even easier say-so in this place, a lawyer who'd defend them in territorial court when they needed one.

"Dangerous Choctaws west of here, Mister Fitzpatrick." King wagged his head. "If you encounter any of them, you'd best shoot them on sight."

Very dangerous. Barnaby, snickering, nudged Annabelle.

"Invite your family inside," King continued. "We won't do any more mocking. I'm in charge of this settlement." He tilted his head at Barnaby. "And Mister Hatch here is my assistant."

Bowing, Barnaby swept his coonskin cap beneath him.

"We're hoping we'll get chartered as a town one day, my good sir," King said, "and we can always use more fine upstanding citizens such as you and your family."

"Where's your house of worship?" Fitzpatrick asked. "Is it having a proper celebration of this sacred holiday?"

King recoiled, feigning shock. "Why, my dear sir. You may be the man we need to help us. We've been needing a church for too long a time. Maybe you can help us build one. What is your religion?"

"Presbyterian," Fitzpatrick said.

"Ah. Shall we discuss it? Not many Presbyterians in these parts I'm aware of. Those of us who've been here since before our country took the region away from Spain are all Catholics. Had to become Catholic, if we wanted Spain to allow us to own land. Baptists and Methodists up in Bassetts Creek, though." King grasped the lawyer's elbow and steered him out of the theater.

Barnaby smirked. Mister King held something good up his sleeve, at least for him and his fellow Ruffians.

Early in the evening, King convened a meeting in his store's office. Gopher drew its window curtains tight. The other Ruffians gathered around a table, their avid expressions visible amidst the dim candlelight. Lucky curled on a large pillow in a corner, napped, and snored.

Although King supervised the proceedings, Barnaby opened the meeting. At first, he regretted Mister King's failure to persuade the Fitzpatricks to settle here, till he and Mister King decided on a plan to take advantage of the fancy-dressed man and his family.

"We're letting them stay in the Ox Yoke for free," Barnaby said. "They say we're being gracious. They're obviously folks of means. Y'all saw the woman's ruby necklace? The man's fancy duds?"

"Sehoy asked me for her necklace," King said.

"I want his coat and hat," a Ruffian cried.

"I'll take his boots," another Ruffian said. "And his high-falutin' wife's emerald ring is somethin' my little woman wants to enjoy wearin'."

Barnaby propped his elbows on the table. "They said they've decided to go on back to Bassetts Creek tomorrow since it has a couple of Protestant churches."

"They may stop at the Maryvale settlement on the way," Gopher said. "We can rob 'em there."

"Not there," King said. "Ambush them on the road, yes, but wait till they're about a half-day's ride from Bassetts Creek."

"Because the man's a lawyer, we don't want him figuring one of us done it. He might get us arrested." Barnaby pointed at Clay. "You lead the robbery. Find two men to go with you."

"Chief Clayton King." Clay flashed a sly grin and pulled at his hair. "Y'all call me Red Hawk."

"Red-headed Red Hawk." The Ruffian's words prompted chuckles.

"Each one of you young men," King said, rapping his fingers on the table, "lend Barnaby and me your ears."

CHAPTER SIXTEEN

Thomas rode alongside Phineas while Dempsey, a blue wool scarf wrapped round his neck, rode ahead. In the sky beyond them, gray clouds drifted. A bright cardinal fluttered into the thinning timber. Evergreens rustled their branches. "Me and you enjoyed us some fine meetings in Bassetts Creek, Phineas." Thomas pulled his wide-brimmed black hat lower over his forehead.

"Fine as a flea on a dog." Phineas chuckled. "Plan on spending a week or two at Maryvale, same as we did at Bassetts Creek."

"My settlement's on the schedule after Maryvale?" Dempsey spoke as he twisted toward them from his creaking saddle.

"It is," Phineas said.

With a heavy groan, Dempsey slumped. "Good ... I think."

"You're doing the right thing, Dempsey, giving back the money you stole and making amends with your folks."

"A hard thing it will be for me, Reverend Steward." Dempsey squirmed. "I didn't lie at Bassetts Creek. I, er, I just didn't share all the dirty laundry in the basket."

Thomas discerned fear in Dempsey's shaky voice. From the things Phineas and Dempsey had told him, Dempsey's parents sounded like unpleasant folks. The two times he'd been to King's Brook years ago, he'd never met them. Should he be scared too? Nothing wrong with being scared. Coming on this mission trip had caused some concern. The future, always uncertain. Especially at this moment, with the Creeks on the brink of civil war and White men such as himself and Phineas trapped in the middle.

"Generous of Bassetts Creek's folks, giving us an offering before we left." Phineas patted his saddlebag. "We'll make a stop at Kana Wolf's farm after Maryvale."

"Kana Wolf?" Dempsey perked up. "She and her husband John stopped by our settlement often. Her uncle, Chief Gray Eagle, and Chief Brave Fox visited too. It sure would've been a pleasure to have courted Kana in my younger years. She is the prettiest thing."

"Why didn't you do it?" Thomas asked.

"My folks, especially Mother." Dempsey spoke over his shoulder. "They hate Choctaws. I used to sneak off to Kana's village. She was always excited by my visits."

Touching his forehead, Thomas recalled his near-fatal encounter several years ago. "Kana ministered to my wounds when a bear attacked me. She's a fine lady."

"That she is, Thomas. That she is." Dempsey slowed his mount for two deer to cross out of some brush.

The trio continued riding in silence for several minutes before Thomas spoke again. "Who'd you figure we'll give the offering to, Phineas?"

"A darling little girl in Maryvale may not have enjoyed much of a Christmas. She wasn't in the prime of health last time I saw her, the same year I met you. Let's hope the little lady is still on this earth. If so, I'll give her parents the offering so they can buy her a nice present. She ought to be going on twelve years now."

"And if the little girl ain't still living?"

"We'll give it to her folks to spend however they choose."

Approaching a sharp bend, Thomas rose in his stirrups. Rattling wheels sounded close.

With his hand raised, Dempsey signaled them to stop. Grunting, he looked to his right.

Who? What did he see? Thomas rose higher in his stirrups and also looked right.

A short, stocky man wearing a red bandana over his nose and mouth emerged from some bushes.

How'd Dempsey see him?

Dempsey urged his horse forward. "I recognize your little limp, Gopher. You can't hide it with a stupid mask."

Shouts up ahead sent Dempsey galloping toward it.

Gopher fired at him, missed.

Springing off his saddle, Thomas strode to the Ruffian. "Give me your gun."

Gopher reached for the small powder horn dangling off his neck.

Thomas snatched Gopher's pistol and with a firm twist of the Ruffian's wrist, wrenched it from him. "Why'd you shoot at my friend?"

"'Cause he's ridin' with you preacher-men." He spat at Phineas, still astride his horse. "Thought we got shed of you years ago, Reverend What's-his-name."

"I ain't easy getting shed of." Like a cat who'd finished off a bowl of warm milk, Phineas licked his lips.

Loud chatter neared. When Dempsey rode back at the head of an ox-drawn Conestoga wagon, he and a young family were engaged in conversation. On its driver's bench, a dark-haired girl in a green winter cloak sat between two adults, whom Thomas assumed were her parents. The man's coat matched the girl's cloak. The lady's crimson cloak had a hood that concealed her hair.

"The other Ruffians took off when they saw me." Dempsey drew rein. "One of 'em was my brother."

The oxen pulling the wagon stopped.

"Clay's Barnaby's number one man." Gopher scowled at the family. "Fitzpatrick here disapproved of our Christmas celebration when he came to our settlement."

"It was an abomination." Fitzpatrick huffed.

Dempsey jerked Gopher's mask. "Take that stupid thing off and do me a favor. Tell my parents I'll be home in a few weeks. And I tell you this. Don't go try robbing anyone else. What I did to y'all was wrong. I'm heading home to give back the money I stole and make amends."

"You're crazy comin' back, Demp." Gopher ripped off his bandana. "Your parents are gonna tan your hide. They'll kill you."

Several seconds passed before Dempsey responded, as though he was considering Gopher's warning. "I'm willing to risk it."

Gopher grabbed his pistol from Thomas and stormed off.

"I'm grateful for your help stopping the robbery." Mister Fitzpatrick gave Dempsey his card.

"My Claudia." Her arm around her young daughter, Mrs. Fitzpatrick hugged her tight against her body, a mother hen protecting her chick. "Those men scared her half to death."

"You'll find nice, friendly folk at Bassetts Creek up the road." Dempsey added a small smile, his teeth showing through his heavy whiskers.

"Paid a visit there weeks ago." Fitzpatrick tipped his hat. "Decided we'll settle there. It's the best place we've been to so far in this territory to open a law practice."

Wagon and riders parted ways, the wagon heading north and the circuit riders south, with Dempsey the preachers' self-appointed protector.

CHAPTER SEVENTEEN

"**P**hineas, my mentor. My friend." Thomas's lungs were ice in the freezing weather. His chest tightened as he bent over Phineas, sprawled on the ground, his head propped on his saddle against a hackberry tree, and moaning. A brisk breeze stung Thomas's cheek. They'd delivered their offering to the needy family in Maryvale after they'd preached a series of meetings, mostly Phineas did, and now this— Phineas was sick.

Sweat soaked Phineas, saturated his clothes, and puddled the ground around him. "My h-head. It hurts. A-aches. M-Muscles a-ache."

Thomas adjusted Phineas's saddle squarer behind his head.

"He's a pretty powerful fever." Dempsey, handing Thomas a rag, spoke behind him.

Don't die on us, my friend. Thomas mopped his mentor's brow.

"A pity I c-couldn't pass into eternity on C-Christmas." Phineas released another moan resembling an injured animal. He rolled onto his side.

"Hush. Ain't your time yet." Thomas smacked his gloved hands. How did those Northern folks survive their winter snows? Glad it didn't snow in the Mississippi Territory.

"I can't face my parents without either of you." Gloom permeated Dempsey's speech. "I may talk brave, but the truth is, I'm powerful scared of 'em. Father and mother can do some awful things. Except to their dog. The one thing Father would never hurt—his dog and other people's dogs."

Thomas uttered a prayer. He wasn't fully trained in the ministry yet, and his sermons seldom stirred a congregation to repentance. Suppose Phineas died? Could he continue this work on his own? Or ride back to Georgia and tell Elder Matthias what happened here? He didn't understand doctrine well enough yet, nor did scripture leave his mouth at the drop of a hat, nor sermons, not like they did for his Preacher in Charge. *Stop worrying about yourself. It's Phineas who needs help.*

"I'm in the good Lord's loving arms." Phineas's frail words, barely audible.

A white-tail doe darted through the brush behind them.

"Still got tinder for your lighter, Dempsey?" Thomas stood. "I'm out of it for mine."

"Ought to."

"Figure we better gather us some firewood and build us a fire."

"Reckon you're right."

Once they'd collected the wood they cleared the area around Phineas and stacked it like a lopsided pyramid.

Dempsey pulled his lighter from his saddlebag. It resembled the back half of a flintlock pistol with a trigger and a hammer for the flint. Although a small candle holder sat behind the lighter's hammer, Thomas held Dempsey's candle for him.

Upon securing the flint in the half-cocked hammer and with tinder in its catch box, Dempsey gripped the lighter's walnut stock. He cocked the hammer back fully and triggered it. The flint struck the frizzen and sheared off steel particles that flew into the box. Its tinder ignited. A flame. A gust extinguished it.

"Dog it." Dempsey reached for another flint in his saddlebag.

After a second attempt, thanks to Dempsey's palm blocking the wind, the candle stayed lit long enough for him to touch its flame to the wood. A blaze shot skyward. Dempsey's breath snuffed out the candle.

FRIDAY, JANUARY 24, 1812
ALABAMA COUNTRY, MISSISSIPPI TERRITORY

Throughout the frosty evening Thomas and Dempsey kept vigil over Phineas. Even though they took three-hour shifts to spell each other for sleeping, winter's misery and worry's mockery robbed their rest. Muttering about lost souls, his late mother's prayers, violin sonatas, and other things, Phineas at last drifted into sleep.

As dawn seeped in and birds stirred awake, Thomas laid his palm on Phineas's forehead. *Still warm.*

Phineas's glassy eyes wandered to him. "Let's get moving. Preaching to do. Got to do the Lord's bidding."

"Your fever ain't broke yet," Thomas said.

"Too many souls perishing." Phineas pushed himself up on unsteady legs, then he crumpled in a heap. "H-Help me, T-Thomas. Help me to my feet."

"No sir," Thomas snapped, adding, "Respectfully, sir. You ain't fit enough at this moment in time. Besides, you don't want other folks catching whatever it is you got."

Phineas coughed. He turned his head while Thomas managed to prop him back against the hackberry tree. "Where's Dempsey?"

"Hunting tobacco." Thomas tossed a stick on the sizzling campfire.

"Tobacco?"

His pink cheeks visible above his beard, Dempsey waded toward them through a thicket.

"Dog it. No tobacco back that way."

Thomas indicated the road. "Try over yonder."

"I am. I am." Dempsey jogged across the path. "Why can't we find it when we need it, dog it." He yelled this as he ducked back into the trees.

Thomas produced his Bible from his saddlebag. "What do you want me to read to you today, Phineas?"

"The Twenty-third Psalm's comforting to my soul."

"All right."

During Thomas's reading Dempsey shouted, "Where is it?"

"Still no tobacco?" Thomas asked upon Dempsey's return.

"No. None on that side of the road, none on this side."

Two cardinals, a male and female by their colors, took flight.

Frustrated, Dempsey puffed. "There has to be tobacco around here somewhere. It's the right time of year for it."

"C'mon Dempsey." Thomas patted the ground. "Sit. Maybe I can find it while you do the reading if you wanna."

"Why y'all keep looking for tobacco?" Phineas coughed. "Tobacco d-don't grow 'round here."

"Keep reading to him, Thomas. I'll find some if it's the last thing I do on this earth." Dempsey hastened off.

"Since you ain't answering my tobacco question, read me Psalm 119." Phineas spoke barely above a hoarse whisper. "By the time you've finished it, he'll be back with what you want. Tired of staying here. Too many souls going to the devil's brew."

Halfway through the psalm, Dempsey's triumphant shout jerked Thomas to his feet.

Dempsey, shaking the plant, sprinted to them from up the path. Its dry leaves were brown on one side and silver on the other.

Thomas, beaming like an athlete who'd waxed victorious in a sporting event, pointed at it. "Tobacco."

"Rabbit tobacco." Dempsey panted from his run. "Lots of it up the road."

A light chuckle from weary Phineas. "Rabbits smoke that stuff?"

"They're pipe smokers, sir," Thomas said, grateful his mentor kept his sense of humor.

"If that's so, I'm fried bacon." Phineas coughed, then chuckled after drawing a harder breath.

"Very medicinal." Dempsey went to his horse, lifted a flap on his saddlebag, and slipped the leaves inside it. "Good for fevers."

"Life Everlasting what I always called it." Phineas coughed again. "Ain't never heard it called tobacco."

"How far is it to Kana's house, you figure?" Dempsey twisted back to them.

After several more coughs, Phineas responded to Dempsey's question. "One day maybe, if we ride hard and don't encounter any trouble. We ain't far from her village. A few miles."

"Figure you can show us the way, I mean, in your condition?" Thomas asked.

"I'll show you where to go." Dempsey hefted a sturdy limb from off the ground. "We'll make a travois and drag him to her cabin. Let's get started. We'll use our bedrolls and blankets for a platform."

"Let's do it."

CHAPTER EIGHTEEN

In her cabin's gloom Kana, a turkey feather mantle draping her shoulders, sat on a stool beside her table, the bright afternoon blocked by shuttered windows, the frigid weather held at bay. The fire Cousin Chilita had made for her in her fireplace—warmth to her body, but it did not warm her icy heart. Chilita had returned to their village, his most recent effort to make her go there having failed. Neither could Red Panther persuade her, nor her uncle or aunt, nor any women of her village. They once promised not to force her to return to Foha, yet still they tried. She wanted no one in her family to live with her. She wanted to be alone, to nurse the ache wracking her soul.

She reached for the longleaf pine needles piled on the floor and began weaving them into a basket. The Great One no longer cared for her. He'd darkened the light that once shone so brightly in her soul. He refused to send her a preacher to answer her questions. He refused to give her a child when her husband was alive. Maybe she *should* go back to her village, to her old Choctaw ways, and her people's religion.

Hoofbeats brought her to a window. When she pushed open a shutter, a cold blast of air swatted her. Riding up the narrow path the man she remembered, Thomas, who her husband rescued from a bear.

A stranger rode … No. *Chief King's son?* She'd not seen him in a long time. A handsome man. Was that the preacher she'd known, lying on a travois? Her throat caught her heart. *No. Great One. No. Preacher Phineas cannot be dead.*

She hurried outside.

Thomas, carrying a short cane table, accompanied Kana into Phineas's bedroom next morning. She carried his breakfast of ham and eggs on a tin plate while Dempsey brought up the rear holding a knife and fork wrapped in a linen napkin.

"My dear Lady Grace." Phineas swung his feet off his cane bed to receive his meal.

"You are better." Placing the food tray on the table, Kana smiled. "I am thankful."

"She told us lots of things happened during our absence." Thomas nudged the table up against his mentor's bed. "Many bad things. John got killed. Figure we're an answer to prayer."

"I'd almost given up on the Great One." Kana leaned forward and touched Phineas's forehead. "The fever is almost gone. The medicine I made with the rabbit tobacco worked." Straightening, she inclined her head at the food. "Eat. I have many questions to ask you when you are well."

As Phineas dove into his breakfast the earth tremored and rattled the cabin walls. A clay vase tumbled off a shelf. Window shutters banged.

Screaming, Kana grabbed the doorframe.

Phineas's fork dropped onto his bed's bearskin covering.

The tremors stopped.

"This is the second time we've experienced these shakes." Phineas recovered his fork.

"An earthquake somewhere," Dempsey said. "Tecumseh got lucky this time."

"Lucky? How?" Phineas resumed eating.

"He told the Creeks he'd stamp his foot and shake the earth when he went home. The comet we saw the other night, he predicted it too."

"Some prediction. I s'ppose scientists up North told him to expect it." Phineas spoke as though nothing out of the ordinary had happened. Between bites, he said, "Yes sir. The Almighty's trying to warn us of a coming judgment if folks don't set their souls right with Him." His brows arched. "Thank goodness for rabbit tobacco too, eh?"

CHAPTER NINETEEN

Twenty yards from his house, The Hideaway, Barnaby stood inside a picket fence enclosing his family's cemetery. Two limestone blocks amidst brown, dead grass marked his parents' graves. He took off his coonskin cap. Annabelle, beside him, clasped his hand, her deerskin glove soft in his cold, naked palm.

Fond memories flooded him. His dear mother passed on for nearly three years. The Ruffians attended her funeral, as did the Kings, The Hideaway's slaves, and their overseer. His slaves' presence didn't fool him. They'd come to avoid the unpleasantries of the overseer's cat-o-nine-tails.

"I miss them." Annabelle brushed a wayward curl behind her ear, her hazel eyes grown duller over the previous years.

"Me too." Barnaby's knuckles rubbed his nose. Lots of fun times they'd enjoyed. Today was his mother's birthday. She loved flowers, especially primroses, but none bloomed during this miserable time of year. He always put some on her grave in spring. "We used to throw parties for Mama on her birthday. You remember? You remember the year I surprised her by celebrating it the day after?"

Annabelle giggled. "I'll never forget it."

"You remember how disappointed she was?"

"Reckon I do. She got herself a good horselaugh out of our joke the next day."

Barnaby squeezed her fingers. "On Papa's birthday, me and him took trips down Mobile-way. You remember us going there? We really enjoyed us a good time fishing in the bay."

"You figure if we talk to your folks, they'd hear us?" Annabelle pulled her dark blue cloak tighter over her lissome body.

Barnaby put his hat back on. At least his heavy beard gave him some measure of warmth. "Let's go inside. I'm freezing. I'll tell Eustis to build me and you a fire."

Eustis always obeyed him, out of fear. Barnaby enjoyed whipping slaves for even minor offenses. Maggie belonged to Annabelle. He'd pay Mister Samuel Mims a social call and buy another kitchen slave to help Maggie in the Ox Yoke.

Ever since Clay and Gopher killed Annabelle's parents, he'd assumed control of the Ox Yoke but took orders from Mister King, who owned it now. Gopher worked in it, and Mister King paid him a decent wage. Annabelle, though, did the managing of it. If he wasn't there or in his blacksmith shop, Gopher or other Ruffians would send word of Dempsey's arrival. He planned something special for him. Mister King approved his idea.

As he and Annabelle stepped onto his front porch, Annabelle glanced back at his folks' graves. "Handsome"— she stroked Barnaby's arm— "don't go getting your dander up at me, but I keep on wondering about what them preachers keep saying."

Barnaby stifled a groan. *Not again.* How many times had she asked this question? He'd lost count. "Saying?"

"About where folks go when they die."

Barnaby opened the door for her, and they entered. "Eustis, build us a fire in the parlor."

The burly slave headed out back to the stacked firewood.

Barnaby wrapped his arms around Annabelle, stroked her curls, and tilted his head against hers. "Still fretting about what you done to that Choctaw?"

"First time I ever killed a person."

"And your parents, your part in helping us kill them by keeping an eye on John?"

Annabelle bit her lower lip.

"Wasn't it done for a good purpose? I got you, and we ain't got no witnesses. Me and you are home free."

"Remember what that horse preacher, What's-his-name, told my folks on one of his visits? That all killers go to Hell. Is that true?"

Exasperated, Barnaby heaved a sigh. "Please, Annabelle. Quit this foolish talk." He slid his fingers beneath her quivering chin. "You ain't going to no Hell because you killed a dumb Choctaw and helped us kill your parents. Every one of them needed killing. Hell ain't a real place. God ain't real neither. He's one of those superstitions like the Injuns got."

For a moment, Annabelle fell silent. "Handsome, when we going to let Judge Toulmin hitch us proper?"

"Darling, ain't us living together the same as me and you being married?" Barnaby, his arms locked around her, drew her lips into his and to satisfy her, their lips locked. His parlor clock ticked off the minutes. Kissing this woman was akin to kissing Mister King's bloodhound. One day, if she didn't quit asking her fool questions about Heaven and Hell, he'd toss her out of his fine house and make her live in the woods. To shut her up once and for all, he might even plant a blade in her bleeding li'l heart.

CHAPTER TWENTY

A nswers eluded Thomas. Each time he responded to Kana's questions as to why the Great One let someone kill her husband, he stammered and wrestled out lame explanations. Some horse preacher he was.

In a private moment Dempsey told Thomas his suspicions, that her village executed the wrong person. "Jasper was lots of things," Dempsey told him. "But I tell you of a truth. The man did not possess one murdering bone in his body."

When Phineas learned of John's death he devoted this Lord's Day, after he recovered, to giving instruction about suffering and persecution. Teaching it proved difficult, though, not for lack of knowledge on Phineas's part but for Kana's constant questions. Each time Phineas answered her, muscle by muscle, her tension eased. At the end of his lesson, he explained to her that John suffered martyrdom for his faith and, because of this, the Great One had a special reward for him in Heaven.

Then Phineas grasped her shoulders, bowed his head, and prayed. "Lord God, Almighty One, Great One, we ain't got the understanding why a person killed our brother John. We ain't got the understanding why our sister Kana, our Lady Grace, ain't never been able to birth children. Your ways ain't our ways, and Your thoughts ain't our thoughts. We are all sinners, and ...."

Phineas's lengthy prayer continued. Kana sobbed, heaved, and gushed tears. At one point, she wailed.

"Much obliged, Lord," Thomas said after Kana's "amen."

Once Phineas finished praying Kana blinked and smiled at Dempsey. "I'm glad to see you again, friend Dempsey King," she said.

Dempsey, a twinkle in his eyes, threaded his fingers on the table. "It has been many years, Kana, niece of the great war chief Gray Eagle."

"Yes. It has."

Thomas's heart backflipped. A mixed-race Creek getting a fancy for a pretty little Choctaw lady. He shared their happiness. Had the Lord created a fine lady who'd fancy him? *Quit thinking about it. It ain't gonna happen.*

CHAPTER TWENTY-ONE

G opher barged into Barnaby's blacksmith shop. "He's ridin' in."

Barnaby gestured at his apprentice to stop turning the forge's crank. When the apprentice did so, its fire shrank from a blazing blue heat to a small orange one. Barnaby set the iron he'd been repairing on an anvil. "Alone?"

"Ridin' with two men. I think one of 'em's the feller we egged years back."

"What's-his-name?"

"May be him."

"The idiot."

What's-his-name. The fool thought it funny when they egged him. Yet every few months after that event he'd return to the settlement's outskirts, wave his Bible, and threaten Hell and Damnation. He was to blame for Annabelle's unfounded fears. Because of that preacher, she kept irritating him with her stupid questions. Barnaby took off his leather apron, hung it on a peg, and pulled on his heavy brown coat. "We're closed for the rest of the day, Phil."

"Sure, Barnaby. Thanks." The apprentice shifted away from the forge.

Barnaby and Gopher rounded a corner and halted at a small log structure. Sure enough, Demp rode between What's-his-name and another man in a black overcoat. *What in blazes happened to Demp? He got religion or something? He's coming back here to get himself killed. Yes sirree. Bang.* He studied the preacher in the black overcoat closer, rocking in his creaking saddle. Slender of build, a brown birthmark on his forehead … He gasped. *Murcher? Thomas Murcher?* Years ago, he'd whipped the tarnation out of Murcher when he'd come to the settlement, a fistfight over his charging him too much to shoe his horse. Barnaby scratched his head. *Murcher's a preacher now?* "I'll be a … He must've drank some crazy water."

"Say what?"

"Nothing, Gopher."

Dempsey and the preachers followed a dirt path toward King's store. Scattered people paused their activities to watch. Concern marked some countenances, curiosity others.

Zander, round knife in hand he used for scoring and paring leather, emerged from his shop.

"Gopher"—Barnaby jerked his head toward the tavern— "go on over to the Ox Yoke and fetch me my pistol. Tell Annabelle he's here. Tell her I said load it."

"Gonna be fun." Gopher took off to carry out Barnaby's instructions.

"Demp, you're dog meat." Guffawing, Barnaby clutched a fistful of his long, heavy beard and twisted it around his fingers.

Once Thomas hitched his horse at a water trough he accompanied Phineas straight to Dempsey, also dismounted in front of his father's store.

"Courage, my friend." Thomas patted Dempsey's shoulder reassuringly. "Me and Reverend Steward are by your side."

"It'll be all right." Slowly, Phineas opened the flap on Dempsey's saddlebag for him.

Dempsey reached into it and pulled out a bulging canvas sack. His musket slung over his shoulder, behind his back, he trudged through the store's door, Thomas on his heels. Phineas followed a few paces behind.

"H-Hello, F-Father. I-I'm home." Dempsey's voice trembled.

A young, redheaded man swerved from the pigeonholes behind a counter where he sorted mail. He flushed. He snickered. "Sooo, the rat has come back. What's the matter, Demp? Preachers protecting you these days?"

Dempsey dropped the bulging canvas sack onto the counter. "Where's Father, Clay?"

"Out." Clay stabbed a finger at the sack. "What's—?"

"The money I stole. I've come to make amends. I earned it back working over in Natchez country."

Clay snagged it. "Father and Mother'll be happy."

"You won't count it?"

"Counting's Father's job."

"We're square?"

"Nuh-uh."

"It's done, and my conscience is clear. You are aware of the war threatening to break out between the Creeks?"

"Uh-huh."

"I attended the National Council in Tuckabatchee when the Shawnee Tecumseh and his warriors were there. Tecumseh gave a speech trying to rile up the village. We made him and his people leave, but he left a man there name of Seekaboo who's rousing a band of warriors who believe their ancient religion. They're eager to fight those of us who refuse to go back to our old traditions and customs, and they plan to fight the White man too."

"Uh-huh." Clay resumed sorting mail.

Dempsey reached for the doorknob.

"Demp." Clay's malicious tone froze Dempsey in his tracks. "I hate you."

Dempsey winced. "We are brothers, Clay, by birth." His hoarse whisper cracked. "It's your choice whether to accept that fact. I accept it, and as your flesh and blood brother, let me tell you the truth. I love you." Hunched, he dragged himself out the door as though the weight of the world's troubles burdened him.

"Love me?" Scathing laughter erupted from Clay's mouth. "Ha!"

Along with Phineas and Dempsey, Thomas, aching for his friend, went outside. He understood the turmoil wracking Dempsey's poor soul, being rejected by his brother, for he himself had suffered rejection more times than he cared to count.

They led their horses past loblolly pines, down a wide dirt path pocked with hoofprints and wagon wheel ruts. At the end of the path a tall, muscular, black-bearded man brandished a pistol at them. "Howdy, Preacher."

"Why, I'll be a cat's kitten." Phineas offered an easy smile. "Barnaby Hatch. Thomas, this is—"

"We've met before, sir. A long time ago. Once or twice." Thomas tensed.

"Become one of those Bible-quoting preachers now, Murcher?" Hooting, Barnaby tossed back his shaggy head.

"I seen the error of my ways, Barnaby Hatch." Working his jaw back and forth, grinding his teeth, Thomas fought his dislike of the man. "So yes, figure I am a preacher now."

"Means you've got noodles for brains. Preaching's against the law in this settlement. Get lost, Preachers. Me and Demp got to take care of things." Barnaby lowered his gun.

"Nuh-uh." Thomas kicked a lump of dirt. "Where he's going, I'm going."

"Thom—"

"Sorry, Reverend Steward. I ain't meaning to sound disrespectful, but Dempsey's our friend, and I'm going with him." Thomas led his horse to a nearby trough.

"I was 'bout to say"—Phineas secured his horse beside Thomas's— "we're thinking the same direction."

"Y'all may be regretting it." Barnaby reached for Dempsey's musket. Dempsey slid it off his shoulder and thrust it into Barnaby's hand.

"Your pistol, Demp."

"I'm not carrying one." Dempsey unbuttoned his coat and held it open for all to see. No sign of one.

"Preachers, tie up Demp's horse. Yonder with yours."

Thomas did what Barnaby said.

"Move it." At the point of his pistol, Barnaby marched them up a woodland road.

For one dreadful mile, Thomas and his friends trudged. Where did this pebbled path lead them? They ascended a small hill. About one hundred yards beyond them, a single-story frame house overlooked two acres of grassland enclosed by scattered loblolly pines and red maples.

"My house," Dempsey said flatly.

"Not anymore," Barnaby said.

A lanky, silver-haired man stepped out onto the raised oak porch. A black-and-tan bloodhound, his tongue lolling, leaned against his legs. Behind them followed a slender woman, her black brows knit into a tight vee and her dark hair a confusion of curls. A bright red cloak concealed her dress.

Thomas's pulse pounded.

The stony man stood as motionless as a statue. Also, the woman. Acrid silence dropped between them, an invisible wall blocking their approach.

The woman's measured paces disrupted the silence, each footfall crunching sticks and pebbles. "You are a disgrace." Her palm popped Dempsey's cheek.

Dempsey flinched, dangled his arms at his sides, and hung his head. "You are right, Mother. I gave back the money I stole. Clay has it at the store."

"How dare you call me Mother." Again, she slapped him, this time hard enough for her metal ring to scratch a red mark on his cheek. "You are not my son. I cast you out of my life."

Dempsey's face twisted as he touched the mark.

She slapped him even harder, this time backhanded.

"Sehoy and I've disowned you." King, his lips curled, shrugged.

Sehoy raised her palm to strike Dempsey once more. "Get off our land. You are not welcome in my house."

"Or my property," King said.

"But—"

"My wife told you to leave, Trespasser." King snarled. "We never want to see your traitorous person again."

"I still love y'all." Dempsey uttered his words like a frail old man. He stretched forth his hand toward Barnaby. "Can I have my guns back?"

"No." Barnaby glared at Thomas and Phineas. "Annabelle's folks died a few years ago. Y'all ain't welcome inside the Ox Yoke no more. I told you once, and I ain't saying it again. Get outta here."

"What about me?" Dempsey asked.

"You?" Wickedness curled Barnaby's lips through his thick whiskers. "Me and you got us some unfinished business."

"What sort of business?" Thomas's voice rose. "Me and Phineas demand to know what sort of business."

Barnaby poked Thomas's ribs. "Y'all want Demp back alive? Y'all best do what I tell you."

Clearing his throat, Phineas nudged Thomas. "Let's do as the man says."

While Phineas dragged Thomas away, Thomas kept glancing behind him. Barnaby marched Dempsey past a large crepe myrtle, down a wooded path.

Phineas eyed them. "Don't you fret, Dempsey. It ain't over yet."

"I'm following him."

"Thinking the same direction."

Careful to maintain a discrete distance, Thomas and Phineas slipped into the woods.

"Going somewhere?" A snickering Ruffian emerged from some brush. "Barnaby figured you'd try and follow."

"Reckon he figured right." As though he intended to leave, Thomas half-pivoted. Then he whirled on the Ruffian to slug him. The man's fist smacked his gut. Pain swooshed Thomas's breath from him as he doubled over and clutched his stomach.

Phineas moved to intervene.

"Back off, Preacher." The Ruffian whipped a big knife from a sheath belted round his ample waist. "One more step, and you and your friend'll be feeding the vultures."

Phineas hesitated.

"Do what my friend says." A second man's feet crunched dead leaves as he approached from behind.

Recovered from the Ruffian's blow, Thomas whacked dust off his sleeves and gritted his teeth. To attack both men, he'd risk his and Phineas's life, and Dempsey's too, because their deaths would leave Dempsey on his own. Unwise to fight them both? *Likely so.*

"All right. Let me get our horses." Sighing, Phineas walked off.

"Make it fast," the man behind them said.

Phineas nodded and continued to the animals.

FRIDAY, FEBRUARY 7, 1812
KING'S BROOK, ALABAMA COUNTRY, MISSISSIPPI TERRITORY

Despite his leather gloves and Phineas's campfire Thomas's stiff fingers, which he held over the campfire's crackling flames, were icicles in the spears of moonlight lancing their somber vigil. Its acrid smoke irritated his nostrils. The intolerable weather compounded their concerns about Dempsey as well as the young Ruffian who guarded them on the packhorse path.

"We've gotta find where Barnaby took Dempsey," Thomas whispered.

Phineas's teeth chattered. "W-We're thinking the-the same direction." He indicated the Ruffian cradling a musket. "Bobby's got his backside facing us."

"We gonna sneak past him?"

Phineas scooted within arm's length of Thomas, closer to the blaze. "Soon as I c-can, I'll ride to the military c-camp at Mount Vernon and bring the soldiers here." He shivered. "Brr."

"Ain't Fort Stoddert closer?"

"Pert near the same distance. Soldiers moved out of Fort Stoddert last year, what-what a person in Maryvale t-told me. The fever hits it, the reason."

"It ain't the fever season.

"S'ppose I'll go to Fort Stoddert first, then, to be sure."

Bobby rolled onto his side. His youthful face, smooth as a boy's, fastened on them. "What're you two yapping about?"

"'Bout D-Dempsey," Phineas said between chattering teeth.

"What about him?"

"What's Barnaby done to him?"

"Why ask me? Quit yapping."

Thomas and Phineas quieted.

For the next few minutes, Thomas surveyed their camp. Back in his evil days he'd have killed Bobby to make his escape. A sinful thing, that. "I'm going to catch me some shuteye, Bobby, so don't go off shooting me while I fetch my bedroll."

Stretching, Phineas yawned. "I'm having a snooze against that p-pine tree yonder, Bobby." He took his bedroll from off his horse.

Under Bobby's suspicious gaze, Thomas spread out his bedding beside Phineas. They'd shifted from the campfire into a darker, though colder, part of their camp, a safer place for them to talk.

"Oughtn't we tell the bishop about everything's been happening?" Thomas whispered.

"I'll write him our r-report from Mount Vernon. Ain't no chance King's going to s-send it to him." Phineas sat up. "Over yonder."

Thomas lifted his eyes in the direction his mentor indicated. "Two of 'em. Enough for both of us."

"Shhh." Phineas crawled toward it, one of two small logs, grabbed one, and crawled back.

Pulling his blanket over his head, Thomas pretended to sleep but caught Phineas pointing at Bobby.

Bobby sat against the tree, nodding, his musket on the ground.

Good. He's almost asleep. Thomas crept to the second small log, slipped it beneath his blanket, and raised it a little to make it, as best he could, resemble his head. On his knees, he crawled to Phineas, the cold ground rough and hard. "Reckon I'm gone. Bobby's pert near asleep."

"I'll be going soon as I'm sure he's wandered off into dreamland. Leave yours and Dempsey's horses here for now."

Thomas tipped his hat and made a wide, stealthy circle around Bobby. Some twenty yards distance, he crossed the path and struck out for the settlement. Hopefully most folks were in bed at this hour.

Guided by heaven's lights, he catfooted into King's Brook. He surveyed his idle surroundings, several log buildings scattered amongst trees, and followed the starlit pebbled path Barnaby and Dempsey took to Dempsey's home. He proceeded past pastures and cows interspersed among timber. After a lengthy stretch he spotted his landmark— the big crepe myrtle.

Pebbles pricking the battered soles of his worn-out shoes, Thomas hastened past the tree and down the road. A mile later, snores lured him to a white structure on a bluff, stark against the full moon's light. High windows. Barred. Thomas's hands clenched. *A calaboose.*

He crept to the tiny jail. At its oak door, a young man swathed in several blankets slept beside a sizzling fire. A Ruffian, he figured, who was supposed to be guarding someone.

Thomas slinked around behind the structure. On tiptoes, he peered inside where Dempsey paced, his wrists bound in front of him by a thin rope, muttering his frustration. "Dog it. Dog it. Dog it."

"Psst."

Dempsey's head twisted toward Thomas.

"What're they doing to you?" Thomas whispered. "Why are you in this calaboose?"

At the window, Dempsey spoke softer. "Barnaby tried shooting me, but Annabelle didn't load the pistol like he'd told her. It dryfired.

He got so mad I thought he'd explode. He went to my father to tell him what happened and came back, swearing he'd make an example of me and hang me tomorrow."

"I gotta get you outta here."

"How?"

"Keep your peepers on the door."

"My what?"

"Your peepers." Thomas touched his eyes. He withdrew to the snoring Ruffian who'd curled his knees close to his chest. Was the jail key lying around him or in his pocket? No sign of it. It must be on his person. Should he risk waking the man to search his pockets?

"Psst." Dempsey's bound wrists gestured from the window.

Glancing to where he pointed, Thomas moved toward the key. When the Ruffian rolled over onto his other side, he revealed it in the dirt beneath him, but before Thomas grabbed it the Ruffian rolled back over it.

Thomas pulled his watch from his vest pocket, flipped it over and over, awaiting another opportunity. Maybe he should waken him, slug the daylights out of him, or lock him in the jail. Yet he hesitated. If the man shouted, someone nearby might hear him. Or, were folks too far away?

By the time the sun peeked over the horizon the Ruffian still hadn't moved.

Thomas stared at the man. He brought back his foot to gently kick and waken him but the man rolled over again, revealing the key.

Thomas snatched it and unlocked the door.

The Ruffian stirred.

Thomas glanced behind him. Still, the man slept.

Dempsey stepped out, Thomas dropped the key back in its place and led him north, to their horses. There, using a knife he took from Dempsey's saddlebag, he freed his friend from his bonds.

"We'll catch up with Phineas." Thomas spoke low enough so as not to awaken Bobby.

"I don't know how I can thank you," Dempsey whispered.

"Being our friend is thanks enough. C'mon. Let's hurry. I figure it'll be broad daylight in pert near an hour."

CHAPTER TWENTY-TWO

Barnaby yanked Annabelle off the dining chair and dodged the boiled egg she flung at him.

"I ain't no liar," she screamed.

He shoved her against the wall.

She winced, hissed. Crimson swamped her battered black-and-blue face.

"You are a stupid li'l liar." Barnaby advanced to grip her neck.

She darted behind the dining table, quaking.

Barnaby stomped to her. "Lying to Gopher, telling him you loaded my gun. You're uglier'n a sow in mud. You disobey me again or tell anyone I hit you, I'll do more'n beat you like I did last night. I'll kill you." He leaned into her. "I swear it, you pig. Stay home today." He tweaked a button on her cotton dress. "Did mice eat what you're wearing? I'll check on getting Demp hung."

Barnaby slammed the door behind him, climbed into his buggy, and drove to the jail. At least Demp spent the night fretting over his demise.

Upon his arrival Barnaby slowed his buggy horse to a halt in front of Clay, awaiting him beside the jail and whose fierce scowl warned him something must've gone wrong overnight. "You sent Loomis home?"

Clay thumbed the jail door. "Locked him in there."

"Why?"

"Demp's escaped."

"Escaped?" The news thunderstruck Barnaby. He peeked inside a barred window. Loomis McElroy slumped cross-legged in a corner on the earthen floor, his head sagging against his chest. "All right, Loomis. Out with it. What happened?"

Loomis, mumbling, didn't lift his head. "Don't know."

"Claims he fell asleep atop the jail key." Clay swept a lock of hair away from his forehead. "Must've rolled over off it."

"And someone came to this jail, got it, and let Demp out." Barnaby's knuckles swiped his nose. "Only way I figure it happened."

"I'll bet money one of those preacher friends of his did it."

"You'd win that bet. And I'd put money on it being Preacher Murcher."

"We shouldn't have let them sleep on the outskirts. We should've made 'em ride on to the next settlement."

"Our mistake. They're probably long gone by now." Leaning into the window's bars, Barnaby snickered. "Hey, Loomis. Hope you enjoy taking Demp's place getting your neck stretched."

Loomis's head snapped up. "You mean—?"

"You committed a capital offense. Hanging at noon today, from the oak tree in front of the Ox Yoke." He shook Clay's shoulder. "Keep an eye on him. I'll get over to your father and tell him the news. Better get Bobby, too, for letting the preachers escape."

"Going to hang him also?"

"Not this time. He's a li'l young and still learning our trade. We'll put the fear in him, though, and make his folks give him a firm talking to."

"Loomis's folks?"

"What about them?"

Clay, slumped, kicked a rock. "Yeah. What about them."

Barnaby, hardened to Loomis's squalls, drove off in his buggy. Despite what he'd said, Loomis wouldn't be hanged either, not yet, not unless Mister King said otherwise, but putting a little fear in his boys was one way to control them.

CHAPTER TWENTY-THREE

"You figure me and you oughta go sermonizing in King's Brook again?" Thomas guided his mount around narrow twists and turns, Phineas ahead of him and Dempsey behind him, as they navigated a path through the thick timber. Squirrels scampered up trees, the piney woods' scent wafted on a gentle breeze, and his horse moved along at a slow, steady clip-clop.

"I s'ppose King and his Ruffians figure one of us helped Dempsey escape." Phineas whipped out his handkerchief and mopped sweat off his brow. "They sure hoodwinked those soldiers and the law officer when they checked into what we told 'em was happening. Told me they found nothing serious."

"In my opinion, sir, there's some mighty fearful folks there."

"Fearful of King and his Ruffians. He may be paying off folks to keep quiet about his doings."

"Reason why nobody's talking, I figure. Folks scared, and folks who can do something about it ain't doing it. Seems the Bigbee and Tensaw regions ain't worth the Mississippi Territory's time keeping law and order."

"Five keys to winning those people, Thomas, the way I see it."

"Dempsey's parents, Clay, Barnaby, and Annabelle."

"We're thinking the same direction." Phineas twisted in his saddle. "What are your ponderings on the matter, Dempsey?"

Dempsey made no response.

"Dempsey?" Thomas peered over his shoulder.

Dempsey, his horse's reins in his lap, kept his serene countenance fixed ahead as though in a daydream.

Finger to his lips, Phineas said, "S'ppose he's got his mind latched onto something prettier."

"Oh." Ever since they'd left Saint Stephens after their meetings there Dempsey rarely spoke, except when Kana's name entered their conversation. At the mere mention of her, he livened up so much neither he nor Phineas worked a word in edgewise.

When they rode onto her yard, Kana dropped her sewing and hurried to them from her cabin's breezeway.

Dempsey swung off his saddle quicker than Thomas and Phineas and doffed his hat.

Her arms outstretched, Kana dove into his embrace. She cocked an eyebrow. "Is it forbidden?"

"From a pretty Choctaw lady?" Dempsey stroked her long hair. "Never."

Smiling wide as the Alabama River, she gave him a huge hug and led him inside.

My oh my. Thomas breathed a wistful sigh. If only a lady gave him such a welcome. Annabelle's figure flashed before him. *Too much attitude. Never her.* Her image vanished.

Wait. Why did he imagine her? They'd only met twice. No girl he knew wanted him anyway, so why did she appear in his mind? Besides, marriage meant quitting the circuit and settling permanent somewhere. Many years ago, he vowed he'd never again risk another girl's rejection after suffering so many. Be a friend to females, of course, but he always took care to keep arm's distance from them emotionally.

When Dempsey and Kana parted, she quickly hugged Thomas and Phineas.

Inside her cabin, she gave them sassafras tea. Thomas opened his mouth to compliment her on the drink, but Dempsey plunged into conversation first.

"Wonderful tea from a wonderful girl." Dempsey smiled above the rim of his cup, held close to his lips.

"Easy to make," Kana said. "You travel with my friends all the time?"

"When it suits me." Dempsey's finger slowly traced the cup's rim, shallow creases emerging on his brow. "How is your uncle doing?"

"He is well."

"I hope I can visit your family again."

Kana beamed. "You will be able to, Mister King. You will. I told my family about your visit here last time. They all wish to see you again."

Engrossed in conversation, Dempsey and Kana caught up on news and shared old memories, even laughing at some of Dempsey's innocent mischief in her village many years ago. Phineas laughed too. Thomas, slumped in his chair, chuckled as a pretense, for his memories wandered to his youthful years, to that day he found himself lost in the Georgia woodlands during a deer hunt. Alone and abandoned, it seemed. A frightful experience, till Cousin Reuben found him after a long search. Whether they intended to or not, Dempsey and Kana abandoned him, ignored him, during their chatter. He shrugged. He was used to it.

"And Father was none the wiser," Dempsey said, wrapping up his stories and snapping Thomas back to the present.

Kana's mirth ceased. "You disappointed my uncle and aunt when you became a Ruffian. It disappointed me too."

"It's all behind me. Forever. I promise. I am a believer in Christ, the Great One, now." Dempsey propped his chin on his upraised fists. "Since our friendship is renewed, we don't need to worry about my parents anymore, do we? They've disowned me and kicked me out of my village."

"That is good, Dempsey King?"

"In a way. Yes. It's good." Dempsey nodded.

While Thomas swilled the rest of his tea Phineas made his way outside.

Thomas stepped off the cabin's breezeway into the cool evening air. "I'd say Demp and Kana's relationship is gonna soon be blooming."

"You ain't memorized the book of Leviticus yet?" Phineas strolled to the hog pen to observe the stock.

"Leviticus?" Thomas scratched his cheek, also stepped to the pen. Was he supposed to memorize the whole entire book? All those rules about offerings and such?

A hog waddled to the fence rail, squealed, grunted, and sniffed Thomas's trousers. *Eew.* What an odor hogs carried.

"A mere joke, my friend. Let's go into the barn where we can study." Phineas cracked open the barn door. "I've been doing a mighty long stretch of pondering. Maybe we shouldn't go back to King's settlement yet. Give 'em time to simmer off after what we done, helping our friend and all." He continued opening the door till it swung wide. "Time for your Bible lesson, my friend."

A half hour later Dempsey, whistling, led Kana, also whistling, into the barn. She swung a pair of pucker-toe moccasins in her right hand.

"Friends," Dempsey said, "Kana has persuaded me to live in her village. Tomorrow, I guess, is farewell."

Thomas scrambled to his feet. Dempsey, moving into her village? A matrimonial relationship soon?

"I told her about Jasper. They executed the wrong man," Dempsey said. "Her uncle and Brave Fox must be told this."

"Thinking the same direction." Phineas stood. "But how do you s'ppose you'll find the guilty ones after these many years?"

"We've decided to leave that to a higher judge, the Great One." Kana pointed at Thomas's battered shoes. Their dusty, worn-out toes were nearly severed from their hole-riddled soles. "Mister Dempsey King spoke to me of your shoes. You were having trouble finding new ones, he said."

Thomas studied the moccasins. "I ain't got the money to have new ones made, Lady Grace."

She thrust the moccasins at him gently. "My husband wore these for a short time. It would be his wish for you to wear them until you can find new White man shoes."

Thomas studied them closer. Too large for his feet, but he'd not tell Kana. "Much obliged. Oughta fit dandy."

Next morning, Thomas and Phineas bid Dempsey and Kana goodbye. Soon after, they struck out for a new settlement and another round of sermonizing. On the way there, Phineas sang hymns and Thomas pondered. What sort of folk lived in the new settlement? Were they rattlesnake mean or sociable like those in Bassetts Creek and Maryvale?

His thoughts drifted to Dempsey. From what he'd learned in Bassetts Creek on his last visit there, the conflict between the tribes in this region had grown more dangerous. Would Dempsey be safe living among Kana's people, or would her Choctaw nation be drawn into it? If it was drawn into it, Dempsey would have to fight and might even get killed. He said a prayer for his friend's protection.

CHAPTER TWENTY-FOUR

King, surveying Hiram Vance's fertile cotton acreage, rode his gray horse at a leisurely gait while Lucky kept pace. Several fat clouds scudded across the azure sky, over this lush land he coveted, two-and-a-half miles from the settlement.

Vance's overseer, Colt Dakin, astride his roan mount and dangling a whip, supervised perspiring slaves trudging behind plows. Dakin's sons probably supervised other fields. He waved at King, who acknowledged him with a smile.

Smiled. Considering the fact that he had lost this prime land to Hiram, the land office in Saint Stephens finally awarding Hiram the grant to it at a dollar an acre, King forced the biggest, toothiest smile possible to disguise his disgust. Thus far, he'd made neither offers nor threats to obtain Hiram's property or at least get some of the man's money. In due time, however, he'd do it, just as he'd done with a few other farmers in the area. The other settlers in these parts feared him. However, acting quickly wasn't his style. Slow and methodical first, then strike fast and hard, one reason why he'd never been caught. He was always careful and thus, never made mistakes. When he'd lost his land back east to the Rebels after the war against Britain .... He gritted his teeth. That'd never happen again. The more land he acquired the more certain he'd be of that fact, the fact that he'd never suffer poverty again. Oh, yes. In due time, either he'd own this land or else collect "taxes" from Hiram or else Hiram and his family would be dead.

"Patience, Lucky boy." King peered over his shoulder at his hound, who'd dropped back. "Pays to be patient. Come along. We're almost there."

Lucky padded quickly to catch up.

No different from most of the dwellings in this region, Hiram's house was a pine-log structure, and though log, not frame like his and Barnaby's and old Samuel Mims's house, it was rather large. He'd been inside it before. A central hall separated four rooms, two rooms per side. Five smaller buildings surrounded it: a smokehouse, a kitchen, an outhouse, a buggy house, and a stable.

Mary, washing clothes in a big barrel, wrung water from a soaked shirt. Her musket lay on a table beside the barrel. "Ma." She dropped the shirt back into the wash barrel. Her close-set brown eyes warily observed his approach.

"What brings you here today, Mister King?" Mary's mother, Laurice, spoke from a clothesline where she busied herself hanging laundry.

"Paying a friendly social call, Mrs. Vance, is all. Is your husband, by chance, home?"

Mary and her mother swapped anxious glances.

They were hiding something from him. Too obvious.

"He'll be back in a spell." Laurice draped a pillowcase over the line.

"How long has he been gone?"

"A day or two. He's supposed to be home today. Sometime." She plucked a shirt from a large basket.

"Gone to Saint Stephens? To the government's trading post there to trade like one of those filthy Choctaws?"

Both ladies shook their heads no … vigorously.

Liars. He feigned a pleasant demeanor. "With your permission, I'll wait for him here. You ladies may continue your chores."

Laurice's forearm swiped her forehead. She gestured at a rocking chair on the porch.

Before he sat in it, two small yapping dogs shot out the cabin's open door and leaped on Lucky. Lucky rolled onto his back with the smaller dogs atop him, snarling and barking in a playful tussle.

While he rocked and waited and enjoyed Lucky's play, a slave brought him a cup of water from the Vances' well. For hours he waited and rocked till the sun started its descent behind the pine forest. Orange, red, and purple splashed the sky.

When he spotted Hiram's wagon approaching at a clatter, King stood. He and Hiram sized each other up. A slave rushed out of the stable to take charge of the wagon's two-horse team.

"Wait." King strode to the back of the wagon, Hiram and their dogs alongside him.

The slave, who stood at the team, stroked the horses' necks. Lucky and Hiram's dogs romped around them and nipped at each other in endless frolic.

Kegs stood on the wagon bed between two large barrels, and a cedar trunk sat two feet from the end gate. As he'd suspected, Vance bought his merchandise at Saint Stephens ... *instead of patronizing my store.* A burning sensation singed the edges of his soul—no illness. Rage. Before he spoke, he waited a couple of minutes to quell his wrath and force calmness into his manner. "Open it." He aimed his forefinger at the trunk.

Hiram glimpsed Laurice and Mary on the porch cradling muskets.

"Don't open it, Richard," Hiram said. "I'll tell you what's inside it. It's fabric for my girls so they can make some new clothes."

"You bought it from the government store up in Saint Stephens?"

"I most certainly did. A new shipment came in from back east."

King regarded the plowed fields beyond Hiram. He knew how he'd get this land, but not today.

"You"—Hiram cleared his throat— "You aren't angry?"

"Why should I be? Y'all be careful, though. If some ill thing happens to you or your family, Hiram, such as outlaws or any such thing, you can depend on me and my boys to protect you if you want us to."

"For a price?"

"Costs money to protect people." King tipped his hat. "Good evening to you all. Come, Lucky boy. We'll ask Zander to make you a special collar tomorrow."

Lucky barked twice, as though he understood.

King swung into his saddle. On the way home, his plan solidified. Come fall, when cotton blanketed Hiram's fields, he'd hit him where it hurt most—his livelihood.

CHAPTER TWENTY-FIVE

Wednesday, July 14, 1812
Bassetts Creek, Alabama country, Mississippi Territory

"Skuze me, skuze me, skuze me." Thomas, coughing through tobacco's haze, wove around the inn's crowded tables and bumped into a couple of patrons. Plopping his journal on Phineas's table, he then placed a small canvas bag in front of him.

Phineas pulled it close. "Finally got our mail, I see."

"Brother Noble sent me a letter. I sent him one today."

"He and his family are in good health?"

"Yes sir. The denomination sent us more religious publications and tracts. Already put them in my saddlebag." Thomas sat. "They sure don't send us much of a stipend, though." He gestured a server forward. "I'd be obliged for some tea, sir."

Phineas raised his fingers like a vee. "Two teas."

The young man strode off for their orders.

"No more complaining about our salary, Thomas. We'll do fine."

"Yes sir." Thomas rebuked himself. Not easy, not complaining about things—the exhausting rides between settlements, poor weather, flooded creeks, and worries about wild animals. He wrote of these in his journal. He drummed the table. "Some hymnals and Bibles have also arrived. I haven't—"

"We'll get them later. Maybe we can sell some for extra cash."

A sudden, unpleasant memory squirmed Thomas. "Bears out of hibernation now."

The waiter brought them mugs of warm tea.

Phineas inhaled the brew's aroma. "They'll be running from us when they spot us."

"Provided they ain't predaceous."

"Ain't no predaceous black bears in these parts."

"Says you." Thomas sipped his tea. *Umm.* This inn brewed it right. "But I will say the sociable folk in this place makes it the perfect headquarters for us."

Phineas drank his tea in greater gulps.

Thomas sipped his slowly, relishing its warmth and taste. They'd missed their annual conference this year. Revivals in several settlements, the reason. On the Alabama River, a new society had formed. Believers there covenanted to hold each other accountable for how they lived their lives. He prayed for the day God would use his sermonizing the way He used Phineas's. "I figure you still ain't found a violin here you can buy."

"And I ain't liking it one bit." Phineas set aside his mug. "I can't sing Haydn or Mozart or any of my favorite composers. They ain't got lyrics in English, far as I know. I can play 'em, though. If I had a violin, I'd make us some extra spending money. Ask folks to drop money in my hat while I played a tune."

"You sing mighty fine without it, and when you do sing, some folks do drop money in your hat."

"Singing without musical accompaniment ain't the same thing. Musical accompaniment's better'n me singing a cappella."

Thomas studied his shoes. Though they were new for him, they first belonged to a local farmer with whom he'd traded his watch in order to acquire them. Fortunately, he and the farmer wore the same size. He wished he possessed some sort of talent like Phineas did to make himself a few extra dollars.

Phineas nudged a pad toward him. "Here's a list of things we'll be needing before we set out again. The Parkers and Greens promised us food for our journey. We'll be needing to get it from 'em first thing come morning."

"I figure we'll be staying with those same folks we stayed with during our previous journeys?"

"Some are old friends, you recollect. Did I leave out anything you can touch your finger on?"

Thomas pulled the pad closer. Everything Phineas wrote seemed in order.

A familiar voice shouted from the entrance—the devout lawyer Adolphus Fitzpatrick, whom they'd saved from a robbery, waving a sheet of paper. "Attention, everyone. Please. Give me your attention. Some important news."

Curious stares riveted on him.

Mister Fitzpatrick faced them from the bar. "I received a letter from my uncle, over in Georgia. He says the war we've been expecting started last month." He thumped the letter. "I knew it'd happen soon. The way the British kept acting, boarding our ships, forcing our sailors to serve on their naval vessels, harassing our commerce."

"Down with the British!" a man yelled.

Fists pounded tables. "Down! Down!"

"If the Spaniards in West Florida and Great Britain forge an alliance, they're liable to invade our region." Fitzpatrick ambled to Phineas. "You two be careful on your mission. My uncle also read an article about some Creeks who killed some settlers in this territory."

"Thank you, sir," Phineas said. "You and your family be careful too."

"We will be."

Thomas groaned silently. The attacks on Whites were becoming more frequent. Neither he nor Phineas owned a means to protect themselves, except for their eating utensils and a knife they used to clean the fish they caught in streams and rivers. A regretful thing his mentor didn't let him carry a gun. Phineas didn't believe in them, said Christians ought not carry one. He disagreed but held his peace on the subject. However, he did pray they'd never need to use one.

CHAPTER TWENTY-SIX

With Maggie seated beside her clothed in a pale blue hand-me-down dress and bonnet, Annabelle drove her buggy to the Ox Yoke, past folks who gawped at her. She battled hard to ignore them. None of their business what happened to her. She'd not been truthful about her bruises. Soon as they healed, Barnaby would smack her again when something lit his fuse. Later, he'd apologize and be a genl'man.

One thing was certain as a mosquito bite, though. If she dared be truthful about their fights, Barnaby would keep his promise to kill her. At least she didn't have to put up with the brute today. He'd gone to Saint Stephens on business. Not sure what sort of business in that small settlement, but she didn't care. From Saint Stephens, the brute said, he'd ride to Sam Mims's place to buy kitchen help for Maggie.

"I hope you're serving beefsteak today." Lemuel reined his horse close to her on his way to his livery stables, half a mile up ahead.

She responded—a curt nod.

Her parents had been brave, standing up to Mister King and his demands. They'd moved to these parts from Georgia to make a better life. Here, her ma and pa lost a son, Elias, three months after his birth. A year later her ma gave birth to her. Had Elias not died she might've had an older brother to defend her. If only she could right the wrong of her misbehavior, if only she hadn't helped get them killed. They were right as rain about Barnaby and his ilk. Up and run away from that disgusting man? How? Where to? Slumped, she uttered an oath. *Trapped.*

"Why don't you tell 'em, Miss Annabelle? About what that man of yours keeps doing to you?" Maggie said.

"I got my reasons. And you keep keeping your mouth shut, you understand me?"

"Yes'm."

Minutes later, Annabelle stopped at Lemuel's livery where Frank unhitched the buggy's horse. She and Maggie continued to the tavern on foot.

"Let's start work." Annabelle whipped off her tan cotton bonnet and set it on a shelf behind the bar. To a Ruffian who'd tended the tavern's registration desk overnight, she said, "Go home. Get some rest."

The Ruffian swaggered out the door.

Maggie set her bonnet behind the bar before she ducked into the pantry, her long curls bouncing behind her head.

Midafternoon, while Annabelle and Maggie wiped tables, Sehoy entered. A few patrons still ate, travelers on their way to Mississippi country, but most had gone. Annabelle stuffed her rag in her white pinafore's pocket.

Her thin lips tight, Sehoy waited till Gopher took dishes into the pantry before she made her approach. "Join me outside, Annabelle. Woman to woman, we must talk." Sehoy whisked herself outdoors.

Annabelle kept after her.

"My buggy." Sehoy hastened to it.

Annabelle and Sehoy climbed aboard. Sehoy drove it around back and reined in its horse at Annabelle's late parents' house. "We will not be seen here. Your key. Give it to me." Sehoy stretched forth her palm and wiggled her fingers impatiently. "Get off the buggy."

Annabelle obeyed. "My key's in the tavern."

Sehoy pulled Annabelle beneath a tall red oak. Lightly, she touched Annabelle's right cheek. "He has beaten you again."

"No. I-I stumbled off a stool."

"Do not lie to me. I know better. We all know better, even my husband. Your scars. How you have changed. You aren't the strong woman you used to be. I like you, but I do not like what I see in you now."

Annabelle, her shoulders sagging, nodded. "What does Mister King—?"

"He says nothing."

"Oh, Sehoy. What am I to do the next time he beats me?"

"Kill him."

Annabelle started, straightened. "Kill? Again?"

"You did wrong by not loading Barnaby's pistol so he could kill the man who claimed to be my son but Barnaby, too, did wrong to beat you. Men who beat their women deserve death." She reached into her beaded reticule and drew out a penknife. "This blade is sharp. Slit his fat throat in his sleep next time he hits you."

"I might get caught. Hung."

Sehoy thrust the folded knife into Annabelle's palm and closed her fingers over it. "After you kill him run to my house, and I will take you to Mobile. I have a White friend there who lives among the Spaniards. She will keep you safe."

"You sure?"

"Yes." Sehoy climbed aboard her buggy, slapped the reins, and drove off.

Annabelle opened the cold knife. Her fingertip traced the dull backside of its tiny blade. She was already going to Hell because she killed John Wolf. She closed the blade. What was Hell like, if such a place existed? Was it as terrifying as the preachers said? Kill the brute the next time he beat her? She stiffened her wobbly knees. Why not?

THURSDAY JULY 30, 1812
KING'S BROOK, ALABAMA COUNTRY, MISSISSIPPI TERRITORY

"Let's see now. According to you, Crazy Wildcat, we ought to build a stockade." King peered out his store window at doves strutting along the ground. His brother-in-law constantly warned him about a war with the White man. Crazy Wildcat worried worse than a woman.

Under the command of his métis chief, William McIntosh of Coweta, the state of Georgia, Crazy Wildcat had become a law mender. He and other menders enforced the Creek National Council's laws and delivered messages to other villages.

"The Creek National Council executed the warriors who killed two White men." Crazy Wildcat rubbed his strong jaw. "We will find the Creeks who massacred a White family in May."

"Where'd it happen?"

"The Duck River."

"Way up in Tennessee, isn't it?"

"It is. Much trouble and death are coming soon, to many. You Whites have angered many who want to kill you. So has our Council, because it has been selling land to the father in Washington for your people to hunt. The White man lets his cattle graze our land. Your people call it trespassing because it's our land, not yours. Some of my people among the Lower Creeks wrote a letter to the governor of Georgia about it. What did he do? Nothing."

"You disapprove of our, er, trespassing?"

"It will not be me who will fight you over land and cattle and that road your people are building through our nation." Crazy Wildcat sidled up beside him. "It will be those Creeks who believe the foolish prophets and carry the red warclubs." His fierceness sharpened on King. "They will kill you. One day soon. If my sister is killed or is harmed because of your foolishness"— Crazy Wildcat flashed his big scalping knife at King— "it will be my pleasure to add your scalp to my collection."

King gripped Crazy Wildcat's forearm and forced it, and the knife, to the Creek's side. "We can always go to Fort Stoddert or Saint Stephens. Your sister will be safe if war breaks out. We'll find refuge if, and when, General Claiborne gives the alarm."

Crazy Wildcat grunted. "The territorial militia?"

"Claiborne got command of it a few months ago."

Crazy Wildcat spat. "By the time they give the alarm many White men, and many of us who will fight on your people's side, will be dead. Be a wise man. Listen to my counsel. Build a stockade."

"I'll take your advice under consideration." He merely said that to shut him up.

"You have seen Barnaby Hatch?" Crazy Wildcat asked.

"He's away right now."

"Last time I saw his woman, she had bruises. She had been beaten again."

"He beats her from time to time. True enough, though she won't admit it. What is your opinion of a man who beats his woman?"

Crazy Wildcat again brandished his scalping knife. Its edge pricked King's left nostril.

"You would be the fool and beat my sister, Richard King?"

"Never. We're in love." *A truth, thank goodness.* He knew Crazy Wildcat harbored no fondness for him and only visited to check on Sehoy out of concern for her welfare. Raising this big Creek's dander would prove to be a fatal mistake. Her brother's advice not to beat her, he would take.

Crazy Wildcat grunted and returned his knife to his belt. "You ever beat her, I will send you to your ancestors."

"Would you send Barnaby to his ancestors for beating Annabelle? And add his scalp to your collection?"

"He is not my family."

"I feel the same way." As he spoke, King hit upon a decision. When Barnaby returned, he'd discuss with him regarding his treatment of Annabelle, and he'd best listen to what he said.

CHAPTER TWENTY-SEVEN

Upon crossing the Alabama River on Samuel Mims's ferry and after a quick visit to the O'Neals, who lived nearby, Thomas and Phineas continued riding up the Federal Road. Phineas's niece had written him a letter asking him to preside over her wedding in Macon, Georgia.

Everywhere they traveled, particularly in this growing Tensaw River region, Phineas sought a violin to replace the one he'd lost. Although they'd encountered several folks who owned one, he'd not found any for purchase, at least none he could afford.

"Maybe you can buy a new violin in Georgia." Even as Thomas suggested this, he'd put a secret plan in motion. Noble's idea. A surprise.

"I hope so."

"What do you figure, Phineas? Have I measured up? My sermonizing. Has it—?"

"You've been doing fine, Thomas."

"One more year riding with you, I figure I'm on my own?"

"S'ppose so. Keep yourself faithful, you'll be accepted in full connection. When you're on your own, each circuit usually lasts a year before the bishop moves you somewhere else."

"Yes sir. Obliged. I'm aware of that."

For several minutes, Thomas and Phineas rode in silence. Blue jays swooped ahead of them and perched in the sprawling canopies of red oaks and white oaks. Cooing doves strutted among the brush. Beyond them, two white-tail deer darted out of the timber. The day waxed warmer. Thomas removed his wide-brimmed black hat, swiped the sweat trickling over his brow, down his cheeks. He unbuttoned his coat.

"Elder Matthias may have passed on." Phineas finally broke the silence. "But me and Elder Wilkes get along. Him and me once worked in neighboring circuits in North Carolina. Keep doing what you been doing. You'll make a fine horse preacher one day. I enjoy your preaching when you do it."

"But—"

"We preached a revival last month, didn't we? In your brother's settlement. You done most of the preaching there. Him and his family enjoyed it."

"I enjoyed our time together, but a society's already there. And my sermonizing. I ain't got your giftings."

"Book of Revelation. Chapter one, verse nineteen." Phineas snapped out the reference.

The verse popped into Thomas's head. "Write the things which thou hast seen, and the things which are, and the things which shall be hereafter."

"Don't judge yourself too harshly. You got the giftings. You're getting better at memorizing the Good Book. It's showing in your preaching."

Showing in his preaching? Phineas's words encouraged Thomas … a little. No eloquence flowed from his mouth, nor could he carry a note in a bucket. Whatever gift he was supposed to possess, it'd never equal his mentor's. His preaching didn't spark that revival. It was God's doings. Besides, the congregation had been accepting of God's holy word.

From a side path, a soothing melody wafted from some trees, causing them to rein their horses to a stop. The glow in his mentor's countenance showed Thomas what he already knew. The music flowed from a violin. Phineas trotted his horse toward the sound. Thomas followed.

In a cool grove of trees, a neatly dressed young man seated on a stool gently drew a bow across a violin's strings. Phineas hummed the tune, dismounted, and let Thomas take his reins. He went to the man. "Joseph Haydn's 'Serenade.'" He clapped. "Beautiful."

The bright-eyed man, his brow furrowed, lowered his instrument onto his lap.

"Well, I'll be a cat's kitten." Chuckling, Phineas slapped his thigh. "Joseph Mims? Is it you?"

"Preacher?" Joseph stood, blinked. "Reverend Steward?"

"Alive and in the flesh." Phineas grinned at Joseph's violin. "My, my, how you've grown. It's been years since I last saw you. Our socializing was so brief a few years ago. I didn't have an inkling of an idea you played a musical instrument."

"Father does too."

"The violin?"

Joseph nodded.

"May I? I lost mine and haven't played one in a long spell."

Joseph clutched his instrument tight against his chest. "Religious music?"

"Not one Protestant note will sound from its bow. My word of honor."

A moment passed before Joseph let him borrow it.

Phineas tucked its chinrest beneath his chin and held the bow over the strings. "Oh, forgive me." He lifted his chin at Thomas. "My associate, Thomas Murcher."

Thomas and Joseph acknowledged each other.

"Johann Sebastian Bach." Phineas set the bow across the instrument's strings. "'Sonata for Violin Solo Number One in G Minor.'"

Thanks to Phineas, Thomas had learned a few things about Bach. It was Phineas's mother who taught him about composers, how to read music, and how to play it. His head cocked as the instrument's neck lay on his shoulder, Phineas moved the bow along its strings, playing the tune. When he finished his little concert, Joseph applauded.

"An excellent musical instrument, Joseph. Where'd you buy it? Mobile?"

"Preacher!" Barnaby, driving his wagon, boomed his greeting. A girl sat in Barnaby's wagon bed. No doubt, a slave. A goateed man trotted his mount alongside him.

"Mister Mims." Phineas doffed his hat in greeting. "Heading over to my niece's wedding in Georgia when I heard Joseph playing a beautiful song."

Reddening, Mims froze. His goatee quivered. "Don't go preaching at us again, Reverend Steward."

"Not this time, sir." Phineas raised his hand.

"He ain't preaching in Mister King's settlement again either," Barnaby said.

"Tried to preach there, did he?" The red in Mims's face receded.

"Tried." Sneering, Barnaby gathered his wagon team's reins. "About all he can do is try. Got to take Suzie back home." He glanced at the girl behind him. "Thank you again for selling her to me, Mister Mims. She'll be a great help in the kitchen."

"Anytime." Mister Mims waved goodbye.

The wagon clattered up the path, onto the road toward Mims's Ferry.

Without another word, Mims headed for his house and Joseph, also silent, mounted his horse and left with him.

"Mister Mims holds more parties than anyone I've ever known." Phineas climbed into his saddle. "Went inside his house once, a big frame one same as Mister King's."

"He don't appear too friendly." Thomas spoke as Mister Mims and Joseph rounded a turn, out of sight.

"He ain't a bad person, long as you don't go preaching to him. Fellow lives for fun, about all. He ain't even much of a Catholic."

Thomas and Phineas proceeded up the path, back onto the Federal Road, and spoke greetings at two covered wagons approaching. More people moving in. Of the Protestant persuasion, Thomas hoped. The thought of his and Noble's plan rested pleasantly upon him. Noble said he'd write their cousin Reuben about Phineas's lost violin. Perhaps the society there could take up a collection for him to acquire a new one. The surprise awaiting his mentor. Problem solved, more music, provided everything proceeded according to the plan.

CHAPTER TWENTY-EIGHT

Barnaby glowered at a squirrel skittering across the grass outside King's office window. The critter moved fast, as fast as Barnaby wanted to escape King's wrath, but he dare not make the attempt. When King coughed, Barnaby pivoted toward him. The man's shrewd eyes resembled a cougar poised to strike.

"Answer my question, Barnaby Hatch," King growled.

Dryness sapped Barnaby's saliva.

Fists on his desk, his boss leaned forward in his leather armchair. "Answer it."

"I don't beat her, sir. She fell."

King pounded his desk, loud as a cannon shot. "Liar. We're all fully aware that you beat her."

"She told you?"

"It's obvious. Her bruises, and the way she's changed."

Barnaby shifted uneasily.

"Look at me when I'm talking to you, Mister."

Barnaby locked on his boss. *Aha.* Mister King suspected the whole time he and Annabelle weren't telling the truth, did he? King might toss him out of town, or even worse, kill him. He wouldn't put anything past the man. Though his insides cringed, Barnaby managed a bold front.

King caught a flitting mosquito and crushed it on his desk beneath his palm.

Barnaby flinched. The mosquito might've been him.

"She should've loaded the pistol like you ordered her to do and shouldn't have lied to us." King slapped at more flitting mosquitoes.

"Y-Yes sir. That's why—"

"Why you beat her. She deserved to be punished."

"But not beaten?"

"Did you hear me say that?"

Barnaby, chilled by King's menacing manner, shook his head.

"Before you beat her again, Mister, ask me for permission first." King drew his horse pistol out of a drawer and laid it on his desk. "I am judge and jury in this settlement. I am the one who pronounces punishments." Cocking his brow at Barnaby, he stroked the big pistol's brass barrel.

Barnaby nodded quickly. It'd been months since he'd seen his boss this riled. "It ain't never gonna happen again, Mister King."

"It better not." He raised his pistol. "Over and done with. Go tell the other Ruffians to meet here tonight. It's time we make plans to do something about Vance's land."

"Y-Yes sir." Barnaby hurried from King's store. *Whew.* He might've been shot today. Next time Annabelle got on his nerves, next time that pig-ugly woman disobeyed him, he'd ask Mister King for permission first and then he'd beat the daylights out of her.

CHAPTER TWENTY-NINE

Hiram Vance's Farm, Alabama country, Mississippi Territory

Ahead of eight other Ruffians, Barnaby afoot led his horse on a lead through a stand of trees. Dusk cooled the scorching day. A chorus of cicadas raised constant racket. Disguised as warriors, they wore buckskin leggings, hunting shirts, and silver armbands. Blankets draped their saddleless horses' backs. This way, the Creeks would catch blame for what they intended to inflict on Hiram.

Nearing one of Hiram's fields, his raised hand signaled his friends to stop on the tree line. Slaves trudged toward their log dwellings. Colt Dakin and his three sons rode horses behind them.

Half a mile away, candle lights shimmered in Hiram's cabin. Were he and his family inside it, or outside? If outside, where? Barnaby remembered the shooting contest Mister King sponsored last year. Among the women, Mary and her mother won top spots. Among the men, Barnaby finished second behind Mister King, whereas Hiram placed third. Those Vance women weren't fools. Their marksmanship made them worthy of his concern.

"Clay." Barnaby spoke in a low voice. "Take two of our boys yonder way." He pointed south, where cattle grazed and a few rested on the grass beside a smudge— smoking green timber meant to keep copperheads and rattlesnakes away—not far from Vance's house. "The minute we set fire to this cotton, start hollering and whooping and scatter Vance's beeves. Keep a sharp eye out for Vance's females. Remember, they're mighty dangerous with their guns."

Clay selected two others to accompany him.

"If any man gets wounded or killed, Clay," Barnaby continued, "drag him off and take him to your father's house."

"Right." In a matter of minutes, Clay and his men positioned themselves on the tree line opposite the smudge.

"Gopher," Barnaby said, "when I give the word, light the torches and tell the boys to load their guns and nock their arrows."

"Gonna be fun." Gopher chuckled.

Bow in one hand and his horse's lead in the other, Barnaby slipped back through the woods, around Hiram's slave cabins and Dakin's dogtrot after he spotted the Dakins, armed with guns, going into a field. They must have expected something would happen tonight. Lying in wait for him, were they? He'd oblige them in that regard. A mile later, he edged into the cotton and knelt to determine his bearings. Hopefully, the Dakins were out of range. Not a single waving stalk betrayed their location.

Grabbing an arrow in the quiver slung over his shoulder, Barnaby nocked the missile in his bow, then loosed a war whoop before he let his arrow fly. It sailed in a high arc to distract the Dakins from the other Ruffians' doings.

Musketry erupted from the stalks. Barnaby shot another arrow, plowed through the cotton to a different spot, whipped his pistol from his trousers waist and started to load it when roaring flames consumed the crop behind him. Gopher and others, wielding torches and whooping, galloped off. The Dakins sprang into their saddles and gave chase.

Once they were out of sight, Barnaby mounted his horse and galloped to Clay's men. From Hiram's cabin, hissing musket balls zipped past him.

Clay and his boys sped their horses in confusing patterns, hoofs thundering, cows scattering. Hiram and his girls missed their marks.

The ladies hit a still target easy, but a moving one proved more difficult. Barnaby made a mental note. Something to remember.

At the head of his companions, Clay disappeared into the trees. The musketry turned sporadic, then died. The Vances stood on their porch, probably feeling helpless at the sight of their blazing field.

Barnaby wished he was close enough to see their expressions, but he dare not risk being recognized. He fired a final glance at Hiram and his family before he overtook Clay. "Let's go tell your father."

"Yes." His fist raised triumphantly, Clay wheeled his cantering horse down a timber path and led the way home.

SUNDAY, SEPTEMBER 13, 1812
KING'S BROOK, ALABAMA COUNTRY, MISSISSIPPI TERRITORY

Through his parlor window, Lucky at his side, King spied Hiram trotting his horse up the road to his house. Judging by his contorted expression and downturned lips, the man appeared awful angry. *Now what?*

Sehoy joined him. "Do you think he knows we did it, Husband?"

"We'll find out soon enough."

"I will get my pistol in case we need it." She swept into the hall. "I will shoot him dead."

Seconds after Hiram hitched his horse to a short iron post, King met him outdoors. Sehoy stood beside him on the porch, and drooling Lucky leaned against his legs.

Hiram inhaled a long, steady breath. "Someone destroyed my cotton last night."

"Sorry that happened." King scratched Lucky behind his ears.

"I'm sure you are."

Sarcastic, isn't he? "We didn't do it, Hiram. Probably some of those Creeks causing trouble."

"A Creek with red hair who rode Clay's horse? I recognized your son immediately when he scattered my cattle." Hiram's hand inched toward the big pistol poking from his cartridge belt.

"Do not do it, Mister Vance." Venom poisoned Sehoy's voice as she brought up her cocked pistol. "Else I will kill you where you stand now."

"I'm sure you will, you little witch." Hiram hesitated before he lowered his hand. "You have no conscience."

"You are right," Sehoy said smugly. "I do not."

"We can always protect you and your land," King said.

"We can protect ourselves."

"Sure you can, Hiram. I can set a guard around your property in case your land is hit again."

"For a price."

King shrugged. "It costs money to protect people."

"I ain't paying you nothing." Hiram mounted his horse and rode away.

His arm around Sehoy's shoulders, King steered her back inside the house. "We aren't done with the Vances, my love."

Sehoy sneered. "Next time, let's kill them."

"Certainly. But killing takes time and careful planning, my wife, if we don't want to get caught."

"Of course." She broke from him and strode down the hall, yelling at two of their servants to hurry up and prepare their lunch.

1813-1814

CHAPTER THIRTY

Hoofbeats brought Billy Weatherford out of a corn field where his slaves were working. At the head of four other braves, a big man astride a brown horse rode toward his house, past his children Polly and Charles playfully wrestling in its yard. He broke into a pleasant smile. His cousin, Chief William McIntosh, Speaker of the Lower Creeks, had come to pay him a visit. Crazy Wildcat too.

The chasm had deepened between supporters of the settlers and those who opposed them. *War.* Billy almost heard the whistle of arrows and the shouts of warriors and the blasts of musketry. Even the smell of blood lingered in his nostrils. He was a métis. Creek blood coursed his veins. The thought of killing his kinsmen in a war on the brink of breaking out sent cold shudders through him.

"Welcome, my brothers, my friends." Billy reined in his gray horse, Arrow, in front of his house and dismounted. "It is good to see you again."

"It is true, Cousin," McIntosh said, dismounting with his men.

Billy gestured at four slaves to take his guests' horses to a paddock. "Come inside. Whiskey, anyone? Something to eat?"

"Not today, Cousin." McIntosh and his braves accompanied Billy into his home. "We thank you."

Crazy Wildcat sat cross-legged on the parlor's red rug and other menders on upholstered chairs and a settee. A small clock ticked on the stone fireplace's white marble mantel. A crackling fire blazed beneath it, behind an iron screen.

Charles and Polly came indoors, greeted their guests, then argued about their wrestling game. Polly was slender, Charles broad.

"I did so beat you, Polly." Charles scrunched his narrow brow.

Polly patted his head. "No, you didn't."

"Don't you pat my head." Charles reared on his toes. "I'm a man."

Polly chortled. "In a few years."

"Enough," Billy snapped. "Go outside and play."

Grudgingly, after waving bye to Chief McIntosh, the children obeyed.

"You've heard the news?" Billy pulled off his deerskin gloves and set them on an ebony table.

"The murders on the Ohio?" Chief McIntosh's dark face twitched when he talked. "The agent to the Chickasaws, Mister Robertson, says some of them committed the crime. Not our people."

"Let's hope he's right."

"If he's mistaken, and it is our people—"

"You and your law menders will catch them and execute them, Cousin." Billy's somber eyes searched the braves. "Many in our towns do not like our National Council dealing out justice. Many do not like your law menders because you carry out the council's will."

"Those who dislike us believe justice and punishment belong to individual towns." Chief McIntosh folded his arms over his powerful chest and shook his head. "They're wrong, Billy. The times are changing. We must change with the times."

"The changing times. It's true. I enjoy my life here." Billy clasped his large hands behind his back. "I fear events are spinning out of control. We are rushing headlong into conflict. We are not thinking things through. Creeks against Creeks, followers of the prophets against our White friends. Men will die. Members of my family, your family, Cousin, will die. Brave warriors on both sides. Over what? Over the road the White men built through our land? Over customs and traditions? We cannot defeat the settlers. I have shared this view with our people many times."

"You still prefer us to stay neutral?"

"We would be wise to do so. We should not fight each other, nor should we fight our White friends."

"But the day will soon come when we must choose a side." The chief grasped a bronze horse statuette off the fireplace mantel and flipped it over in his palm. "We come from the same clan. Our families wield lots of influence among our people. We'll have to either choose the prophets' side, Josiah Francis and High-Head Jim and others. Or else choose the settlers' side. We'll both be leaders in the war lurking on the horizon."

Billy received the bronze horse from his cousin and set it back on the mantel. "You'll take the settlers' side."

McIntosh straightened. "You'll fight with us too, Billy? You will help me lead our warriors?"

"I am not a chief."

"But your influence among our people is great."

Billy scratched behind his right ear, opened his mouth to speak, and paused, unsure what he'd do when the time came to fight. "Let me show you the new horses I bought in Pensacola."

CHAPTER THIRTY-ONE

"**S**top." Annabelle darted out of the Ox Yoke and overtook the Ruffians as two of them, wrenching Phineas's and Thomas's arms behind their backs, drove them forward. Barnaby quick-stepped ahead. Gopher banged cadence on a snare drum. Two fat feather pillows rested in Clay's arms, clutched against his chest.

When Annabelle spotted their destination, she gasped. An enormous barrel of pine tar stood at the end of the path beside a smoking pot of coals. *Oh no.*

"Death to preachers. Death to preachers," the swaggering Ruffians chanted.

Thomas, grimacing, writhed in their grips. Phineas, however, stared straight ahead as though on a Sabbath-day stroll.

Striding back and forth behind the small cluster of spectators, Annabelle kept pleading. "Y'all have to do something. Have to help them."

"You do something, girl," Mary Vance said. "I don't much fancy my pretty little self getting tarred and feathered. Anyway, I ain't got my gun to shoot 'em."

"Where's your pa? Your ma?"

"They ain't here." Mary frowned at the unfolding events.

Annabelle understood Mary's frustration, the reason for her outburst. She couldn't fight so many Ruffians by herself. Without her musket, she was as helpless as a newborn kitten.

Patience Morgan, slightly hunched with age, touched Annabelle's arm. "Our men want to help, dear. Most of us like them preachers."

"But the men are scared of them Ruffians." Annabelle made tracks for the livery stable. In front of its open doors, Lemuel observed the vicious parade. "Mister Cooper. You're a big man." She tugged his arms. "Help them preachers. Please."

Lemuel's complacent demeanor shifted to her. "Why'd you take a liking to them all of a sudden when you used to hate them so much?"

"I realized the error of my ways. Get some men. Fight. Don't let them preachers get tarred and feathered."

"Get out of here, girl. You're blocking my view."

Arms folded, Annabelle harumphed and stayed put.

Lemuel inched past her.

Frank, mucking rake in hand, emerged from behind a stable door. "Aww, Miss Annabelle. Don't you understand what'll happen if we try to stop it?"

Annabelle muttered. The men in this settlement, all a flock of chickens. Well, she'd not let it happen. Hiking her dress, she whisked herself away. She remembered meeting Thomas a few years back and his and Barnaby's brawl, but against so many today Thomas didn't stand a chance.

The Ruffians shoved Phineas and Thomas against the bitter-smelling tar barrel. Gopher, his drum lowered to the ground, dipped a hog-bristle paint brush into it.

"Not yet." Barnaby raised his palm. "I gotta make a proper announcement for those witnessing this glorious event." He buttoned his shirt's top button before he kicked up his little speech's volume. "Mister Richard King has pronounced a sentence on these breakers of our 'no preaching' law. We're gonna tar and feather them and kick them off our property. Permanent."

Huzzahs from the gang.

Dead silence from the spectators. Annabelle elbowed a path through them. "You can't do this, Barnaby."

"Reckon on stopping us?" Barnaby assessed her, cracked his knuckles, and swiped his nose with his ham fist.

"It-It ain't right."

"They broke the law, Miss Lawson," King yelled. He and Sehoy filled the doorway of a recently completed log building, one of King's projects. "Listen to what Barnaby said. It's my sentence on these vile lawbreakers."

Thomas snarled. "You're gonna answer to me if you tar Reverend Steward."

"Barnaby'll smash your face," Clay said, yawning, "and make your nose crookeder than it is already."

Thomas gritted his teeth. "When I get outta this, you insult me again, I'll—"

"It's all right." Pity oozed from every fiber of Phineas's being. "Go ahead, Barnaby. Do it. But please be merciful to my friend Thomas. Let him go."

"I do what I wanna." Barnaby tweaked Phineas's cheek.

"All right." Defeated, Thomas slumped and sighed. "Go ahead and do it to me too. I ain't gonna fight it no more."

Annabelle gaped. Thomas, giving up, so quickly? It didn't surprise her when she'd learned he'd helped Dempsey escape, but to surrender in this situation? Without a fight? He wasn't the man she'd once known, albeit she'd known him briefly. And a preacher now. Maybe that's why he didn't fight harder.

"Strip them naked, boys." King strode down a stone path.

"Make them look like birds." Twirling her indigo parasol, Sehoy kept behind her husband in no great rush. "Tweet, tweet."

Upon her departure, Annabelle dragged her trembling feet. The preachers' screams mingled with the gang's scathing laughter. Someone stripped off their clothes. Someone else either poured or painted hot tar on them. Loads of feathers would follow and cling to their bodies. She'd witnessed it before—a dreadful sight. What was it about Thomas and his friend, who subjected themselves voluntarily to such treatment?

Back inside the Ox Yoke she asked Maggie's new kitchen helper, Suzie, to bring her a beer. Simmering, she sat at a table and sipped it. Sehoy and all who knew her said she was no longer the feisty female she used to be. She slammed her tankard on the table. After what she just saw … "Hit me again, Barnaby, you big lout. I got Sehoy's penknife. I'll slit your fat, flabby throat."

From this moment on, she'd follow her ma's and pa's ways. She'd treat each person and traveler fairly, even preachers. That'd stick in the brute's craw. "I'm sorry, ma, pa. Maybe I can make up the wrongs I did to you this way, by treating folks right."

Outside, the drum rolled steadily, its rhythm a dirge. Barnaby chanted. The Ruffians echoed him on their way past.

She clenched her hands on the table. Her fingertips dug into her palms. They were driving the preachers out of the settlement. Annabelle twisted toward the bar. "Maggie."

Maggie poked her head out of the pantry.

"You and Suzie go fetch me a big kettle of water. The biggest kettle we got."

"Yes'm." Calling Suzie's name, Maggie hastened out back to the well.

Minutes later, Barnaby exploded through the front door and, quaking, banged his fist on Annabelle's table so hard she feared he'd break it.

"Stupid sow." Barnaby raised his arm to slap her. "Why'd you try stopping our fun?"

Annabelle huffed. "Them preachers ain't done nothing worth tarring and feathering."

Seizing her shoulders, Barnaby gave her such a powerful shake she flinched, and her neck hurt. "They tried doing it this afternoon, you dumb sow. Stood on a street corner, What's-his-name howling his religious songs. Travelers dropping money in Murcher's hat."

"They got a right."

"Ain't nobody's got a right breaking our laws."

"Our laws are stupid."

"No." Barnaby aimed his fat forefinger at her. "You're the one who's stupid."

Annabelle studied his finger. *Slap me. One time. I dare you.* "Y'all at least give them their clothes back?"

"Birds don't wear clothes." Barnaby stalked out. The door slammed behind him.

Annabelle snatched her bonnet, tied it on her head, and exited the back door to the kitchen. The murmurs of the tavern's boarders entering the building quickly faded. After she put on thick gloves, Annabelle and Suzie hefted the kettle by its handle and hastened into the woods. A glance behind her assured Annabelle no one followed.

"Where we going?" Suzie asked.

"To them preachers. Hurry."

"How you know where they is?"

"Yonder. That path."

"You sho' that's where they is?"

"That's what someone said."

"Who?"

"Someone who followed them to their camp two nights ago. The next path, Suzie. On the right. Hurry."

Frank, holding the preachers' clothes, brushed aside a spider web as he emerged from a thicket.

"How'd you get them things back?" Annabelle, panting, nodded at Suzie. They set the kettle on the ground to catch their breaths.

"Weren't easy." Frank gave her the clothes. "The Ruffians made me give 'em a week's pay first. I promised 'em I'd use these clothes as rags."

"Humph! Barnaby and his hogs always find ways to take other folks' money."

"You ain't mad at me for not helping 'em on the street?"

"You done good, Frank. Can't let them Ruffians figure out you and your folks been calling on the preachers at night. You ain't full grown enough yet to fight them."

Frank dug into his trouser pocket. "Brought soap too." He tossed the small bar of lye soap into the kettle of warm water, then received the clothes back. "I'll help 'em get off their feathers and tar long as I can. Mister Cooper believes I've gone home to eat. Father'll come later and help 'em scrape it off if he can do it without someone catching him. He also gave me some lard to help 'em. It's at their camp"

"Bandages?"

Frank nodded. "Father says he'll do the bandaging for 'em when he gets off work for a spell."

Annabelle touched his arm. "Maybe you'll become like my folks one day and stand up to them Ruffians."

"Miss Annabelle, way back when Reverend Steward first came here and the Ruffians egged him, I was seven years old. I saw 'em do it. It made me and my folks mad, except my folks were too scared to help your folks fight 'em. They've sort of been blaming themselves for what happened to Mister and Mrs. Lawson."

"They'd oughtn't blame themselves. If anyone deserves blaming it's me. My fault in more ways'n one."

Frank scowled. "I hate King and his bossy little woman. This place needs religion."

"I ain't going to argue that truth." In some ways, though, Sehoy King was an ally and a friend. *Get rid of her too?* "Let's go back to the tavern, Suzie, before Barnaby the Brute shows his ugly self. We got travelers and boarders to feed."

During her walk back to the Ox Yoke Annabelle pondered the preachers, especially Thomas Murcher. She must get to know him better, beyond being a mere acquaintance from years back. Her folks would've approved of him now that he'd changed and even been as amazed as she was at what happened in his life. A true genl'man, him. Not bad looking, either. Was there a way to escape Hell like he said earlier today? Suppose God did exist. Would He forgive her murdering heart? The way he and Reverend Steward behaved today, when Barnaby did them wrong, how were they able to withstand such treatment? She needed an answer.

Beneath a cool inky sky Thomas sat on a log, a plate of beefsteak in his lap courtesy of Annabelle. From the day they first met in the year '07, a change in her attitude had occurred, for when she brought them their food she also brought brightness instead of bitterness.

Across the sizzling campfire opposite him Phineas sat and, having eaten, played a tune on the violin Cousin Reuben's society presented to him when they passed through his town on their way back from the wedding in Macon. Phineas's astonishment at this gift—an event forever etched in Thomas's memory.

Beneath their clothes, bandages swathed their scarred chests, arms, and legs. Moths flitted around the lanternlight between them. Distant coyotes howled a poor imitation of Phineas's songs.

As his scarred hand poked a morsel into his mouth, Thomas winced at the pain inflicted on him. A terrifying experience. The tar the gang painted on him burned, not badly, but still hurt. The ugly spots on his flesh, the blisters, presented more fodder for scoffers regarding his physical appearance. He regretted flaring up at Clay. Not exactly Christian conduct, but Phineas made no mention of it.

"Accept the way God made you, Thomas," Phineas told him on more than one occasion. "We're fearfully and wonderfully made, the Good Book says."

Fearfully and wonderfully made. The refrain often played in his mind. Was he rejecting the work God did when God created him in his mother's womb? Yes, he figured he was, but accepting himself proved no easy task. He hoped Phineas avoided King's Brook for a spell. Another insult from Clay and the painful burns on his flesh … Thomas choked on his irritation. No, forgive Clay. He must forgive everyone who'd hurt him and accept the way God made him, two very difficult tasks.

Phineas set aside his violin on a bed of pine straw. "One positive thing did come out of what happened to us today."

"And what might that be?" Thomas cut his meat into manageable portions.

"We made some new friends in Annabelle and Frank's family. Being tarred and feathered was a stroke of Providence."

Providence? Thomas took a swig of water from his canteen. It never failed that Phineas saw Providence at work in every event in his life. Maybe he ought to learn how to see things more the way Phineas did. "If so, it sure wasn't pleasurable." Rising to his feet, Thomas indicated three lanterns approaching. "The Oglesbys."

Zander, squinting at Phineas, lifted his lantern toward him. "Do you feel better, Reverend Steward?"

"Don't feel like much of a bird now." Phineas, his palms on the earth, shoved himself to his feet. "Complaining don't help nothing."

"And you, Mister Murcher?" Mrs. Oglesby held her lantern toward Thomas.

"Terrifying, but figure I'll live," Thomas said.

"You didn't act scared." Frank unslung his canteen.

Thomas balled his hands into tight fists. "Kept it inside and called on the Almighty."

"It's awful what they did to you." Reaching into a canvas sack, Mrs. Oglesby pulled out a bottle. "I brought you some egg whites for your burns and blisters."

Phineas received it. "Thank you, dear lady."

"Here." Zander let Thomas have his canteen. "Also, some cool water for your burns."

Thomas examined his scarred wrists and welts in the lanternlight.

"Reverends, we've been pondering on our situation here," Mrs. Oglesby continued. She lent Thomas a clean cloth gotten from her sack. "If we could take care of King and his rascals, get them arrested or something, we can establish a Methodist society in this place."

"I'd prefer showing 'em the way to salvation." Phineas indicated a stool. "Annabelle brought us this small bit of furniture. Please, Mrs. Oglesby, please sit."

She did. Frank and his father sat on the ground. From a bush, frogs croaked. All around them, cicadas' fussing increased.

"Annabelle's sure been changing." Mrs. Oglesby nudged her spectacles up to the bridge of her nose.

"She sure has." Phineas plucked at the pine straw beneath his violin. "We can't let the way they treat y'all continue."

"How?" Mrs. Oglesby asked. "How will we stop them when they don't let you preach?"

"Y'all keep coming to Thomas and me in secret. Find folks who're really interested, they can visit us the way you do. At night. In the woods. We get us enough people to help build us a brush arbor, we can do our preaching right here on the outskirts."

Zander and his wife clapped softly. Frank mouthed a barely audible "hurrah."

"Every time we visit, we'll send word before we come here."

"But King runs the post office in his store, Reverend Steward," Zander said.

"Then I'll send you a letter from Saint Stephens or some other settlement, with the approximate time we plan on coming back so you can tell folks to get ready. This here will be our secret meeting place."

Zander snapped his fingers. "Excellent."

Thomas's heart somersaulted. Sermonizing outside the settlement. No one and nothing could stop them. He hoped their secret society prospered. He could not, would not, let the devil's side win, and he knew Phineas shared his hopes. Time was long overdue, them standing up to those Ruffians.

Phineas opened his Bible and began teaching on Nicodemus's nighttime interview with Jesus.

CHAPTER THIRTY-TWO

Monday, April 19, 1813
Samuel Mims's Farm, Alabama country, Mississippi Territory

Gentlemen and ladies whirled and glided to Joseph Mims's music. Around various outbuildings, Ruffians and their girls strolled Samuel Mims's grounds. Some walked arm-in-arm to Boatyard Lake about five hundred yards to the southeast. Mobile, captured from Spain by an American army without a shot fired. Mister Mims was there when the event happened. Upon his return to the Tensaw region, he'd spread the news throughout the region and invited friends to this celebration. The O'Neals, the Moniacs, the Kings, the Ruffians, and others, enjoying a grand time. Except for Barnaby, who grunted at the dancers and tossed wine onto the grass. He didn't want to be here.

Clay, seated in a chair on Mister Mims's porch, whispered something in a young girl's ear. Her knitted brow indicated she was listening intently.

Barnaby, however, nursed his black disgust. No matter how much he'd begged her, Annabelle refused to come. Alone without a woman. Embarrassing. He shrugged. He wasn't much of a dancer anyway. Coming here turned out to be a mistake.

Young David Mims, Mister Mims's son, approached. "You aren't dancing, Barnaby?"

"Do you see me dancing?" Barnaby snapped.

"I didn't mean—"

"Don't take it personal. I got lots on my mind."

"Forgiven and forgotten." David cut a slice of pound cake and set it on a plate. "Annabelle?"

"She refused my invite. I caught her reading a religious tract some preachers gave her." Before he'd tarred and feathered them.

"You two breaking up on account of her sudden religious inclinations?" David slid a piece of cake into his mouth.

"Ain't sure yet." Barnaby cut himself a slice. He'd beat her to death if she got too uppity pious, and he'd kill the Kings if they tried stopping him.

Monday, April 19. 1813
King's Brook, Alabama country, Mississippi Territory

During her return to the Ox Yoke bearing a glass of water she drew from the tavern's well, Annabelle cocked her ear to the gleeful chatter out among the trees. Under Thomas's guidance people engaged in building a brush arbor for an evening of preaching. Since the Ruffians were away, they figured this was the best time to have it.

Thomas. She blinked. When she told him about Barnaby's beatings his nostrils flared and he breathed fast and loudly, clearly angry. He'd prayed with her, asked God to stop Barnaby's meanness, and prayed for Barnaby's soul.

She passed through the pantry into the tavern's dining area and placed the water before Phineas. "Rev'rend Steward, since them Ruffians and their gals ain't around, I got me some questions."

Phineas sipped his water. "S'ppose Providence brought Thomas and me back at the right time." Phineas took another sip.

Annabelle fingered a tiny pink bow decorating her dress's white bodice. Did she really want answers? Her stomach wrenched. No. Yes. She must know. Worries tormented her sleep, not to mention how much her head throbbed most all the time. "Do all murderers go to Hell?"

"Murder is a sin. All sinners go there."

"Ain't you a sinner?"

"Every man, woman, and child is. We've all done wrong."

"Ain't you fearful of going to Hell?"

"Was at one time, Miss Annabelle." Phineas's finger traced his water glass's rim. "I ain't anymore. Jesus died for me. He died for every one of us sinners. When we make Him the Lord of our life, He forgives us."

"What does that mean?"

"Forgiveness?"

Annabelle bobbed her head eagerly. Maybe she wouldn't go to Hell, if—

"It means, dear lady, that when a sinner repents of his waywardness and trusts our Savior and what He's done for us on the Cross, dying for our sins, we will become, in His eyes, as one who ain't never sinned. He shed His blood for us."

His sharp brown eyes chilled her veins, as though he probed the darkest shadows of her soul. She squirmed.

"Do you know of a person who killed somebody?"

She shook her head quickly. "N-No. Only a question I've been chewing on." If she admitted her guilt Gray Eagle would have her scalp. The front door's click snatched her out of her dreadful thoughts. *Thomas.*

"Sir," Thomas said, "some folks at the arbor got a question I can't answer. Maybe you can."

Upon quaffing his water, Phineas offered Annabelle his arm. Together, they accompanied Thomas to their meeting place. *A way out of Hell?* A hint of hope sparked.

Behind the brush arbor's back row, Annabelle stood alone next to one of the upright poles supporting its roof, thatched with straw and boughs of pine. She wanted no distractions from the preaching. For the first time since her childhood, she prayed from the depths of her ache and asked God to show her whether He really existed.

Up front, Phineas strolled back and forth playing a song on his violin while the few settlers who traveled here from nearby farms sang from hymnals Thomas and Phineas had passed out. Annabelle didn't join in, but not because she didn't want to. She knew how much folks enjoyed her musical gift by the way they'd flocked to the settlement's theater whenever they knew she planned to entertain them. She just wasn't in the mood right now. She surveyed the little congregation and did a quick head count. Most folks in the immediate region attended. Between her and the Oglesbys, they'd "arm-twisted" and persuaded a few of them to come. Others showed up voluntarily.

Singing swelled to the arbor's roof. Joyful songs and shining faces. King's Brook settlers, free from Mister King's tyranny, if only for a spell. As the songs faded to quiet, Thomas stepped forward and Phineas sat in the front row.

For a moment, Thomas swept the congregation seated on benches. Opening his Bible, he read aloud. "'Two are better than one; because they have a good reward for their labor. For if they fall, the one will lift them up his fellow; but woe to him *that is* alone when he falleth; for *he hath* not another to help him up.'" He lowered his Bible.

Annabelle wriggled as though she sat on nails.

"Friends," Thomas said, "I just read y'all a passage from the book of Ecclesiastes. It's one of the wisdom books in God's holy word. And it's full of wisdom. And we can beat the Ruffians in this place, 'cept one person can't do it alone because two are better than one, like the Good Book says. If we all do it together and help each other—"

"Annabelle's parents fought them," Mary shouted two rows from the front. "Got them killed."

"You Vances shoot better'n anybody here," a man said. "Y'all kill them. We won't say nothing."

"We're farmers, not murderers." Hiram spoke from his bench. "I'll defend my family if they try killing us, but I don't cotton to going around hunting for folks to shoot. No, sir. I did consider it once, decided I'll never do it."

"Nary a one of y'all tried helping my ma and pa, that's why they got killed," Annabelle shouted.

"How'd you figure a Ruffian did it, Miss Lawson?" Lemuel spoke from beside his wife. "We never found their bodies."

"We all know they did it, Lem," Hiram said. "Once we find the proof, Judge Toulmin can do something about it."

Her cheeks burning, Annabelle waved her arms. "All y'all men, cowards. All y'all. Y'all let these good preachers get tarred and feathered and—" She bit her tongue when Phineas stood and lifted his brows in a warning. No sense stirring up a bee's hive when folks needed to be of one mind in this fight. She quieted.

Murmurs rippled throughout the congregation.

Zander stood. "Thomas is right. Listen to him. Who will they kill if we all unite together? They ain't got a settlement to boss around and extort money from if they kill every one of us."

"One or two of us may get ourselves killed." Abe Wade spoke from the third row. "If'n he kills ever one of us, he'll get all our land."

"Which is what he wants," a man next to Abe said.

Patience Morgan, gathering her ankle-length cotton skirt, swiftly moved between the aisles. Although small in stature, she held the fierceness of a tigress on occasion. "Listen, y'all. I been living in this here territory well-nigh ten years, and I been ashamed of how we all been acting. The Good Book says we *can* stand together, and if one of us falls we *can* help each other. We *can* help each other against our heathen masters." She raised a wrinkled, aged fist. "I'm going on seventy years next month. I done my time on God's good earth. I'm willing to be the first to die if them evildoers care to kill me. I say"— she pointed at Thomas— "we take a vote, sir, if you think it's fitting. To stand together and defend ourselves and our land, or we don't. Like Zander said, they ain't got a settlement to boss around if they kill all of us."

Phineas assumed a position beside Thomas. "A vote, that we join together against the Ruffians?"

"Let's do it," Zander said.

"Folks in favor of standing united against the Ruffians," Thomas said, "raise your hands."

One by one, people raised them.

Annabelle silently counted the votes. Unanimous. *Oh no.* They'd started jabbering about their plans against the Ruffians. No one preached because they didn't give Thomas or Phineas the chance. Her sobs painful, she bolted from the arbor, almost knocking over a torch. No answer to her prayer. God didn't exist. Next time Barnaby fell asleep, she'd slit his fat throat with Sehoy's knife.

Thomas spotted Annabelle striding from the meeting. He fussed at himself. Why didn't he preach first, before discussing what to do about the Ruffians? He ought to start farming again. Last letter Noble sent him, he'd bought more cotton acreage. "Annabelle." He chased after her.

Annabelle's strides quickened into a jog.

Puffing hard, Thomas pursued her till he caught up. "Annabelle. Stop."

She jogged faster, widening the distance between them and sending a wayward possum skittering into some brush. "I don't believe in God."

"What?"

She whirled on him. "No such thing as a Supreme Being. I prayed tonight and asked Him a question. I said I'd believe in Him if He answered it during the preaching. He didn't. I'm going to the Ox Yoke for a beer. You want one?"

"Wait a doggone minute, Miss Annabelle. I'm here. Me and you are alone. Me and you can talk private-like. Don't you figure my being here at this moment in time is God's answer?"

The muscles in Annabelle's face and neck relaxed. "One answer, Thomas Murcher." Her weak voice quivered. "The question's been bothering me a powerful long time."

"What question?"

"Will God …" She swiped a tear. "Will God send murderers to Hell? I know what Rev'rend Steward said. How do you opine on the subject?"

With a spring in his legs, Thomas hurried ahead. "C'mon. Let's scoot inside the Ox Yoke. Phineas will do the sermonizing given the chance. He's better'n me at it anyway."

Once inside, he helped her light candles and oil lamps before they sat at a table. An urge prompted him to reach across it and grasp her hand. He squashed it.

"In the first particular, Miss Annabelle," Thomas said, "God is a God of love. He don't send folks to Hell. A person's gotta wanna go there."

"Huh?"

"The Bible says God created Hell for the devil and his angels, not people."

"Murderers? Ain't they going there? Why would they want to go there?"

"They shouldn't wanna go there. I've dreamed about Hell. Nightmares, I oughta say. It's a horrible place. A person who goes there has to wanna go there. It's their choice. As the Bible says, 'choose ye this day whom ye will serve.'"

She brightened. "You mean I got to pick where I go? I think Rev'rend Steward said something about, about repenting or something."

Thomas gentled his manner. "Do you understand what that word means? Repentance?"

"Turning—"

"Confess your wrong doings, your evil ways, to God. Quit doing them and put your trust in what Christ did for you. That's what I did, why I ain't the orneriest man who ever lived like I was that day we first met, back when me and Barnaby fought each other. Choose today who you'll serve, Miss Annabelle. The Lord gave us the freedom to choose the road we'll take."

Annabelle leapt from her seat. "Oh. I understand it now! Clear as sunshine." She danced around the table and seized Thomas's coat sleeve. She desperately pulled at him. "Please, Thomas. Please help me do it. Help me choose the right road."

Laughing, Thomas asked her to sit. When they finished talking, he led her to faith. As she bowed her head, tears gushing onto her dress, she began, "Dear Lord G-God above, I done some mighty evil things and …." After their prayer, she nervously surveyed the tavern as though people watched them even though they were alone. "I'm the one done the killing. I killed Kana's husband and blamed poor Jasper for it."

"I know." Although shocked by her deed, Thomas maintained a neutral expression. Her brokenness needed mending. Besides, in his evil days, he'd almost killed a few folks himself, so he had no right to judge her.

Blinking back tears, Annabelle recoiled. "How?"

"You were so upset about it, and sobbing so hard, you said it during your confession and repentance. Figure you kept it so pent up inside, you didn't realize what you were saying. You blurted out the whole story and forgot I was here. Barnaby and Clay killed your folks."

A sudden pallor overwhelmed her.

"No, no, Miss Annabelle. I ain't judging you for it, and God's forgiven you."

"I can't prove they killed my folks, but they did do it. Nothing that'll hold up in court except my word against theirs."

"They'll answer to the Almighty Judge in Heaven for their evil doings."

"What if I tell Barnaby and Clay I'm willing to forgive?" Her brightened face fell. "I got to tell Chief Gray Eagle what I done. He may scalp me when he finds out."

"Me and Reverend Steward'll talk about it. He'll have an idea what to do."

Annabelle, sniffling, said, "Thank you." She stiffened. The veins in her slender neck bulged. "Barnaby will kill me when he comes back, when he learns what I done."

"Miss Annabelle, before he lays a paw on you, he'll have to deal with me first."

"This time, your fighting won't be fisticuffs. This time, he'll kill you."

"It's a chance I'll take." Soon as Thomas spoke, the gravity of his opposition to Barnaby and Annabelle's well-being smacked him. He must find a way to stop Barnaby's abuses. The one thing riling him, above everything else—abuse. Years ago, he'd vowed not to let it happen to anyone—man, woman, or child—nor to him ever again.

Thursday, April 22, 1813
King's Brook, Alabama country, Mississippi Territory

Every night, while Phineas traveled to other settlements for a series of meetings, Thomas preached in King's Brook's brush arbor.

From each corner of the vicinity and a few miles beyond, settlers poured into Thomas's meetings where Annabelle led the singing.

Awestruck, he sometimes paused his sermon to watch God move. People shouted. Some wept. A few folks fell flat on the ground, crying. Many professed faith in Christ. Why, it was unbelievable. His preaching had never affected congregations this way before. All doubt about his calling swept aside. At last, God used him to bring real revival.

On top of this, the powerful change in Annabelle, no one could deny. Sweet-spirited and kind, she treated each person with respect. The wonder God wrought in her profoundly affected everyone who knew her. The tavern became the ministry's local headquarters where he and Phineas prepared their sermons and offered counseling.

Thomas, pondering tonight's sermon, dipped his quill pen in his lap desk's inkwell. Maggie and Suzie puttered around the pantry. Annabelle wiped tables.

"Lookee here, ever'body," Barnaby boomed as he barged through the tavern's front door. "Preacher Thomas is back for another tarring and feathering." Swinging his powerful arms across his bulky stomach, Barnaby bore down on Thomas like the bear that charged him years ago.

Thomas twisted in his chair, stood, and spoke in an even tone. "I came here to preach."

Barnaby swiped Thomas's lap desk on the floor, spilled the pen, and splattered ink. "It's against the law."

"Against your law. Not God's."

"Leave him alone." Annabelle rushed over.

"You taking up for this crazy man?" Barnaby roared.

"I-I ain't the same person." Annabelle trembled like a leaf in a gale.

Sweaty beads dripped off Barnaby's scraggly beard. He cracked his knuckles. "Changed, huh? What've you changed into? A hog?"

Crimson swamped Annabelle's face. "Go ahead and insult me, you big ogre." She retreated a step. "I'm-I'm finally sure I ain't going to Hell no more."

"Hell? There ain't no such a place." Barnaby exploded into horselaughs and whacked Annabelle upside her head faster than Thomas could stop him.

She fled into the pantry with Maggie.

"Do not hit her again." Thomas arose from his chair.

"Say, Preacher Man." Barnaby picked at the buttons on Thomas's coat. "I ain't heeding your lousy advice."

"Do not touch her. Do not hit her. She's a lady. Gentlemen do not hit ladies."

"I ain't no gentleman." Barnaby jabbed Thomas's ribcage, then sprinted into the pantry.

Thomas stayed on his heels.

"Stupid woman." Barnaby cursed. "Got yourself a li'l religion now, do you?"

Her back against the pantry cabinets, Annabelle wagged her finger at him. "We've been having preaching in the brush arbor too. You ought to try a little of it."

"Don't need no religion. Don't need no god. And I ain't no ogre."

"You're uglier'n an ogre." When Annabelle caught Thomas's worried eyes, her mouth clamped tight.

"Death comes to us all, Barnaby." Thomas softened his manner.

"You'll die before I do, Murcher," Barnaby said, snarling, "cause I'm gonna kill you."

Thomas waved off Barnaby's foul breath that reeked like rotten fish.

Barnaby flung him against a wall.

Ugh. Pangs exploded inside Thomas's head.

Barnaby raised a fist to slug Annabelle, but Thomas threw his arms around his barrel-size waist from behind and tugged him clear. "Stop it. It ain't right."

"Take your lousy paws off me, Murcher. On the street. Me and you'll finish our business once and for all."

Lowering his arms, Thomas recalled a few things he'd learned from his and Barnaby's previous fight, that day when Barnaby whipped the dickens out of him. Maybe this knowledge would be useful this time around. "Just me and you, and if I win, you quit beating her."

"I'm gonna win." Barnaby flipped up a lapel on Thomas's coat. "And when I do, you leave outta here permanent else you're a dead man."

Thomas shed his coat, laid it on the back of a chair, rolled his sleeves up above his elbows, and made for the door. He paused to peer over his shoulder. A little stooped and biting her lower lip, Annabelle clutched the pantry door's jamb and gave a slight shake of her head. Thomas's reassuring smile responded to her concern. Maggie and Suzie peered past her.

Right outside the door, Barnaby awaited him. The moment Thomas stepped out the brute wrapped his arms around him, hefted him high, and tossed him into a horse trough. Warm water sloshed over the trough's sides. Barnaby's guffaws erupted. "Murcher, let's me and you get at it."

Spitting out the stale liquid, Thomas scrambled from the trough. He sauntered to Barnaby.

Barnaby glowered and raised his fists. His first punch smacked Thomas's face with the power of a cannon ball. Recoiling, shaking off his new headache, Thomas dodged Barnaby's next punch and charged. His fists contacted Barnaby's thick chest.

Laughing, Barnaby tossed back his head. "You hit like an old woman."

His fists lowered? Thomas plowed two blows into Barnaby. Punch after punch Thomas forced him back. His knuckles ached. He drew blood and stayed in too tight for Barnaby to use his longer arms. Harder, faster Thomas jabbed. Briefly, Barnaby withdrew and threw a swift left hook.

Thomas rolled beneath Barnaby's arm and followed up by plowing a fist into his armpit.

Barnaby swayed.

Thomas roared into him and rolled sideways when Barnaby threw an uppercut. Thomas's fists landed square, bloodied Barnaby's nose.

Each time Thomas slugged him, cheers from spectators drowned the Ruffians' shouts.

Thomas licked blood off his lips. They bobbed and weaved and danced and jabbed, swapping blow for blow. Barnaby swung a left hook.

As he ducked low to dodge it, Thomas flew back onto the stone street when Barnaby's right uppercut connected with his chin. Groaning and spitting blood, his spine vibrated. Barnaby threw himself at him.

Thomas rolled clear, scrambled to his feet, and sprang atop him fast as a cat on a rat. Seizing a lock of Barnaby's hair, Thomas jerked it. "You will quit hurting Miss Annabelle. Understand?"

"Get off me." Barnaby groaned and kicked his legs.

Thomas twisted Barnaby's right outstretched wrist beneath his body. Growling, Barnaby squirmed.

Thomas thrust his other arm beneath Barnaby's right armpit, up around Barnaby's body, and pressured his neck. "You ain't gonna hurt Annabelle again." He shoved harder on Barnaby's neck. "You will not touch her. You will not hurt her."

Barnaby grunted.

Thomas rolled forward and, with a bit of effort, flipped Barnaby onto his back. Barnaby spat.

Straddling him, Thomas pinned his shoulders.

"Better do what Reverend Murcher says," Zander said. "Since you're so cold and your conscience so seared, we all pity you. We'll make sure you don't hurt our dear Annabelle again."

"Off him, Preacher." King, brandishing his cocked horse pistol, moved up with Sehoy. "Hatch won't be causing any more trouble."

Thomas got off Barnaby.

Ashen, Barnaby stuttered. "M-Mister K-K-King, I—I—"

"You committed two sins, Barnaby Hatch," King said, his coldness roaming to Annabelle who stood outside the Ox Yoke's entrance. "Sin number one, you didn't get my permission to beat Annabelle. Sin number two, you let this beanpole preacher make a fool out of you."

"S-Sir, I—"

"Leave us," Sehoy said. "A man who beats his woman deserves death. The next time you set foot in this place, I will take personal pleasure in killing you."

Barnaby, swearing, stormed off.

King steered Clay who, supremely confident, swaggered. "Citizens of King's Brook, here is the new leader of the Ruffians. My son."

"Don't think so, King." Zander gathered Constance and Frank close on his flanks.

"No one here will pay you or your Ruffians any more of your so-called protection money." Mrs. Oglesby nudged her spectacles higher up her nose.

"Oh, you'll pay." King shrugged. "This is still my settlement."

Zander shook his head. "No, we won't. You ordered Annabelle's parents killed because they stood up to you. Well, we're all standing up to you too."

"Not a one of you can prove it." King's pistol shifted to Zander. "I will kill the next person, man or woman, who challenges my authority."

Abe Wade squeezed through the crowd. "You can't kill all of us, King, because if you do, you ain't got nobody to push around and get money from."

Lemuel joined the tanner shoulder to shoulder. "I ain't paying you anymore of your rent money either."

King pointed at Lemuel's wife. "Your husband—"

"Was seeing a young Spanish lady in Mobile." Lemuel's wife lifted her round chin. "Lem told me. He's sorry for seeing her behind my back, and I've forgiven him, something I'm sure you don't understand. 'Sides, she's moved to Mexico. Your power over us is gone."

"Try anything else," Zander said, "we'll all search for the proof till we find it and report you to the authorities."

Approaching hoofbeats drew the crowd's interest—Phineas.

King and Sehoy stalked off.

Clay shot a "you're dead" look at Thomas, then went with them.

"What happened?" Phineas's gaze roamed the settlers.

"We beat 'em, Rev'rend." Annabelle did a little dance, her tangled hair bouncing on her narrow shoulders.

"Every one of these fine settlers here, and the good Lord," Thomas said.

"And you, Thomas." Admiration swelled her countenance.

Embarrassed by Annabelle's compliment, Thomas turned from her pretty eyes.

"All right," Phineas said loudly. "Let's begin the serious business of building a church here."

Mrs. Oglesby wrapped her arms around Frank and her husband. "We're all ready to do it, Reverend."

Phineas pulled some venison jerky from his inside coat pocket. Deep in thought, he slowly unwrapped it. "I reckon I'd better go call on Chief Gray Eagle first." Phineas steered his horse back in the direction from which he came. "I'll be back in good time."

Everyone bade him farewell as he trotted off.

Annabelle's lips quivered. "T-Thomas, do you … you … reckon … reckon Gray Eagle will scalp me for what I done?"

He'd never met Gray Eagle, though he'd heard Kana talk about him. The future … Thomas's pulse quickened. "Let's pray about it, Annabelle. Pray long and hard."

"Yes." Annabelle bowed her head. "Let's do."

CHAPTER THIRTY-THREE

"Gray Eagle's here." Thomas announced the Choctaw's arrival from Mrs. Oglesby's front porch. His fingers touched his forehead to shield his eyes from the sun's merciless blaze. The chief, erect on his horse, rode at the head of six braves.

Thomas sucked in a long breath. Thank goodness, none of them wore warpaint. Two beaded necklaces hung from the chief's thick neck, over a white hunting shirt. He also wore a black breechcloth and buckskin leggings.

"Reverend Steward's with him," Mrs. Oglesby said. "Dempsey, and … Why, that's Kana. I ain't seen her in a dog's age." She dashed onto the street to greet them but they, stern of visage, continued past without acknowledgment.

Phineas tipped his hat. "Hurry to the Ox Yoke, Thomas."

"On my way," Thomas said.

"I'm going too, Reverend Murcher." Mrs. Oglesby snatched her bonnet off a small porch table.

In silence, they trod there. Mrs. Oglesby, he knew, shared his concern about Annabelle's fate.

By the time they arrived, the chief closed on the Ox Yoke's bar and Annabelle emerged from the pantry, Maggie and Suzie with her. Thomas opened his mouth to speak but shut it when Kana raised her finger at him to keep quiet. Dempsey stood next to her. Behind him, Mrs. Oglesby breathed ragged breaths.

"Ch-Chief Gray Eagle, I-I know I did wrong," Annabelle stammered.

Gray Eagle gestured curtly at two braves. They strode around the bar and flanked her. One of them clutched a tomahawk at his side.

Dempsey and Kana sidled up beside the chief.

People filtered into the tavern and others, seated at tables, held expressions running the gauntlet from worry to fear to shock amidst the taut tension.

Gray Eagle's big fist hammered the counter. "We will take you away, White woman. Choctaw justice for killing my niece's husband."

Annabelle lifted her trembling chin. "I'll go with you."

"We will execute you for your crime."

Sniffling, Annabelle stretched forth her shaky arms. "I'm a killer deserving of your justice. Here are my wrists. Take them. Bind them. I've forgiven the men who killed my folks, and God has forgiven me for my crimes." Her soft orbs wandered to Thomas.

Thomas gasped. *Don't go. No. She's repented.*

The brave on her left seized her thin arms, and the brave on her right whipped a rawhide strap from his sash. Three times, he wrapped it over her wrists, cinching it tight, eliciting her wince.

Thomas started to speak out but again, he caught Kana shaking her head at him, so he stayed mum. Despite Annabelle's brave words, her quivers and sobs betrayed her fear.

Phineas leaned into Thomas's ear. "We better do something."

Thomas nodded his agreement.

"Wait, Uncle." Kana stepped forward.

Dempsey rocked back on his heels. "Chief Gray Eagle, I've known this Annabelle woman since we were children. I grew up in this place, you recollect. You've known her too, but not as long as me."

"Tell us. What is your conclusion?" Gray Eagle's stern eyes never wavered from her.

"My conclusion, most honorable Chief, is this. This woman is not the woman she used to be. You have heard the White man Phineas speak to us in our village. He's told us what happened, how she has changed." Dempsey inclined his head at Annabelle. "A few weeks ago, she'd have cursed you and fought you. You are aware of how she once used to be. Now you see her change for yourself. Annabelle Lawson, you are a believer in the Almighty now? The Great One?"

"Yes." Annabelle, her demeanor solemn, pointed at Thomas and Phineas. "These preachers of the Great One's word showed me the Way. I'm sorry for what I did. It was wrong. A sin."

"She speaks the truth," Phineas said.

"Still, she must be punished." Gray Eagle glared at her.

Kana, grasping her uncle's arm, spoke softly. "She's already being punished. Her conscience is killing her. Let the Great One deal with her deeds."

For a moment, Gray Eagle hesitated. He nodded at the two braves beside her. One of them cut loose Annabelle's bonds.

Kana enveloped her in a sisterly hug. "The Great One commands me to forgive you, Annabelle. And I do." Hugs from weeping Maggie, Suzie, and Mrs. Oglesby followed.

CHAPTER THIRTY-FOUR

Billy Weatherford and his brother-in-law, Sam Moniac, trotted their horses up the narrow road on their way to Billy's house. They'd been to Mississippi country trading cattle with the Choctaw, but as they approached a stream Billy drew rein. Up ahead, Peter McQueen sat in a circle with Josiah Francis and other prophets and warriors, passing a gourd from one to another, drinking from it. Others sang.

McQueen, shirtless, wore a buckskin breechcloth and leggings. A black porcupine hair headdress with two feathers sat upon his shaved head. Francis wore no headdress. His hair, and the other warriors' hair, resembled a Mohawk's—shaved bald except for an upraised tuft at the back of his scalp. Every man's chest bore red and blue tattoos of various shapes and designs.

"It appears they're drinking the *assee*," Sam said when one warrior doubled over and retched.

Settlers called the *assee* the Black Drink—a tea made of boiled holly leaves, a purgative. Why were they drinking it here? Billy scrunched his brows. Purifying themselves for war?

"It doesn't bode well." Sam, bullish of build, rose in his saddle.

When he spotted his new wife, Supalamy, seated among them with Polly and Charles, their backs facing him, Billy's breath hitched. Prisoners? Supalamy's and Polly's hair were styled in topknots, the traditional Creek female fashion. Charles didn't move. Too frightened, perhaps. No, not prisoners. Supalamy's sympathies lay with the prophets' cause. In the Choctaw town of Chickasawhay, where he'd delivered his cattle, he'd secretly sought to persuade one of their district chiefs to help fight the settlers but he, like Pushmataha, refused to take up arms against the White man. Billy nudged his horse forward. As he and Sam dismounted, McQueen and Francis approached, Francis wielding a red warclub.

McQueen bared his teeth like a rabid wolf. "You ready to kill White men, Yellow Billy? Eh? Go to war with us?"

"It's not a wise move." Billy spoke this not only because he believed it but also for Sam's benefit, who knew nothing of his meeting in Chickasawhay. "We cannot defeat the White man. I have spoken on this matter many times."

"Chief Peter McQueen"—Sam tossed back his head indignantly— "this mixed-race man will not join you false fools."

"So we shall kill you both. Eh?" McQueen snickered. "You will go first, Yellow Billy."

"Sam, you will be next." Francis smirked.

Sam snatched the prophet's warclub, whacked him upside the head, sprang into his saddle, and galloped off in a cloud of dust.

Francis staggered.

Billy sighed. *Be safe, Sam.*

"You are on our side?" McQueen asked.

Rolling his neck, Francis massaged his head. "You didn't leave us, Yellow Billy."

"Supalamy is on your side. I will join you too." Perhaps he could help save the lives of the women and children. He was honor-bound to fight with his fellow warriors. "I don't approve of this war or what you're doing. It will destroy you, and many will die. But you are my people, and I will share your fate."

Billy moved into the circle of warriors, clasped a gourd, eyed his wife. She nodded her approval and, with his children, silently watched. While he drank the *assee*, others sang ritual songs. If he were not a man, he would shed many tears for his people and his family who would fight on the side of the Whites. Although he knew the war's outcome, if he must die with them, he must die. They were his blood.

CHAPTER THIRTY-FIVE

"**P**hineas. What's happening?" Thomas pointed when the sharp odor of burning wood struck him.

Dense black clouds swirled over treetops near the Alabama River. Panicked birds scattered in flight. Above the roar of a blaze, a crash echoed. Thomas and Phineas galloped to the fire.

Orange flames rocketed from a log cabin, rolling up, devouring its square pillars and spiraling upon its roof. Shutters exploded off windows. Its porch buckled.

Fist over his mouth, Thomas coughed in the noxious smoke. A piercing cry threw him from his saddle.

Phineas, too, sprinted toward the plea but Thomas, younger and faster, outran his mentor, shrugged off his coat, held it over his face, and approached the door.

A grizzled old man stumbled out. "M-My wife. C-Creeks." He collapsed onto the dirt, clawed grass, and sobbed in guttural, gut-wrenching bursts.

Thomas grabbed the man's legs and Phineas his arms. They dragged him clear of the conflagration. Thunder shaking earth reverberated behind them.

Thomas pivoted. A mounted warrior wielding a red war club charged him from out of the timber and swung the deadly weapon at his head. Thomas ducked and dodged the club by a hair. Another warrior, then another one, charged on their mounts. Gunshots echoed.

His attackers jerked their mounts leftward and galloped into a field. Other mounted warriors gave chase.

Thomas fingered around his scalp for blood. Phineas struggled to his feet.

"Are you all right, sir?" Thomas asked, not finding any blood on his hands.

Phineas whacked dust off his trousers. "Gunshots saved us, scared 'em off."

"Reckon so."

More gunshots from the woods.

Thomas strode to the sobbing farmer, dirty and slumped against a stump, his clothes blackened by smoke. "They k-killed my w-wife."

Phineas wrapped his arm around the old man. "I'm sorry, friend."

A fiery implosion quaked the sky. The cabin tumbled into a mound of charred rubble, burying the man's wife somewhere beneath its smoldering embers.

A big man astride a black horse approached at the head of a small band of men. He didn't carry a warclub, but instead, a scalping knife and a tomahawk. Two pistols sat in bucket holsters draped on his horse's neck. He halted his mount, as did his men whose hair varied in lengths and styles.

"We executed the fools who attacked you," the big man said.

"Why'd they do it?" The old man's voice cracked. "I ain't done nothing deserving what they done. They killed my wife, burned my crops."

"I am Crazy Wildcat, a law mender of the Creek Nation." Dismounting, the big man stretched his muscular arm toward his men. "We are all law menders. Your attackers followed the false prophets. Chief Big Warrior, Speaker of the Upper Creeks, challenged them to come to the village of Tukabatchee and prove their powers."

"I figure they didn't come." Thomas's words sounded sarcastic in his ears.

"They killed our messenger who delivered our challenge. Burning farms along this river is how they answered us." Crazy Wildcat's gruff manner succumbed to tenderness as he knelt beside the sobbing man. "I am sorry we did not arrive in time to stop this from happening."

The man nodded.

Thomas inhaled deeply. So, war had come to their doorstep. Constant chatter of it had, unfortunately, turned to action.

"Who are you? What are your names?" Crazy Wildcat straightened.

"Ministers of the gospel," Phineas said.

"I have heard about preachers." Crazy Wildcat huffed. "I have no interest in your Christ. I do not even believe my own people's religion. My sister doesn't either. She hates preachers. I do not hate them, but I do not trust their religious words."

"What would your sister's name be?" Phineas asked.

"Sehoy. She is married to a White man named King."

Thomas started. "Richard King? In the Tombigbee Valley?"

"He is the man." Crazy Wildcat squinted at Thomas till a flash of recognition sparked in his eyes. "You are the one who brought great dishonor to Barnaby Hatch?"

Thomas stammered. "I, uh, I took no pleasure doing it. I was defending Annabelle, not myself."

"I'm glad you did it. I do not respect men who beat their women. It is the way of a coward. What Barnaby did was his concern, not mine, which is why I did not interfere."

"Uh, I made it my business to protect her." Relieved that the Creek didn't demonstrate displeasure, Thomas breathed easier.

"What you do is what you do." The big Creek flashed a grin. "We are friends now."

"Friends, Crazy Wildcat." Phineas shook the Creek's hand. "Very good friends. You saved our lives."

On wobbly legs, the old man managed to gain his feet. "I've lost everything. My house, my wife."

"We'd be pleased to have your company," Phineas said.

His vacant stare fixed on the grass, the man shook his head. "N-No. Not sure, not sure what to do."

"Do you have family nearby?" Thomas's words came out gentle.

Everyone waited for the terrified man to regain his composure. "My cousin lives in Mississippi with the Chickasaws," he said at last. "He's married to a Chickasaw woman."

"The Chickasaws are on our side." Crazy Wildcat gestured to his five mounted men behind him. "Three of my warriors will travel with you there to keep you safe."

The man gripped Crazy Wildcat's hand in gratitude.

"First, sir, we must have a proper burial for your wife." Phineas hurried to his horse and got his Bible out of his saddlebag. "Thomas and me'll be heading back for the Tensaw where things are, we hope, a little safer. S'ppose our work in these parts is done for a spell."

Crazy Wildcat and his warriors helped Thomas and Phineas dig the grave. How were things safer? Thomas tossed aside a shovelful of dirt. If they were in a war, and if White folks were pulled into it … His shovel smacked a rock. *Dear Lord, protect us all.*

CHAPTER THIRTY-SIX

Barnaby tilted back further in his rocking chair, his fingers clawing its arms, its mournful creaking playing a dirge on the floor. Had it not been for the tiny flicker of the oil lamp on his table, total blackness would shroud this room. Its drawn drapes killed the moonlight. The entire house, not a sparkle of candlelight anywhere. He'd grown accustomed to this darkness, the silence, the sporadic hoots of owls or a coyote's lament.

Eustis had gone to his cabin for the night, his domestic responsibilities done. Alone. An outcast from society, thanks to losing that fight with Murcher and Mister King's threat. His blacksmith business, sold to King at the point of a gun.

He stroked his aching right biceps. He'd whipped too many slaves today. Tomorrow, he'd let his overseer perform that duty. Whipping them vented his bitterness at the world.

The chair creaked louder on the floorboards. Faster, he rocked. He'd find a way to get even with King and his dirty little Injun wife. Oh yes. They'd offered a handsome reward to anyone who killed him if he dared show up in King's Brook again. No doubt, he'd become an outcast to all who knew him. The day after he'd fought Murcher and lost, King and Clay paid him a visit and warned him of that fact.

Tomorrow, he'd have Eustis go with him to pick up supplies in Saint Stephens. No one there knew what happened two months ago, at least he hoped such was the case. On previous trips there, not a soul had mentioned it to him. Only a smattering of folks lived there. Word might have gotten round to them. However, it was a chance he'd take.

At sunrise the next morning, he dressed and went to Eustis's small log cabin behind his house. He knocked on the butler's door. "Eustis. It's me. Open up."

No response.

Barnaby rapped harder. "Come on out. This minute."

Still, no response.

"I'm gonna whip you, boy." Gritting his teeth, Barnaby kicked the door open.

Inside the cabin's tiny room, the dawning day spilled through a window. Eustis's cot was empty. His shoes, which he always kept under it, were gone. No suspenders, no hat, no shirt, and no trousers anywhere. Hot blood rushing to his head, Barnaby roared. "Eustis! Escaped!" He bolted outside and spotted the butler's tracks imprinted in the ground's soft red dirt, going in the direction of King's Brook. If he pursued him … He shook his head. "Go on, Eustis. I ain't getting myself killed on account of you. I'll buy myself another butler when I get me the chance."

After he told his overseer he was leaving and left him in charge of things till he returned, he hitched his horse to his wagon and struck out for Saint Stephens. He expected to arrive there within hours.

WEDNESDAY, JULY 21, 1813
SAINT STEPHENS, ALABAMA COUNTRY, MISSISSIPPI TERRITORY

Barnaby parked his wagon at the log trading post inside Fort Saint Stephens. On the limestone fort's parade ground, two companies of perspiring militiamen marched one behind the other to the cadence calls of other men. None wore uniforms, so he had no idea of their ranks.

A tobacco-chewing man stepped out of the post.

Barnaby thumbed them. "Looks like the militia's training today."

The man spat a stream of tobacco. "For the fight that's coming."

"I knew things around here were getting bad."

"More'n bad. You ain't heard the talk?"

"I've been on my farm the last few months."

"Good thing they ain't raided you yet."

"The Red Sticks?"

The man bit off another chaw and worked it back and forth between his cheeks. He spit it on the ground. "They've been raiding lots of plantations in the region. Sam Moniac's farm got hit bad. James Cornells's farm too. Cornells's wife got captured and taken to Pensacola, but rumor says he got her back."

When the marching stopped and the militiamen grounded their muskets, Barnaby identified Clay in the second rank, his tousled red hair unmistakable.

"A band of them Creeks went to Pensacola to get arms and ammunition from them Spaniards." The man stomped on a roach skittering past his feet. "They're wanting to fight us. Moniac and Cornells gave us the alarm, said Peter McQueen and Josiah Francis were their leaders."

While the man palavered away, Barnaby made a path to the militia. Dismissed from their drill, the men meandered about, chattering. As Clay passed him, he muttered, "I'm killing you soon as I get the chance, Barnaby."

Before Barnaby responded, his former friend joined others in a building up ahead.

A tall, slender man, his light brown beard dropping halfway down his chest, approached. "Barnaby Hatch. It's been a while since we last saw each other."

"It has been, Benjamin Smoot." Barnaby had a passing acquaintance with Smoot but no more than that. He grabbed his musket out of his wagon. "Hear trouble's brewing. Moniac's and Cornells's farms were raided. You reckon on fighting McQueen's men who done it?"

"Soon as Colonel Caller and his boys arrive. I've been elected a captain."

"Congratulations. Is Clay in your company?"

"Captain Heard's. Want to join us? We can sure use you."

For a moment, Barnaby considered Smoot's offer. By enlisting, he'd have a chance to kill Clay and protect his farm at the same time. "Thank you, Captain Smoot. That's a good idea."

Smoot clapped him on the back. "Let's go. You can sign the enlistment papers. I'll swear you in."

On the way to Smoot's quarters, Barnaby's brain stirred. He'd write his overseer to tell him what he'd learned today and inform him he'd signed on to fight. This gave him the best opportunity to kill Clay without getting caught.

THURSDAY-TUESDAY, JULY 22-26, 1813
ROAD TO PENSACOLA, ALABAMA COUNTRY, MISSISSIPPI TERRITORY

During his wait for Caller's militia Barnaby didn't speak to Clay nor Clay to him. The hatred sizzling inside him burned like a slow fuse. He'd kill Clay during the battle and make people think a Red Stick did it. The Kings and the Indians—he loathed them both. Sehoy King, working her hardest to act like a White lady. Stupid woman. *Sehoy's a cow.*

A few days later Caller and one-hundred-eighty men arrived. The march continued toward Pensacola. They crossed the Tombigbee in canoes while their horses swam to its opposite bank. Along the way, they made camp at the cattle pens owned by Billy Weatherford's brother-in-law, David Tate.

An hour later a man of medium build, wearing a fine straw hat, rode into their camp at the head of a company of mounted militia. He sat erect with his shoulders squared. Though beardless, a drooping brown mustache framed his wide lips. Barnaby recognized him immediately— Dixon Bailey, a métis who lived in the Tensaw district.

Unlike Caller's militia, Bailey's militia rode in two perfectly spaced columns. Once they entered the camp, he dismounted and barked several orders to his company. His militiamen swung out of their saddles, assembled shoulder to shoulder and at Bailey's command, they did a sharp "right face."

"Sergeants, dismiss the men," Bailey said.

The sergeants repeated the orders. The men broke ranks.

A sword dangling from his hip, Bailey marched to Colonel Caller and saluted. "Captain Dixon Bailey, sir. We're ready to fight."

Caller didn't return the salute. "Glad to have you join us, Captain. Mrs. Tate has invited us to dine with her tonight. I trust you and your officers will attend it."

"Thank you, sir. Gladly."

Judging by Captain Bailey's and his men's conduct, Barnaby couldn't help but compare them with Caller's force. Bailey must've spent lots of hours training his boys. Despite their lack of uniforms, they marched and conducted themselves in a professional manner whereas Caller's men behaved like amateurs.

On the twenty-sixth day of July Caller called a halt at the main trail to Pensacola. Again, they made camp. Eager conversation about their pending ambush rippled through the ranks. Yet Barnaby didn't speak a word. He rarely spoke to anyone during the march. All he wanted to do was kill Clay … at the right moment. This battle provided him with that right moment.

TUESDAY, JULY 27, 1813
ROAD TO PENSACOLA, ALABAMA COUNTRY, MISSISSIPPI TERRITORY

Barnaby sat alone beneath a tree finishing off some beef jerky and glared at Clay, drinking coffee with his messmates in a grove of oaks. His blood simmered like a kettle of water over a fire. No one had ever rejected him before, not the way ole King and his Injun wife had done him. It'd been three months, three whole months of torture by an ache that'd only heal once he achieved his revenge.

Hoofbeats caught his interest. He stood. A small group of men Caller had sent to Pensacola to spy on the enemy, minutes earlier, rode back into the camp. Within earshot of Barnaby, they reined in their mounts at the colonel, who arose from a stool. "You boys returned awful fast."

"McQueen's warriors are camped a few miles up the trail," one spy said. "They don't know we're here. They're eating lunch."

"Good work, men. Now we can take them by surprise." Caller rushed from officer to officer and gathered them for a conference in a grassy area where their horses grazed.

Meanwhile, Clay swaggered to Barnaby. "Appears we're going to have a fight in a few minutes, Hatch. I hope you're ready to die."

Standing, Barnaby thinned his lips. "Not today." He poked Clay's ribs. "I joined this militia for one reason. So I can kill you."

Clay snickered. "You're the reason our gang disbanded. You're the one who's going to get killed today. I'll make my father proud." He pivoted on his heel to leave when Caller announced the battle order.

Barnaby, with Captain Smoot's company, took the front right flank. Captain Bailey's men the front center, and "Big" Sam Dale's boys the front left. For fear the enemy might hear them, no one uttered a sound.

They trod a few miles toward their objective. At the top of a hill, the scene below brought the militia to a stop. In a bend of Burnt Corn Creek packhorses aplenty grazed, burdened with what Barnaby suspected contained tools of war. Warriors gathered sticks and built fires for cooking. Other warriors were already eating.

Because he never met him, Barnaby was unable to identify McQueen among those men. Each warrior possessed a tuft of hair at the back of his shaved scalp. One man did wear a porcupine hair headdress. Perhaps he was McQueen.

Whispered orders passed from captains to sergeants to their men. Quietly, they assumed their battle positions, Barnaby in the second rank of Captain Smoot's company. He knew little about soldiering, and the captain never had much time to train him. He raised his musket.

His sword lifted in the front lines, Caller yelled, "Charge!"

The ranks swept down the hill toward the enemy camp. Startled, the Red Sticks dropped pots and pans and meals and made for the creek. Musketry rattled. A warrior fell. Clay and others chased them into the water. They splashed and swam to the other side into a canebrake.

"That was too easy," Barnaby told a militiaman, seizing a packhorse's bridle.

"If they all fight this badly," the militiaman said, leading another packhorse away, "it'll be a short war."

Blood-curdling whoops pierced the sky. Dropping the packhorse's reins, Barnaby whirled, dropped to his knee to load his musket. The hair on his neck stood straight.

Captains Smoot and Bailey shouted orders. Their companies, and Sam Dale's, pivoted toward the onrushing enemy splashing toward them from across the creek. Shoulder to shoulder, their musketry cut loose. Caller's panicked militia scattered in full flight.

The enemy's musket balls flew wildly. Smoot's company and the others out front kept up a steady fire to buy time for their fellow militiamen to escape. Barnaby knelt, checked to be sure his flint was in his musket's hammer, then triggered a round.

Shouting and waving their deadly war clubs, the Red Sticks closed. Barnaby stood. A ball struck his right shoulder, another one his left thigh. He tossed aside his gun and took off as fast as his wounds and heavy legs could carry him. Panting, staggering, he stumbled away from the action. With his strength exhausted from loss of blood, his legs surrendered. He hid beneath some brush while others fled the field. Captains Smoot's, Bailey's, and Dale's men withdrew in more disciplined order.

Breathing hard and despite his ebbing strength Barnaby ripped off his sweaty shirt, a tourniquet for his wounds.

Militiamen continued to stream past. Some ran, others plodded. They'd left their horses behind.

He clenched a shirt sleeve between his teeth to tear it apart.

"There you are."

The remorseless voice snapped up Barnaby's head. "You found me, eh, Clay?"

"I found you. Remember what I said." He aimed his cocked pistol at Barnaby's heart.

"N-Now w-wait a minute, Clay." Barnaby wriggled back against a tree. "I-I'm wounded. You wouldn't shoot a wounded man, would you? It ain't playing fair."

"You're right. I wouldn't shoot a wounded man, but I do show mercy to wounded animals. I put them out of their misery." He squeezed the trigger.

CHAPTER THIRTY-SEVEN

"We sure got ourselves into a heap of trouble at this moment in time, Phineas." Thomas steered his mount into the tree line to let a long column of covered wagons hurry past, dust flying beneath creaking wheels and odiferous sweat coating the horses and oxen drawing the vehicles. Yapping dogs chased each other in play. Curled up cats napped on wagon benches or on people's laps. Somber faces, panicked faces, children and babies weeping in their mothers' arms. He figured this scene repeated itself throughout the Tombigbee and Tensaw regions. Probably on the Alabama River too. Even before the militia's recent defeat at Burnt Corn Creek, settlers began building stockades in anticipation of war.

Phineas guided his horse back onto the post road.

Thomas fell in behind him. He craned his neck. Up ahead, somewhere among the wagons, was Mrs. O'Neil, at whose house they'd heard the news from her husband who'd fought at Burnt Corn. They'd ambushed some Red Sticks returning from Pensacola who they believed carried arms and ammunition obtained from the Spaniards, but the Red Sticks routed them.

When word of their defeat spread folks started pouring into stockades, such as this one around Mister Mims's house. These fanatical Creeks wielding their red warclubs had declared war on the settlers and all who supported them.

"I hope your muscles are ready," Phineas said. "S'ppose we'll be helping build Mister Mims's stockade."

"I don't know nothing about stockades, sir," Thomas said.

"Nor I, but we got to do something to help these frightened folks. Folks around here need us."

"I figure he'll be agreeable to what we're doing." Thomas's mind ambled to Annabelle. He hoped she came here. Within minutes, he rode through Fort Mims's eastern gate and thrust her from his thoughts. War had begun. Souls hung in the balance. "Dear Lord, help us in this time of trouble. Show me and Phineas what we can do."

"Amen," Phineas said.

Thursday, August 5, 1813
Fort Mims, Alabama country, Mississippi Territory

On a little over an acre of Samuel Mims's property Thomas, Phineas, and settlers labored like bedeviled ants on a plowed-up hill, preparing for a battle they hoped never came. Sweat poured off men digging narrow trenches for the palisade. Perspiring axe-men made tall pickets for it by splitting pine logs. Nails were pounded. Lumber sawed. Tiny clapboard houses were thrown up around Mister Mims's single-story frame house.

Every day, more terrified settlers and their slaves sought refuge in this stockade, their wagons bulging with food and worldly goods. Amidst swarms of mosquitoes, swamp stench permeated the fort. Its commander, Major Daniel Beasley, a heavyset man with a fleshy, florid face, delivered orders here and there. Soldiers under his command busied themselves with erecting an adjacent stockade outside the east gate.

Ever since Beasley's arrival two days ago, Thomas puzzled as to why General Ferdinand Claiborne, commander of the Territorial

Militia at Fort Stoddert, dispatched him here. Beasley never made his men drill, nor did he enforce anything in the way of discipline and to top even this, the arrogant man loved his liquor.

While men planted the pointed split-log pickets upright in the palisade's trenches Thomas worked alongside Mister Mims. Mims's brother David and Phineas cut wedges to form one-half of a picket's loophole.

Women hurled themselves into work as well. They washed clothes at nearby Boatyard Lake, kept their children out of the way of the hard-working men, and cooked meals from supplies obtained from their farms.

By way of flatboat, soldiers from Fort Stoddert brought food to Fort Mims's military garrison. Oblivious to the danger, people's pets roamed the grounds. The odors of the unwashed spread throughout the stockade. Only the métis inhabitants, in keeping their penchant for cleanliness, bothered to bathe on a regular basis in Boatyard Lake.

"It's good your wife's in Mobile, Mister Mims." Thomas helped him heft a picket onto sawhorses.

"And I'm mighty glad she is." Mister Mims cast a wary eye at Phineas. "No preaching in this stockade, and we'll keep things around here peaceable. Our predicament is too serious for us to argue religion."

"Life and living's a serious matter, Mister Mims." Phineas slapped the picket. "Let's do this." He raised his ripsaw for Mister Mims to measure it.

Thomas joined John Randon and Randon's slave, Jimmy, a lanky awkward youth. He grabbed Randon's timber in its middle and helped them carry it toward the palisade.

Jimmy stumbled and dropped his end.

"Quit dawdling, boy," Randon growled.

"He didn't mean to drop it," Thomas said. "Maybe me and you are moving too fast."

"Stay out of my business, Murcher. I own Jimmy. No one messes with my property."

Thomas bit back a retort. No sense stirring up a man's wrath during a crisis. Jimmy huffed.

As they lifted the picket again Thomas spotted another covered wagon clattering into the fort. Richard King, perched on its bench with Sehoy, drove it in. His bloodhound Lucky, wearing a brown leather collar, poked his wrinkled head out between them. Afoot, their slaves brought up the rear. After King parked, he hastened to Major Beasley who was studying a chart spread out on a table.

Once he set up the fence rail, eagerness for news about Annabelle sent Thomas to them.

"More of us may be coming," King said.

Major Beasley squinted. His whiskey breath stank. It was a wonder that, despite his slight slurs, he spoke clear enough to be understood. Thomas winced at the distant memory, how in his evil days he used to drink whiskey almost every Saturday night.

"General Claiborne's orders?" Beasley asked.

"He told my settlement to quit building its stockade and to seek refuge in certain ones. I came here because Mister Mims and I are friends."

"Too many fortifications to defend stretches ush thin." Beasley set down his bottle.

Intoxicated commanders don't help none either. Thomas quelled his irritation.

"Do you always keep the gate open?" King thumbed at the east gate.

"Telling me my bushness, King?"

"I'm just saying, Major—"

"I'm in command here." Beasley waved his whiskey bottle at King. "Sho, if I shay the gate shtays open, it shtays open." He banged his fist on the chart table and swilled more whiskey. "Keeping the gate open makes it eashier for people to come in and go out."

It also made it easier for the enemy to get inside, Thomas told himself.

Turning, King bumped Thomas. "What'd you want, Preacher?"

"Is Annabelle coming?"

"Why would I care?" King stalked past soldiers arguing over a card game.

TUESDAY, AUGUST 10, 1813
FORT MIMS, ALABAMA COUNTRY, MISSISSIPPI TERRITORY

Thomas mounted Mister Mims's gallery. Hundreds crowded beneath the brilliant starlight. Some people sat on wagons eating corn and sweet potatoes obtained from their farms, others engaged in conversation. Children and dogs romped the grounds. Major Beasley's Mississippi Volunteers played cards with General Claiborne's men whom he'd dispatched from Fort Stoddert. Not a care in the world did these folks have. A pitiful thing Mister Mims didn't let him and Phineas preach. One sermon, at least. But no. Not a single concern about their eternal destinies did these people possess, for they figured their lives lasted forever.

He started to announce a hymn Phineas planned to play when Mister Mims, seated in a rocker, struck up a waltz, or at least that's what Thomas figured. He truly had no idea. Many couples danced, men's arms around their ladies' waists, twirling and spinning across the beaten ground. Lucky led other dogs in a chorus of howls. Several cats echoed meows. Phineas, standing behind Mister Mims, lowered his violin with a scowl.

Thomas shared his mentor's disgust at the dancing and revelry. Maneuvering and squeezing between the dancers, his elbows bumping some, he passed through the inner east gate to the outer gate, the expansion Beasley's soldiers had begun several days ago at last completed to keep the officers' quarters and enlisted men's quarters separate. He stopped at a mound of red clay and twisted toward the inner gate, staring at the party.

"We'll have us one dickens of a time closing these gates if we're attacked." The speaker, a youthful soldier on sentry duty, left the guard house to speak with him.

"Agreed," Thomas said.

"The major wants to keep it open. But supposing he's wrong. Supposing we are attacked?"

"A grave consideration."

A young man of a light brown complexion with black muttonchop whiskers approached—Doctor Thomas G. Holmes. When they first met, Thomas learned the doctor was of African Irish descent — his mother Black and his father Irish— which accounted for his slight Irish accent. He, too, had been at Burnt Corn Creek. "Beasley's no real soldier, Namesake." Namesake was the nickname the doctor gave him on account of they shared the same first name. "He was a sheriff in the Natchez region before this war. Also, captain of the county militia. A friend of General Claiborne too, if the rumors are accurate. He once served in the territorial legislature, what I've been told."

"He ain't got business being in command here, Doctor Holmes," Thomas said.

"Although I'm a mere assistant surgeon in this sorry place, even I possess enough sense to keep this gate shut." Doctor Holmes surveyed the fort's merry occupants. Outside the gates, he looked both ways. Woods, cane marsh, brushy ravines. "When General Claiborne inspected us a few days ago, he ordered Beasley to build more blockhouses."

"Shucks, the one we got now ain't finished yet, Doc," the sentry said.

"Sad, but true." Doctor Holmes's feet crunched twigs as he backed into the fort, Thomas and the soldier with him. Holmes continued. "This place being where it is, having so many swamps around it, it's no wonder Doctor Osborne and myself have lots of sick folk requiring us." His thin brows formed a straight line. "We don't have much in the way of medicine. Bleeding them, giving them a little whiskey or wine is about all we can do. Yes, sir, Namesake, I'd say we're in a mighty serious pickle in this place."

"I sure 'nuff hope we aren't attacked." The soldier lowered his musket to pull a snuff box from his shirt pocket.

A clattering wagon and a horse's snort ended their conversation. Thomas tensed. *Hmm.* Three women in it— Maggie, Suzie. He broke out in a delighted grin. "Annabelle."

"Thomas. Thomas." Excited, Annabelle slapped her team's reins and hurried through the gate.

Clay, brandishing his pistol, popped up from some behind some crates in the wagon's rear. With a wicked grin, he cocked it halfway. "Ready to die, Preacher?"

WEDNESDAY, AUGUST 11, 1813
FORT MIMS, ALABAMA COUNTRY, MISSISSIPPI TERRITORY

Murmurs and laughter awakened Thomas. He scratched his head, rolled onto his side, and shoved himself up onto his feet. His back ached from sleeping on the hard earth. Breakfast at Fort Mims. The food was tolerable but not their situation. He was a rat trapped in a pest-ridden cage. Swamp air and foul-smelling bodies packed together. And disease.

Along the western wall, Lucky tramped about sniffing earth at the head of smaller dogs as though on guard duty. Like the east wall, the west wall had two gates. Unlike the east gate, the west wall's inner gate stayed closed, but its outer one remained open.

In keeping to their early morning routine Captain Dixon Bailey's sister, Peggy, led other métis women and their children to Boatyard Lake for baths, this time accompanied by Annabelle, who'd befriended them. She returned in time to eat.

Thomas brought his plate of eggs and bacon to Annabelle's table. "Mind if I join you?"

Annabelle, chewing her food, patted the seat beside her.

A shabby man rose from his spot. "I'm in no mood to listen to you two yappin'."

"Since you think that way, go ahead and leave us." Annabelle slapped her hand over her mouth. "Oops. That came out the wrong way."

"It certainly did," a woman said. She shot to her feet to accompany the man.

"I'm sorry," Annabelle yelled after them.

But the couple hastened over to Mister Mims's smokehouse to gab with someone drinking something from a mug.

"Don't fret about it, Annabelle. You can apologize to them later." His head bowed, Thomas blessed his food.

"It's a sorrowful thing, these people acting so carefree 'round here." Annabelle reached for a fork.

"Indeed." Thomas scooped up a spoonful of scrambled eggs. "A lot of them ain't giving mine and Phineas's words and warnings much listening to."

Annabelle set aside her fork and wiped her fingers on a napkin one finger at a time.

"Any news about Barnaby?"

"He was wounded in the fighting at Burnt Corn and died a couple days later, if Clay spoke truthful."

"I'm not sure I believe him."

"You don't believe he's dead?"

"Oh, I believe he's dead, else he'd be here. Thing is, I ain't sure it was his wounds that killed him."

"You think Clay done it? Killed him, I mean?"

"King put a price on Barnaby's head, didn't he? Said he'd kill him if he came back to the settlement. Him and Clay hated each other after I defeated him in our fight." Thomas scooped up more scrambled eggs. "A regretful thing, Barnaby dying before he turned from his evil doings."

"Clay told ever'body Burnt Corn weren't much of a fight."

"Captain Bailey told us about it." Thomas sliced his bacon. "He was there too. The captain said some men quit chasing McQueen's warriors and began stealing their packhorses and looting what they left behind. Not his men, though, the captain said. Said his men were better disciplined. Anyway, that's when McQueen's warriors counterattacked and scattered them."

Annabelle reached for her mug of milk. "Peggy Bailey said most ever'body mustered themselves out of the militia and went home. 'Brother Dixon's no coward,' she says. She's proud of him." Her attention drifted to Clay, seated at another table eating with his parents. "It ain't 'cause you whipped the tarnation out of Barnaby why Clay's aching to kill you."

Thomas grunted. "Still figuring that way, is he?"

"It's 'cause when you took a stand against him and his family, them Ruffians lost control of ever'body, and he hankered after taking Barnaby's place. 'Cause of you, he said there ain't no more gang."

"I don't figure he'll do anything at this moment in time. Too many folks packed in here. He'd get caught easy as apple pie."

Annabelle flashed a sunshine smile. "We're all mighty grateful to you and Reverend Steward."

"We're just glad those Ruffians won't be bothering y'all again. Where've the Oglesbys gone?"

"To Mobile, where they said they was heading. Zander's brother moved there from Georgia soon after the Spanish surrendered the town. The Vances and Lem's family went to another fort. Ain't sure which one."

Thomas cut a small portion of bacon. "What about the Ruffians?"

"Scattered to other forts. I thought some were coming here. Reckon I was wrong."

Doctor Holmes plopped on the bench beside him. "Here I am, Namesake Thomas, my friend."

"How are the sick folks?" Thomas stuck a few more portions of scrambled eggs into his mouth and chewed.

"Not faring very well," the doctor said. "A child got his foot cut on a nail, one dog bite, and as you are already aware, lots of cases of fever."

Annabelle gasped. "Yellow fever?"

"Let's hope not, Miss Lawson. My guess is, and Doctor Osborne concurs, there's a better chance it's dysentery. Quite a few feverish folks have suffered other symptoms. Nausea. Stomach pain." Doctor Holmes slapped a mosquito on his brown knuckles.

Two children ran up to them, a skinny sandy-haired boy of about eight years and his younger sister, a tiny girl of about three years of age—Robby and Helen Heathrow.

The boy tugged Annabelle's cotton sleeve. "Will you play with us, Miss Lawson?"

"Play?" Annabelle raised her voice in a pretense of excitement. "Does your ma mind, Robby?"

Robby pointed at his mother, a tiny, smiling woman waving at her from her clapboard house.

"Let's do it." Annabelle pushed her food aside and patted Robby's sister's head. "What game you wanna play?"

"Pick-up sticks," Helen said.

"No, Helen," Robby said. "Jacks. We wanna play jacks." The boy reached into his pocket and produced a canvas bag Thomas figured contained the game pieces.

"I reckon we can play both." Annabelle grasped their hands. "One game at a time. Let's go on over to your place." She cocked her brows expectantly at Thomas. "Won't you join us?"

"I … er …"

"Play pick-up sticks with me, Mister Murcher," Helen said, pleading.

"Oh. Why not." Thomas winked at Helen. "Y'all go on ahead. I'll play pick-up sticks with you in a quick minute."

Helen giggled. "I'm going to beat you. I'm going to beat you."

"Oh no you won't, Helen." Thomas chuckled.

As Annabelle and the children strolled to the children's mother a boy called to her from the northern pickets in front of the log loom-house inhabitants called the "bastion."

"Miss Lawson! Miss Lawson!" The boy caught a ball Phineas tossed him. "Come here!"

"Wait your turn, Mitch. I'm playing with Robby and Helen first." She peered over her shoulder at Thomas. "Reckon I've gotten a mite popular in this place. With the young'uns at least. Hurry up and join us, Thomas. Please don't be long."

"I'll be there." Thomas's gaze followed her as she sauntered off with the children. Every day, she blossomed prettier, a rose bud opening one petal at a time to a hearty spring. She always insisted he be with her as often as possible. A close friend, she'd become. In fact, his only female friend, at least among ladies who approached his age. "Never knew till we got here how much Annabelle loved children, Doctor. Kept it hidden from us beneath all the tough talking she used to do."

Doctor Holmes leaned forward. "Let's pray she'll survive this war. Pray all of us will."

"Amen." Thomas frowned. At the thought of Annabelle falling victim to arrows and tomahawks, queasiness gripped him. "Doctor, I got a bad sense about us being here. A mighty bad sense of some ill event."

"I share your feeling, Namesake. Not much we can do about it though, is there?"

"Not much. Please excuse me, sir. I have a promise to keep to little Helen."

"Understood, my friend." Doctor Holmes resumed eating.

SATURDAY, AUGUST 14, 1813
OTHLEWALLEE, ALABAMA COUNTRY, MISSISSIPPI TERRITORY

No longer clothed in the garb of a White man but instead, wearing a breechcloth and moccasins and his head shaved, Billy Weatherford sat beneath an arbor on Othlewallee's square where a sacred fire burned. He listened to his fellow leaders discuss their plans against the settlers, their vengeance for the militia's surprise attack at Burnt Corn Creek.

"Yellow Billy," a chief said, "what do you think? They are building a fort around Samuel Mims's house. Should we attack it and Fort Pierce?"

"I know Sam Mims," Billy said. "Those forts are two miles apart."

"Is it wise for us to attack them?" the prophet Paddy Walsh asked.

Billy scanned the eager braves awaiting his response. These followers of the prophets never heeded his warnings. They couldn't defeat the Whites in this war. A different plan took shape in his mind. "Fort Sinquefield is a better target than Fort Pierce. Some runaway slaves from Fort Mims told me that fort is weak too." His finger drew a line in the dirt as he explained his idea.

"It is a good plan," Josiah Francis said once Billy finished. "I will help you with further details."

"Josiah Francis, you will lead the attack on Fort Sinquefield," another chief said. To Billy, he added, "You and Paddy will lead our attack on Fort Mims. Paddy, you will attack under Billy's direction."

Billy and Paddy nodded at each other.

"We'll send the other towns on our side the 'broken days' with a message to meet us at Flat Creek." Billy stood. *Broken days, bundles of twigs.* Every sunrise, each town would break off a twig from a bundle till the appointed time for their gathering there, on the lower Alabama River. "I must check on my woman and children."

The chiefs and prophets bid him a cheerful goodbye. Step by step to his cabin, he studied the darkening sky. A storm brewed. Dreary weather, like the dreariness burdening his soul.

CHAPTER THIRTY-EIGHT

Inside the first level of Fort Mims's half-built blockhouse Thomas gathered with Phineas, Annabelle, and Doctor Holmes to pray. Maggie, Suzie, and another slave named Hester joined them along with Robby and Helen's parents. While they talked to God others made merry or passed out of the fort on various errands. Young couples danced; children played. For them, their eternal destiny promised no consequences.

"Shut up, you flock of fools." Clay barreled into the blockhouse, his parents with him and drooling Lucky at their side.

"Listen to my son," Sehoy snapped.

King, grinding his teeth, glared at Hester. "I saw you pet my dog this morning, girl. No one, I mean no one, pets Lucky unless I tell them they can."

"I was looking at his collar, sir." Hester glanced at the dog. "He's sho' wearing a nice collar. Is that his name on it?"

"Look at me when I'm talking to you."

Hester's head pivoted in King's direction. Her tight fists on her wide hips, her squinty eyes challenged his glare.

Shaking a finger at her, King delivered his warning. "Let me catch you petting Lucky again, I'll make sure your master whips you."

Hester stalked off.

"Come back here, Hester. I'm going to tell Mister Steadham. He'll whip you."

Without a glance back, Hester jostled through a crowd to a well where other slaves gathered.

King puffed out his exasperation. Lucky sat on the ground, leaned against him, and panted.

"Stupid girl," Sehoy scoffed. Next, she leveled her wickedness upon Thomas and Phineas. "Those who believe my people's religion and their prophets are dangerous. They are deceived." Her thin lips twisted in a sneer. Her hard stare bore in on Annabelle as though she'd slit her throat. "All religion is false. You people who talk about your religion are also deceived. Annabelle Lawson, you disappoint me. You, too, have fallen for false words. We are no longer friends."

Annabelle thrust back her shoulders. "Go ahead, Sehoy. Kill me. You want to do it. I ain't scared of dying no more."

"Religion, Mrs. King, is dangerous," Thomas said, "'cept religion and true faith ain't in the same bucket."

"Ain't you noticed the change in me, Sehoy?" Annabelle offered a sweet, gentle smile framed by small dimples. "I ain't such a bad person no more. And since I been here, I've found my true calling."

Sehoy spit at her feet.

"My calling's working with young'uns, Sehoy. The children here love me. Can't you see what love is by watching them? Watching how them young'uns love?"

"Love. What is love?" Sehoy marched off to Mister Mims's smokehouse.

"You're all touched in the head." King tapped his temple to emphasize his insult, then departed with Sehoy. This time, though, Lucky didn't follow. Instead, he sniffed Thomas's legs and feet.

"Preachers, I'm serving notice. Soon as this trouble's over, you're both dead." Clay stormed off behind his father.

Thomas gritted his teeth. None of them would likely live long enough for Clay to try to kill him. His irritation eased when he patted

Lucky's head. "Good boy." He offered his knuckles for the hound to sniff and slobber on. Lucky reminded him of dear Perro, whom the predacious bear killed many years ago.

Annabelle's fingers threaded Thomas's, tightening her grip and throbbing his pulse. She let go to stroke his shoulder. "I'm proud of you, Thomas. You are a fine genl'man."

"Yes, you are," Helen and Robby's mother said. Their father nodded.

"Uh, I, uh." Thomas fled the blockhouse and disappeared into the milling crowd. A riddle, Annabelle was. One great big, beautiful riddle.

An hour later, at Mister Mims's request, Annabelle stood on his porch and, accompanied by two violins and three guitars, moved into a song. Thomas caught his breath. God's marvelous handiwork. Her angelic singing drew people closer to listen. Sunlight glinted off her sparkling eyes. Thomas gulped. Twice. On several high notes, her soft gaze lingered on him. He looked away. A blush rushed up his cheeks.

In the stockade, he'd observed her closer. She helped as many folks as possible, took a personal interest in their needs, and cared for their children. A good wife she'd make. For whom? For himself? Because she'd grasped him earlier? Because she stroked his shoulder and complimented him for no reason? Because her gaze on him lingered during her song? *No.* She was being nice. That was all.

"Whiskey. Whiskey," the sentry at the east gate cried.

In his haste to the whiskey wagon ahead of the human stampede, Major Beasley knocked Thomas to the ground.

"Ouch!" Thomas sat up, snatched his hat off the ground, and massaged his sore head.

Two hours later Thomas caught John Randon's slaves, Jimmy and Mark, walking out of the stockade. "Where y'all heading?"

"Got told to check on Mister Randon's cattle," Mark said in a scratchy voice, in the peculiar sound boys made when growing out of childhood into manhood.

"Want me to go with you?"

"Naw, sah. We'll be fine."

"You two be mighty careful."

"Sho' will." Mark headed out the east gates, Jimmy at his side.

Thomas set his foot on a hard mound clay and wiggled the outer gate.

"What'd you think you're doing?" Beasley, his sword jangling on his hip and his arm cradling a whiskey bottle as though cradling a puppy, strode out of his tiny clapboard cabin.

Thomas wiggled the large gate again. "This gate. Don't you figure it'll be hard to shut fast if the Indians attack us?"

Beasley tilted back his head as the bottle touched his lips.

"Sir?"

Beasley clutched his bottle tight against his chest.

"Sir, with all due respect, if we're attacked—"

"Attacked?" Beasley tossed his empty bottle into some brush. His arm swept toward the scene beyond them. "Where's the threat out there, Murcher? You see it?"

"The enemy might be lying in wait till the right time. In those trees and marshes over yonder. Or in the ravines."

"Quit spreading rumors. We're all sick and tired of false alarms. I've given Doctor Holmes fair warning, and your fiddle-playing friend Reverend Steward. This time, I'm warning you. You will not stir panic."

"Major, the folks in this foul-smelling pig pen ain't scared enough. Their carefree attitude, and yours, is appalling. People only live once on this earth."

"Stop preaching at me, *Reverend* Murcher." Beasley spun on his heel to leave. "I intend on living a very long life. No more false alarms about Injuns and such."

"Indians! Indians!" Jimmy and Mark cried, sprinting into the stockade hollering at the top of their lungs.

Gasping, Jimmy's chest heaved and his breaths came hard. "'Bout-'bout twenty of 'em. Maybe more. Wearin' war paint."

Beasley jerked Jimmy off his feet.

Thomas scowled. Major Beasley, their first-rate idiot.

"You better not be lying to me, boy." Beasley slapped Jimmy.

"I-I ain't." Jimmy stomped his foot insistently. "I seen 'em. H-Honest."

"Out in them woods yonder." Mark's head bobbed fast.

Striding to the white tents where soldiers played cards, Beasley gave the order. "Captain Middleton, send out your scouts."

"Yes sir." The captain sprinted to his company and relayed Beasley's command.

The scouts quit their checkers and card games, grabbed their pistols, and swung into saddles while chattering excitedly about "killing us some Injuns." Within the minute, they trotted their horses out of the fort.

A drum rolled. Militiamen scrambled for their muskets and assembled at various posts.

Settlers darted into their makeshift homes and ducked beneath wagons, their weapons loaded and drawn. Frantically, Thomas scoured the stockade in search of Phineas and Annabelle.

Billy perked his ears. Hoofbeats. Murmurs. On the road. Other warriors stopped eating and listened too. As stealthy as cougars creeping up on prey, he and three of his braves crawled through the woods to investigate. Twigs and stones scraped his bare chest and rubbed his feet through his moccasins. Two scouts rode toward a creek he and his braves had forded a short time ago, six miles from Samuel Mims's plantation. Their intense conversation deflected their attention away from him.

A warrior eased up at his elbow. "Let's kill them, Billy." The warrior kept his voice low.

"Yes," another warrior whispered. "Kill them now."

Billy shook his head no.

Soon as the scouts passed, they dropped back to their camp where Billy conferred with his chiefs and prophets.

"If we kill them," Billy said, "it'll alert the fort we're here. I'll choose two warriors to go with me tonight to spy on it. Paddy, be sure our warriors finish their meals and rest. Tomorrow, we attack."

Paddy Walsh beamed. "It will be a great victory."

Billy maintained his grave demeanor. Friends and family were inside Fort Mims. His half-brother, David Tate, might be among them, for David's plantation wasn't far away. He stifled the screams threatening to explode. Tomorrow, many would die, much bloodshed on both sides in the coming battle. If he must die too in this lost cause, he'd die with his warriors … bravely.

Minutes after Middleton's cavalry detachment trotted back into the fort Thomas stood beside Phineas and Annabelle on Mister Mims's porch. He gripped one of its columns and leaned against it, his interest dominated by the unfolding events. "I wonder if they found anything."

"We'll learn the answer soon, Thomas." Phineas cleared his throat. "Very soon."

A lieutenant dismounted. "No sign of 'em, Major."

Upon the lieutenant's announcement hundreds swarmed Jimmy and Mark. Insults and threats stormed at them. The wide-eyed, stuttering boys quaked.

Annabelle squeezed Thomas's fingers as she squeaked out a cry.

A warm yearning spread through him, to wrap his arm around her, to calm her … No. She probably didn't realize she'd grabbed him on account she'd suffered a fright. While he continued to witness Randon's wrath and ill-treatment of Jimmy and Mark, his blood boiled hotter by the second.

John Randon shouted in Jimmy's face. "You filthy liar. Scaring us, telling us you saw Injuns."

"I-I did see 'em," Jimmy stammered.

"Me too, sah," Mark said in his scratchy voice. "I did. I did. I swear it."

Randon thumped the youths' heads. "Stop lying."

Jimmy and Mark cringed.

Two crows perched on the inner east gate, then winged into the surrounding trees.

"Out of my way." Beasley, sweating profusely and oozing a foul odor, jostled through the throng. "I'm whipping the daylights out of both of you." He marched Jimmy toward the whipping post on the fort's south side. "Changed my mind. I'm only whipping you, Jimmy boy. Make an example out of you for the other rumor mongers."

Thomas's hands constantly opened and closed. Phineas's crimson cheeks quivered. At Annabelle's wagon, Maggie's and Suzie's brows lowered. Hester, seated with them, muttered oaths. Thomas raised his fist and silently called out to God. Jimmy and Mark were just as human as they were. No man, woman, or child deserved this abuse.

Phineas nudged Thomas. They jumped off Mister Mims's porch and sprinted past Beasley to block the major's route.

"Get outta my way, Preachers," Beasley snarled.

"I seen 'em," Jimmy shouted. "I ain't lyin'. Mark seen 'em too."

"Perhaps, Major," Thomas said, "the scouts didn't look hard enough."

"Jimmy and Mark are ignorant. That's reason enough to whip 'em." Beasley shoved Jimmy past him.

Atremble with rage, Thomas waved off Beasley's stench. Words simmered in his brain, exploded out his mouth. "Major Beasley, you are the dumbest, laziest, cruelest human being I have ever known in my whole entire living existence."

Beasley kept moving Jimmy toward the whipping post.

"You are an intoxicated skunk!" Thomas added, louder.

Still, Beasley ignored him. When Thomas cast a side glance at Phineas, Phineas shook his head. All right. He'd apologize later for his outburst. At this moment, he hankered after slugging common sense into the man. Beasley would be the reason for these people's deaths and perhaps his own and Phineas's and Annabelle's when the Creeks attacked this so-called stockade.

Shrouded by a cloudy evening and noisy cicadas muffling their movements, Billy and two warriors crawled from a ravine. Since sunset, they'd watched the fort. Provided they reached its palisade unnoticed, he could assess the situation better for himself. A sentry stood at the west gate, his back facing them.

They crept across a lengthy stretch of land and peeked through the rough, uneven diamond-shaped loopholes. Lights flickered in Mims's house. A few other lights glowed in crudely built shelters. Someone played a violin. A lady nearby told children a Bible story. Laughter, talking, and people just carrying on as though oblivious to dangers. He muttered to himself. No woman, no child, must die tomorrow.

Using his hands, he measured the loopholes. About four feet from the ground. A serious mistake these settlers made in this stockade's construction. His warriors could shoot them as easily as the warriors inside the fort could shoot his braves. They'd capture these holes and catch the warriors inside in a crossfire. Not even the sentries were alert.

Upon his return to their camp Billy assembled his chiefs, prophets, and warriors. What he planned to say might not deter them, but his conscience and sense of honor compelled him to make a speech and a request. Although scalps of women and children were acceptable trophies in times of war, they weren't acceptable for him.

Billy addressed them in Creek. "Friends, warriors, prophets, the scouts did not spot us. The fort's sentries aren't alert. The people in the fort are not aware we're close. We will attack at noon, the way they attacked us at Burnt Corn when many of our friends were eating. We will succeed. In the morning, we'll make final plans for our attack. Lots of fighting to do tomorrow …."

His warriors— almost a thousand strong—followed his gestures as he paced.

He wrapped up his speech by making his most important request. "Only fight the fort's warriors. No woman or child is to die."

An icy stillness pervaded his audience. Paddy Walsh sneered.

Drawing a deep breath, Billy continued. "We will capture the women and the children and take them back to our nation as slaves. But they are not to be killed. No female or children's scalps tomorrow.

Only the warriors' scalps for trophies. Get some sleep. We will fight hard tomorrow. We will win."

The warriors grinned and murmured words of victory. No shouts of triumph, lest those in the fort or a scout discovered them.

As Billy struggled to sleep beneath his blanket, he tossed and turned from an onslaught of torment. Tomorrow, he'd be responsible for the slaughter of friends and family members. A coyote howled, its eerie cry a harbinger of death. He rolled onto his side with his elbows tucked beneath him. Two more coyotes howled, harbingers of bloodshed.

CHAPTER THIRTY-NINE

Monday, August 30, 1813
Fort Mims, Alabama country, Mississippi Territory

Morning till Noon

"**I** kinda hate asking you this, Peg, but can I borrow your towel again?" Annabelle pushed wet tendrils behind her ear. "I'll wash it for you next time we come here."

Peggy Bailey pulled a clean tartan dress off a clothesline hanging between two trees beside Boatyard Lake. From beneath her pale blue bonnet, tousled brown hair smothered her shoulders. "I don't mind washing it again. Take it." She draped the dress over a table and quickly folded it.

Annabelle picked up the towel from a shorter table, wrapped it around her hair, and gave her locks a rough scrub. It was nice to be clean again after so many days in stinky Fort Mims. She loved bathing in the lake, and she loved having a new friend in Peggy. Even though Peg was Catholic, she harbored no ill will toward Protestants. They got along well, like sisters.

Five métis ladies behind them washed clothes over a large barrel of soapy water. Four others paced the lake nursing their infants. Six women, laughing and tossing a bar of soap to each other, chattered and bathed in the lake.

Annabelle dropped the towel, picked up her brush, and brushed her long hair in smooth strokes. "Thomas is a real gen'lman, ain't he, Peg?"

Peggy nodded as she placed the neatly folded dress in her laundry basket. "As fine a man as my brother Dixon."

"Do you think he fancies me?" Annabelle's brush made another pass through her hair.

"Of course he does. Y'all are friends, aren't you?"

"That ain't what I mean."

Peggy went to the clothesline for a second dress, a white calico one embroidered with tiny pink flowers. "Oh. You're talking about love."

"Yes. Does he love me, you figure?"

"Do you love him?"

Annabelle licked her lips. *Uh*. Good question. Did she more than fancy Thomas? Did she love him? At one point a few years ago, she'd fancied Barnaby. He'd treated her good, even during their growing-up years, always full of flatteries and bringing her gifts from his trips to Mobile. Her father's words struck her: *Likin' and lovin' ain't the same thing*. A true statement, she discovered. She didn't know Barnaby like she thought she did. That temper of his. That rage. He'd never abused a woman till they started living together. At least, she never saw him do it. Her liking him never grew into love. Instead, it turned into hate, as much hate as he'd grown to have toward her.

Ever since the day Thomas defended her against Barnaby, the bravery he'd shown, his manners, and her loneliness in his absence … Yes. Her feelings for him ran deep, as deep as the deepest well. "Know something, Peg? I think I do."

"You think?" Peggy laid the dress on a table beside the basket and, arms folded, faced her.

"No, Peg. I do. I'm sure I do love him. I–I have no doubt."

"Good. Never show a serious shine to a man you don't love." She took Annabelle's hands. "Dear, please be patient. Some men take longer than other men to notice a girl." She stroked Annabelle's cheek. "Give him time, Annabelle. He may only be shy."

"Shy? You mean I gotta go after him hard?"

"No, no." Smiling gently, Peggy pulled away from her. "Some men get scared off when we come on to them too strong."

"What should I do, then?"

"Keep being his friend. Show him how much you care by doing little things for him. He'll catch on soon enough. Once he catches on, you'll learn whether his liking you has turned to the same love you have for him."

"I hope so." Annabelle hiked her skirt an inch above her ankles. "I'm heading back to the fort."

"I'll be there in a few minutes." Peggy yanked more clothes off the line, then went to her other friends washing their garments.

On the way to the fort, Annabelle's imaginings roamed to the future. What was it like, being the wife of a preacher, wed to a man whose calling demanded lots of travel and weeks and months away from home? What would it be like to be the dutiful wife of the Reverend Thomas Murcher? If he didn't show an interest in her beyond friendship, it was all over between them. Over for good.

Upon her return from Boatyard Lake, Annabelle's fresh scent attracted Thomas like nectar did a hummingbird. From the fort's western sector, an ear-ringing crack exploded.

"Oh no. Not again." With her eyes squeezed, Annabelle leaned her head on Thomas's shoulder. "I-I can't bear to watch."

Thomas's blood sizzled through his veins. *Stupid major.* He wished he could slug him to kingdom come and burn his whip.

Pop! Crack!

Before the crowd of witnesses, Beasley lashed Josiah Fletcher's young slave, Henry, whose wrists he'd bound to a whipping post. Crimson saturated Henry's bare back, his flesh ripped to pieces. Earlier in the morning, the slave had accompanied Jimmy to check on the cattle. Thus far, Jimmy had not returned, but Henry brought a report claiming he saw Red Sticks about a mile away. Beasley scoffed. However, Fletcher didn't because he said Henry never lied. After he and Beasley quarreled over the matter Fletcher, reluctantly, agreed to Henry's undeserved, and savage, punishment.

"A shame." Phineas eased up beside them.

"A terrible sin against humanity, it is." Thomas wagged his head.

"Poor, poor man." Annabelle, though she didn't look at the whipping, lifted her head off Thomas. "Beasley ain't nothing but a big ole brute. Another ole Barnaby, that man is."

"God's gonna judge us one day for owning and whipping folks." Thomas noted Beasley's slight tottering, his whip raised.

"You're absolutely right," Phineas said.

"Figure Jimmy's coming back, Phineas?"

"I hope not, for his sake."

Thomas's teeth ripped apart some venison jerky. Had it not been for the major's abusive treatment of Henry and the horror he sensed looming over this stockade, he might've enjoyed its spicy taste. "They're attacking us today. Those Creeks are out yonder, for sure. Mister Fletcher said Henry spoke truthful. I believe him."

Phineas winced when Beasley's whip cracked another lash on Henry's bloody, scarred back.

Henry loosed a scream.

"No sense telling the major." Phineas cringed at the whip's next pop. "He won't listen. 'Sides, he's pert near drunk."

"Shouldn't we tell the folks?"

"Of course, Thomas, 'cept I don't have lots of faith they'll pay our words any mind."

An hour later, after roaming the stockade giving warnings, Thomas played ball with Robby at the west wall, where Annabelle sat cross-legged on the ground playing checkers with George Hardy. Piano and violin music flowed from Mister Mims's house.

Peggy strolled through the west gate bearing her laundry basket heavy with clean clothes. "One more load," she said, approaching Annabelle. "Brother Dixon's." She briefly paused at Annabelle's game. "Who's winning?"

"I am," George said.

"He's a good checkers player," Annabelle said.

Chuckling, Peggy moved on.

Thomas held the ball Robby tossed him while he watched Peggy go to the north wall where Captain Bailey met her outside the loom-house bastion. The captain set a large basket of dirty clothes in her arms. Peggy seemed like a decent girl, the same as her brother. He appreciated her befriending Annabelle.

Peggy passed Thomas and Annabelle on her way out. "Be back in a few hours."

Annabelle waved goodbye.

An hour passed. Hunger pangs stabbed Thomas. "Let's quit for a spell, Robby. Ain't you getting hungry enough to eat a whole possum?"

"With all the teeth stuck in his head, Mister Thomas." Robby grinned hugely.

Thomas steered the boy to a clapboard house where Mrs. Heathrow and Annabelle prepared corn Mister Heathrow and three of his slaves had picked from their field upriver. Soon, Helen joined them.

"Miss Lawson's been awful kind to my young ones, Reverend Murcher." Mrs. Heathrow's soft voice lilted. "To every child here. I'm thankful the parents who dislike you at least let them listen to the Good Book."

"I figure it keeps them occupied when they get tired of playing." Thomas glimpsed the open east gates. They'd be here ... today ... the Indians. An icy shudder rattled his bones.

"I enjoy your Bible stories, Miss Annabelle." Helen spoke in her tiny voice. "Who did you say built a big boat?"

"Noah, dear." Annabelle patted her head.

"It was Ben Mattis who thought you were talking about Abraham, wasn't it?" Robby said.

"Yes." Annabelle touched Robby's shoulder.

Mrs. Heathrow scanned the murmuring crowd. "Where's my husband?"

Phineas jogged to them and rubbed his stomach in a circular fashion. "This feller's on the brink of starvation."

A galloping horse, James Cornells astride it, commanded theirs and everyone's curiosity. He reined in his mount inside the outer east gate. "They're coming. Thirteen of them. In the woods."

Staggering to Cornells, Beasley gripped the horse's bridle. "You only saw red cattle, man."

"Well, those red cattle will sure give us a kick." Cornells whisked his horse around and galloped off.

Thomas sprinted to the east gates to close them, shoved the outer gate, grunted, shoved again.

A drum roll announced the garrison's mealtime.

"Injuns!" the gate sentry hollered, firing his musket before sprinting into the fort.

Men, women, and children knocked against each other, tripped over each other, and darted every which way in panicked confusion.

A thousand shrieks. War whoops piercing air. Bare-chested warriors in breechcloths, some painted black, and others red, charged the fort swinging tomahawks and war clubs. Heart in his throat, Thomas zigzagged to the Heathrows' clapboard house. He turned once to spot Beasley staggering to the east gate.

From the north, from the south, devilish whoops reverberated. Red Stick gunfire erupted from the southern and western walls' loopholes. Settlers clasped their stomachs and chests, collapsed in bloody heaps.

Thomas ducked inside the Heathrows' tiny house and shot up a quick prayer. His stomach twisted into a tight knot. *Outnumbered. Surrounded.*

Afternoon till Evening

Thomas sprinted through the fierce fighting in search of Annabelle.

A warrior lunged and slugged his jaw. The blow smashed him hard. He stumbled. The whooping warrior sprang atop him. His club's blade smacked the dirt beside Thomas's ear. Thomas seized his foe's wrist to shove it away., then Lucky and another big dog pounced on the warrior, knocked him off Thomas, and sank their teeth into the Indian's legs.

Scrambling to his feet, adrenaline pumping, Thomas raced through a hail of musket balls and arrows. From wagons and outbuildings and Mister Mims's house, settlers and mètis battled their attackers and fought hand-to-hand. Wails of women and children. Cracks of musketry.

Gunsmoke's sharp smell stung Thomas's nose as he barged into Mister Mims's house. In its parlor, Phineas consoled a sobbing elderly woman. He ducked in and out rooms, bumping elbows and squeezing through a crush of terrified folk. No sign of Annabelle, nor of Maggie or Suzie.

Bolting out the door, Thomas sidestepped two braves swinging red warclubs, seized the arm of one and flung him against the other. A third Creek charged him with a tomahawk. Again, Thomas sidestepped and after a short struggle he disarmed the brave, knocking him unconscious with his fist. The first two attackers lay at his feet, shot in the back. The warrior's tomahawk in hand, he lit out for the wagons, dove beneath one, and smacked the ground. A man lying prone beside him loaded and fired his pistol with deliberate accuracy. One Creek after another fell to the man's marksmanship.

"Monsters." Thomas's adrenaline pumped fast. Slaughtered women and children. Demons whooping and dancing. It reminded him of the nightmares he used to suffer about Hell. A side glance— Maggie's and Suzie's bodies, sprawled on the ground near one of the wells. His fist pounded earth. "Monsters. Monsters."

The blood-thirsty horde retreated out of the fort through a barrage of gunfire.

Legs wobbly, Thomas crawled out from beneath the wagon. Once he tossed the tomahawk into a well, he worked his way past bloody corpses and stepped over shattered bodies. A few warriors lay among them. Slumped behind the east gate, Major Beasley's body. Next to him, a whole company of shot-riddled and tomahawked militiamen. "God," Thomas muttered, hot tears seeping and the stench of blood sharp. "Dear Lord God, why?"

Maybe none of this would've happened had the major owned enough sense to keep the gates closed. Souls gone into eternity, most without the Lord. He wiped moisture from his eyes.

"Major Beasley's dead, so is Captain Middleton." Captain Bailey waved his straw hat. "I'm the senior officer here now."

Thomas listened closely.

The captain stood on Mister Mims's porch. Mister Mims and Phineas joined him outside. "We killed their prophets while they danced and chanted," Captain Bailey announced. "That's why they retreated. They didn't believe we could kill their prophets, but we showed them different." Bailey waved his pistol. "But they'll be back. It's do or die for us now. Every man and woman who has a gun, or can handle a gun, load it. Get ready to fight again."

"We'll kill them all," King shouted, raising his musket amidst cheers.

"Death to them." Clay brandished his pistol.

"The soldiers know their assignments," Captain Bailey shouted. "To your posts. My men, the north pickets. Move."

Soldiers and militiamen scrambled to their sectors— the guardhouse on the west, riflemen to the southern pickets. Bailey led his men past the loom-house bastion where the palisade extended outward, toward the woods and away from the main wall.

White settlers, métis, and slaves hastened into their makeshift houses or posted themselves on or beneath wagons. Others crouched behind barrels and overturned tables, loading their weapons fast. A few, such as Doctor Holmes, carried shotguns.

Thomas's eyes shifted back and forth. *Dear Annabelle, please, be alive.*

Weeping distracted him. Robby and Helen were bending over their slaughtered mother. He stooped beside them. "There, there, now." What could he say to these dear ones? How could he comfort them? Maybe, in dire times such as these, it was better to say nothing if he didn't have the right words.

Annabelle, dirty and powder-stained, stooped at his elbow. Trembling, she rubbed Robby's back.

Thank you, Lord. Annabelle's still alive.

"They're orphans now," Annabelle whispered shakily. "Their pa got killed in the attack. They don't know this yet."

"No grandparents? Or relatives?"

Annabelle shrugged. "I ain't sure. We going to get attacked again?"

Sighing heavily, Thomas nodded. "I fear we are."

Slumped in his saddle astride his gray horse Arrow, Billy rode away from the O'Neals' house about a mile from the fort, his slaves following afoot. There he and his warriors had conferred about resuming their attack. He'd advised them to end it. They'd humbled the White man, and they'd lost lots of braves, but as he expected, no one listened. Many Whites remained alive in the fort. His warriors intended to kill them to the last man, woman, and child.

Billy clenched his eyes as though to dispel the horror he'd witnessed. In fact, he'd seen too much. His friends and members of his family— dead. Innocent women and children—butchered. He'd not seen his half-brother David Tate, nor did he find him among the dead. "Go away!" he thundered at the tortured recollection of David's slain wife, Mary Louisa. He steered Arrow up another road. He'd ride to David's plantation to deliver the tragic news about her death.

A bark twisted him in his saddle. A black-and-tan bloodhound wearing a dusty leather collar followed him. One of his slaves patted the dog's head. The hound might be a good hunting dog, so Billy dismounted.

The hound's wide collar held large letters stamped on it. Not the best reader, Billy read the word slowly. *L-U-C-K-Y.* He guessed it was the dog's name. Stooping, he lifted the dog's dirty forepaws, inspected his hind legs and head for injuries, and found none. "You sure lived up to your name, good boy, but your owner's probably dead." Billy straightened. "Want to come with me, hunt rabbits and deer when the war ends?"

Lucky barked as though he approved.

"Let's go, dog. There's been enough bloodshed here."

Barking twice more, Lucky fell in with Billy's plodding slaves.

⁓

"Can you shoot, Reverend?" Captain Bailey met Thomas at the northern pickets.

"Did lots of hunting in my day," Thomas said.

Bailey thrust a Brown Bess musket into his hands, followed by a cartridge box. "Stick that muzzle through the loophole and wait for 'em. Can you kill an Injun?"

Before Thomas answered, the captain posted a squad at the loopholes and another squad in front of the loom-house facing the east gate.

Thomas poked his musket's muzzle through the loophole. Could he kill a man? No. But how to get himself and his friends out of this fatal fix? Also, Robby and Helen. He withdrew his musket and peered through the loophole. Woods blocked their path to Boatyard Lake and, about fifty yards closer, a fence. He slumped against the pickets.

Doctor Holmes plopped on the ground next to him, his double-barrel shotgun in his lap.

"We gotta find us a way outta here." Thomas glanced left and right. "Where's Phineas?"

"He's praying with people in Mister Mims's house." Doctor Holmes indicated Thomas's musket. "He refuses to pick up a gun, says it violates his conscience."

"Guns don't violate my conscience, but killing a man sure does. Wish I knew if God's gonna judge me if I gotta kill men when I'm trying to protect other folks. I oughta be praying with folks too, but Captain Bailey says he needs me here since I can shoot. What about Annabelle?"

"She's with Robby and Helen in Mister Mims's house too. I told her where you were. Ole King and Clay are knocking out a hole in the gentleman's roof. They plan on fighting from it." Quaking, Doctor Holmes cupped his ears. "I can't get these awful images out of my head. The slaughtered women, the babies, the mutilations, the—"

"Stop. Please." Thomas turned to the doctor. "Major Beasley was a drunken fool. He's to blame for all this."

"These poor people's blood is on his head. A fact." Inhaling deeply, Doctor Holmes tapped Thomas's knee. "We're going to escape."

"How?"

"Here she comes." The doctor stretched forth his hands at Annabelle, sprinting to them with an axe, the Heathrow children with her. Her sweaty, tangled hair pasted her dirty cheeks. Blood splattered her calico skirt. She puffed hard from her run. Doctor Holmes received the tool. "You found one. Splendid." He held it toward Thomas. "This is how, my friend." The doctor proceeded to pound the axe against a picket.

Annabelle lowered herself eye-level with the children. "Now, young'uns, y'all stay with me. We're getting outta here quick as lightning when the time's right."

The children clung to her skirt. Helen sniffled and Robby, shaky and struggling with his emotions, chewed his lower lip.

"Get Phineas. Tell him we're escaping. Get him out of that house." Thomas grabbed a paper cartridge from the cartridge box, bit off the musket ball on its end, and kept it in his mouth while he emptied a few grains of powder in its flash pan.

Annabelle and the children started to leave when screaming warriors surged into the fort, a deadly tidal wave leaping corpses and flooding the stockade. A crossfire from captured loopholes erupted from every sector except the north pickets. Men, women, and children sprinted to their posts, firing at the enemy in a desperate bid for survival.

Adrenaline pumped hard through Thomas as he finished loading his gun, pulled its frizzen over the pan, cocked the weapon's hammer, and thrust its muzzle through his loophole. Praying that if he hit someone it'd be nothing more than a slight wound, he squeezed the trigger. Annabelle's prone body shielded Robby and Helen beneath her.

Thomas peeked over his shoulder. Gunsmoke swirling amidst iron balls, Captain Bailey's disciplined men stood shoulder to shoulder and put up a stout defense. Women loaded guns for the men. Time and again, the Red Sticks charged the captain's line. Time and again, Bailey's gunfire repulsed them. While the whooping and shooting continued, Doctor Holmes snatched up his shotgun. Thomas loaded another round and triggered it through his loophole.

"The bastion. The bastion." Captain Bailey, yelling, pointed his sword at the loom-house.

A fistful of survivors snatched up their fallen friends' guns as they poured into it and another house. Desperate musketry pop-popped from windows. Braves returned fire through the swirling, acrid smoke.

Thomas swerved from the palisade and squeezed off another ball from a corner behind Bailey's loom-house. Doctor Holmes's axe kept whacking away, knocking out an escape.

Minutes later, the Red Sticks turned to looting and scalping. Scattered hand-to-hand confrontations continued. The stench of blood, of death, permeated the stockade.

"All's lost!" Captain Bailey shouted to those around him. "Escape how you can!"

Thomas tossed aside his musket and wept for those who'd fought alongside him, their frozen eyes open in death. The injured people's agonized cries chilled his spine. Roaring fires consumed Mister Mims's house. Thomas's fingertips wiped his glassy eyes. Poor Phineas, his mentor and friend, perished inside it.

Still atop the children, Annabelle lifted her head.

Doctor Holmes crawled forward. "I've loosened enough pickets. Some warriors are at the fence blocking our retreat."

Thomas peeked through a loophole. "They might be leaving."

"They're waiting for us. Be sure of that."

Captain Bailey, pressing a rag against his bloody shoulder, hurried to them, Hester on his heels.

"My man Tom's coming too," Bailey said, gasping.

Briefly, Doctor Holmes examined the captain's wound. "I'll tend to it later."

Thomas shoved aside the loosened pickets. Doctor Holmes and Hester ducked out and made for the lake.

From various points in the woods, musket balls showered them. Two Red Sticks charged. Two blasts from the doctor's double-barreled shotgun dispatched them. He kept running.

Hester clambered over the fence and stumbled from a ball striking her, but she continued at breakneck speed toward the swamp.

Thomas uttered a quick prayer.

Captain Bailey exited through the gap next. Another shot rang out from the timber. He stumbled, fell, got up, stumbled again, crawled, got up, kept going. Bailey's slave, Tom, carried his feverish son Ralph through the gap, into the woods.

"Annabelle, you and the children." Thomas nodded at the gap.

She rose on tiptoes and kissed his forehead. Gripping Robby's and Helen's hands, they ducked out. Thomas followed at a sprint.

Creek gunfire cut loose. Annabelle and Robby clambered over the fence. Thomas hefted Helen over it. Several balls pierced his coat. Their legs pumped hard and fast till they gained the dense swamp and threw themselves into a clay hole beside the doctor. Thomas's head hit it hard. He got a foul taste of its clay and spit it out. Peering above a thick, fallen tree, Thomas spotted three Red Sticks searching for those who'd escaped. He ducked his head behind the tree.

"They're heading this way," Thomas whispered.

"Quiet," Doctor Holmes whispered back. "They won't notice us here if we keep low."

"We'll swim downriver to Fort Stoddert when darkness settles in." Thomas whispered this once the enemy passed beyond earshot.

"I reckon that's wise." Annabelle put her arm around the children.

"Uh, there is one slight difficulty I forgot." Doctor Holmes reached for his shotgun.

"Problem?" Thomas arched his brows.

"I got so worried about escaping and trying to figure out a plan, Namesake, I forgot I can't swim."

"Neither can we," Robby and Helen said.

"Huh." Thomas scratched his head. "I figure we do got us a bit of a predicament."

"Why are you two talking so calm about this?" Annabelle said.

Doctor Holmes drew his gun flush against his side. "Because we must consider things clearly if we expect to get out of our precarious plight."

Exhausted, Thomas rested his head sideways on the hard earth. "We'll figure a way. Won't we, Doctor Holmes?"

"Let's put our brains together and work out something. The sooner we're free from this horror, the better."

"Sooner ain't soon enough." Annabelle drew Robby's and Helen's dirty bodies closer.

"Shh." Doctor Holmes ducked lower behind the fallen tree. "More coming within range."

Thomas dared not breathe till the Red Sticks passed. During this moment, he realized what Annabelle did right before their escape. She'd kissed him. No girl had ever kissed him before, except his mother. His pulse galloped amidst his tingles.

Evening till Midnight

Doctor Holmes, Thomas, Annabelle, and the children lay prone in the clay hole. Flames illuminated the night sky, brightening it like a cloudless day. Roaring fires consumed the boatyard and the fort.

Thomas reflected on Phineas, his mentor's bravery, his humor, how fast he quoted scripture, and how gifted he was at preaching. Although he missed Phineas, the fact that his mentor now resided in Heaven comforted him. A scripture floated through Thomas's mind: *And the world passeth away, and the lust thereof, but he that doeth the will of God abideth for ever.*

The will of God. Phineas certainly did that. The others who'd perished, who'd been so careless about their souls, Thomas ached for them. Rolling onto his side, he admired Annabelle, asleep with her arms around the children, also asleep. The Lord had certainly changed her into a beautiful lady, inside and out. From the depths of his heart and down his arms, longing moved his hand toward her waist … He jerked it back.

Midnight came. The fires died. Fort Mims burned to the ground. A drizzle sprinkled the earth, as though the Lord wept for those who'd entered eternity today.

"Thomas." Doctor Holmes tapped him. "Wake the children and Annabelle. We'll move on before it gets light. We're taking the high ground."

Thomas whispered "wake up" in Annabelle's ear.

Turning to him, she rubbed her sleepy eyes.

Those small, pink lips of hers, those dark lashes fluttering and sweeping up like an angel's wings. A strange yet warm emotion swirled inside him. *Kiss her?* Not wise. She'd get offended. Even ridicule him. "Wake the children. The doctor says it's time to get moving. We're taking the high ground. And keep the children quiet. We're gonna have to go around some enemy camps."

Annabelle wakened the children and, whispering, explained their plan. After a desperate prayer, they were on the move again.

CHAPTER FORTY

Ragged and footsore from dodging enemy camps and living off mutton, roots, and water, Thomas straggled into Mount Vernon, the military cantonment atop a hill three miles from Fort Stoddert. Tuckered out and weak, his knees buckled him onto the hard ground in the unforgiving heat. He licked salty sweat trickling over his lips. He panted … hard. His lungs and stomach ached. He needed bread, venison, anything to sate his malnourished cravings.

Helen crawled onto his lap, wrapped her small arms around his neck, and nodded off quickly.

Chatter closed on him. A few fellow survivors approached. Josiah Fletcher, Henry's master, dragged himself ahead of the other despondent men.

"Sorry to wake you, my little dear." Thomas peeled Helen from around him and put her on the ground.

With a tiny grumble, Helen stood.

Annabelle and Robby sat, slouched, against a wagon's wheel.

Doctor Holmes, seated on a barrel, rose to greet them.

A gray-haired man in a blue army officer's uniform observed the subdued reunion as he emerged from a log building.

Groaning, Thomas struggled to his exhausted feet.

"Is Hester here?" The doctor scanned the premises. "I saw her shot after she ran out of the stockade, but she just kept on running."

"She was a marvel," Thomas said.

At the mention of Hester's name, Annabelle and Robby joined them.

"She's under good care." The gray-haired man spoke from the porch. "Hit in the arm. She's in our hospital." He ambled to them. "I'm General Ferdinand Claiborne. Hester arrived here first and gave me the alarm. She stole a canoe and paddled here."

Thomas shook the general's hand. "The name's Thomas Murcher, sir."

"I'm Annabelle Lawson." Annabelle poked Robby's shoulder and urged him and Helen forward. "These young'uns are brother and sister, Robby and Helen Heathrow."

The general winked at them. "A pleasure making your acquaintance, children." To Annabelle, he said, "You and the children will stay with Major Kennedy and his wife. I believe they have enough room in their quarters. I'll be dispatching the major and a few men to Fort Mims tomorrow to count and bury the dead."

"General," Doctor Holmes said, "may I go with him? I am a physician, sir. My services might be required."

Claiborne nodded. "Permission granted."

"May I go too?" As he made this request, Thomas hoped he'd find Phineas's body and give him a good Christian burial.

"Permission granted as well." Claiborne propped his hands on his hips. "I suppose you're all hungry."

"General"—Thomas grinned—"I'm hungry enough to eat a whole possum …." He waited for Robby to finish his little saying.

"A whole possum with all his teeth still stuck in his head." A broad grin broke across the boy's dirty face.

Laughter and backslaps as General Claiborne led them past a row of barracks to another building whose sign directed them to the mess hall.

Doctor Holmes clapped Thomas's shoulder. "Since Hester's under good care, we'll check on her after we eat. I can't examine a patient on a growling stomach."

"I'm so glad she survived." Dreaminess emerged from Annabelle's exhaustion when her gaze drifted to Thomas.

Thomas drank in her clear hazel gems. Girls. They always addled his brain.

CHAPTER FORTY-ONE

After the Red Stick victory at Fort Mims, Thomas and others fretted over reports riders brought into Mount Vernon on a regular basis. Their raids continued against settlements. Settlers fled their farms to help the militia fight skirmishes with the enemy. The Creeks held the advantage in this region, or so the settlers here believed.

Till things took a turn for the better—an offensive. According to what General Claiborne told his men, their armies planned to hit the Red Sticks from three directions. General Andrew Jackson marching south from Tennessee, General John Floyd marching west from Georgia. General Thomas Flournoy, commander of the Mississippi Territory's Seventh United States Military District, ordered General Claiborne's army north with orders to maintain a defensive posture. Thomas accompanied Claiborne's army as his chaplain and Doctor Holmes, his surgeon.

When they reached Weatherford's Bluff, a high limestone outcropping on the Alabama River, Thomas and Doctor Holmes helped build a stockade dubbed Fort Claiborne. This spot wasn't named for Billy Weatherford, a militiaman told him, but rather for his uncle.

Thomas's muscles throbbed at the end of a day's labor. He stretched his arms high, then pulled some beef jerky from his saddlebag. He poked it into his mouth and chewed. Though eating it every day bored him, he had little choice in terms of a meal, for General Claiborne's army suffered a shortage of food and supplies.

Based on his observations, Thomas considered General Claiborne competent. Regular army troops, dragoons, militia, and Choctaw warriors commanded by Pushmataha and Gray Eagle reinforced them.

"Annabelle," Thomas whispered, before he realized he was talking to himself. Her magnificent brunette hair, gentle heart-shaped face, and a smile so brilliant it lit up a dark night. For some reason, without her, he felt like half a man.

He'd taken her and the children to Mobile to stay with the Oglesbys. From a letter she'd written him, Robby and Helen's cousins lived in Charleston, but the current war with Britain needed to end before they could go there. Annabelle promised him she'd return after things got, in her words, "peaceable again." On a few occasions, he'd visited her and the Oglesbys. With each visit, his constant yearning to be at her side warred against flashbacks of rejection. They'd laughed together and strolled the small city's streets. She even cooked him a tasty meal or two. For the first time in his life, he'd eaten baked trout. *Miss Annabelle, you'd better come back.*

Thomas started. Where'd that thought come from? He reached into his saddlebag for more jerky. Most traveling preachers he knew didn't get married. Because of the numerous difficulties they encountered and always being on the move, Phineas considered marriage unwise.

Slowly chewing his jerky, working his jaw back and forth, he watched scattered groups of regular army soldiers and militiamen converse and eat hardtack. Doctor Holmes and two officers messed together outside one of the stockade's three blockhouses. A few yards away, warriors laughed and swapped stories. Dempsey ate with his messmates Red Panther and Chilita. Thomas sauntered up to them.

Red Panther chuckled. "The jerky doesn't suit you, my brother? We're all tired of pork and hardtack."

Thomas received a hardtack cracker from Red Panther

"We're proud of our chiefs." Red Panther pointed his hardtack at Lieutenant Colonel Pushmataha, resplendent in his fine blue uniform, golden epaulettes, and silver spurs. He'd been given that rank and uniform after the Army accepted his request to join the fight. Except for his army boots, Gray Eagle wore Choctaw clothes. They were engaged in a discussion with General Claiborne.

"We're glad they're with us." Thomas dunked his hardtack into a bowl of water.

"We who fight under Pushmataha and Gray Eagle can teach the Red Sticks a lesson or two on our own." Dempsey's fist smacked his palm.

"When do you figure we'll finish building this stockade?" His hardtack moistened and soft enough to eat, Thomas pulled it from the bowl.

"In not many days," Red Panther said. "Pushmataha says we'll attack Econochaca, the Holy Ground. This fort is to be a supply depot for General Jackson's army. He's somewhere close by, is what someone told me."

"Chief Gray Eagle says General Jackson fought battles at Talladega and Tallushatchee," Dempsey said.

"Perhaps our Cherokee brothers joined the general." With his knife, Chilita cut his softened hardtack into two halves. "It has been reported to us that Chief McIntosh, a few months ago, made a trip to their nation to persuade them into an alliance."

"They fought with Jackson in those battles, if the report our general received from him is accurate." Wiping his hands on his deerskin leggings, Dempsey next placed a hand on Thomas's shoulder. "My friend, I have an urgent matter we must discuss."

Thomas detected Red Panther's and Chilita's gleams. *Urgent? Serious?* "Let's go to the river for some privacy and discuss it before the sun sets."

On their way out of the fort, Thomas caught Red Panther's and Chilita's amused expressions. Quite odd. But maybe …? If his suspicions proved correct, he most certainly did want to hear what Dempsey had to say.

Thomas accompanied his friend to a cannon facing the Alabama River.

Dempsey, his elbow rested on the big gun, gushed forth his request as eagerly as a little boy begging for candy. "We want to get married."

"You and Kana?" Thomas asked.

"Who else?"

Ah, suspicions confirmed. For a few moments, Thomas considered his friend's request and tried to remember the questions Phineas often asked young couples in love. "How does her father feel about this?"

"Her parents are deceased. Gray Eagle and Panola raised her. In Choctaw culture, it is uncles and aunts who raise their children. Not the parents."

"Do they approve?"

"Kind of."

"Kind of?"

"They like me, Thomas." Dempsey straightened. "They always have liked me, and like me even more since I'm no longer part of a gang."

"So, what's the problem?"

"We don't want to live in her village. Choctaw custom says when a man gets married, he leaves his village to live with his woman."

"I recollect John told me that. Choctaw men can't marry women in the same village."

"A fact. I don't want to live in Foha forever. Neither does she."

"Uh." Thomas tugged his chin. "Reckon that does present sort of a predicament." He brightened. "What about her farm?"

For a moment, Dempsey observed an alligator lumbering along the opposite riverbank. "We discussed that possibility. Gray Eagle and Panola will accept our living on her farm, but"— he shook his head— "but too many memories there of John. Kana and I, we both want a fresh start. In Providence."

"Providence?" Thomas's brows arched.

A confident grin broke through Dempsey's heavy beard and mustache. "A new name for King's Brook. Soon as this war ends, we and the other settlers plan on applying for a charter for it to become a town. We're calling it Providence. That's where we want to live."

"And what will you do there?"

"Farm my father's land. Since my family's dead, guess his house and acreage belong to me now. I'll settle it legally at the land office in Saint Stephens. Maybe Mister Fitzpatrick, with his legal skills, will help us." He gripped Thomas's arm. "If I can obtain Gray Eagle's and Panola's permission for Kana and me to move there, will you do the ceremony for us? After this war?"

"My good friend, why, I'd be pleased to." Soon as he spoke, Thomas wondered. Could he do it? Yes, but maybe not as quickly as they wanted. *Wait.* He wasn't in full connection with his denomination yet, and those marriages he'd participated in, he'd merely helped Phineas tie the couples' wedding knots. Suppose, though, the conference didn't receive him in full connection. If that happened, he couldn't keep his promise to them.

Dempsey punched Thomas's shoulder lightly. "I knew you would, my friend."

They headed back to the stockade.

I hope I can do it, Dempsey. I sure as sand hope so.

An hour later a muscular man wearing heavy leather boots, brown trousers, a long woolen coat, and a cocked hat cantered in. Sam Moniac. Thomas and Phineas stayed at his inn on several occasions during their travels. He remembered seeing Sam at Mount Vernon when he brought his family there after the Red Sticks raided his plantation. A man of great wealth, most people in these parts either knew him or had heard of him.

Sam tipped his dusty hat at Thomas and Dempsey, then dismounted beside a small campfire.

"Hello, Sam," Dempsey said.

"Hello, Demp. Excuse me." Urgency in his stride, Sam hastened to the general who conversed with a few officers on the other side of the fire, within earshot of Thomas.

"About time you joined us, Moniac." Claiborne turned from his officers.

"General," Sam said, his fingers touching the brim of his hat, "I'm offering my services as your guide to the Holy Ground."

"We can use your services, of a truth." Claiborne walked with Sam to a post where horses were hitched. "How far is it?"

Sam hitched his horse. "About one hundred forty-five miles thereabouts, General. Best to avoid the trails."

"We'll go straight through the piney woods then. We're moving out first thing in the morning."

Sam unscrewed his canteen. "I'm an early riser, sir."

"Excellent."

CHAPTER FORTY-TWO

Shouting, Billy Weatherford bolted upright in bed clutching his head. Soaked in sweat, he shivered, not because of winter's weather but from his nightmare—Fort Mims. Women and children, friends and family— their scorched arms outstretched, pleading for their lives. The stench of blood, the reeking smoke, the blazing inferno. "No! No!" His words echoed throughout his small cabin. He groaned. From his stomach to his throat, icy fingers twisted deep inside him as though wrenching out his heart. For what seemed an eternity, he begged the nightmare to leave.

He hurled his pillow at a wall, swung out of bed, and pulled on his leather leggings and a breechcloth. He next threw on a cloak and slipped into his moccasins. Snatching his roach— his porcupine hair headdress— off a deerskin-covered table, he roared. "Fort Mims. Leave me alone." The terrifying memory refused flight.

Supalamy darted into his room. His children peered at him past her doeskin dress.

"Are you all right, my husband?" Supalamy asked.

Billy steadied his unsteady voice. "Another nightmare."

"I hope they'll soon pass and you have no more," Polly said.

"Me too." He patted the black topknot on Polly's head. "I must go speak with Josiah."

"Breakfast will be ready when you return," Supalamy said.

Billy mounted Arrow and proceeded along a path past numerous cabins and wigwams in search of the prophets' leader, Josiah Francis. Situated on a high bluff overlooking a bend in the Alabama River, the Holy Ground stood in an isolated spot. No road led into it. Creeks and swamps surrounded it. The prophets' incantations assured its inhabitants that magic would kill any White man who dared approach.

"No sign of the soldiers yet, my brother." Francis met Billy on the edge of the lower village.

"They'll be here." Billy dismounted. A warrior led Arrow to a crude paddock.

Francis shrugged. "Let the White devils come. Our magic will protect us."

Billy gestured at him and some nearby warriors. "Come."

Other prophets and warriors flocked around him, too, as he led them to the bluff. "If the White soldiers attack us, they'll try to cut off our retreat across the river here by posting men on the riverbank." Billy pointed. It was quite a distance below them. Some fifteen or sixteen feet, he estimated. "Some may cross the river to cut us off."

"Retreat?" Francis scoffed. "My brother, you talk as though the White man has won. Our magic will kill him before he sets foot on this sacred land."

Those around Billy expressed their agreement but Billy, unwilling to take chances, headed for the village's upper section. "Follow me, my brothers."

"Where are you taking us?" Francis asked.

"Econochaca Creek."

Francis jerked him to a halt. "Why?"

"To offer counsel about what we should do in case our magic fails us."

"You aren't the head man of this village," a sinewy prophet snarled. "We follow Josiah's words."

His lips pursed, Billy studied those awaiting his response. "All right, Josiah Francis. This is your village." He continued to the upper town. Stakes in the village square and the numerous scalps that hung from them and the firewood stacked beneath them provoked his frown. Francis burned his captives on those wicked things during rituals. All his efforts to stop the prophet from doing this had failed. Nothing he did or said made them listen to reason, so why did he keep trying?

He maneuvered a path through the trees, to a stream bank flowing into Econochaca Creek. Scattered trees and stumps on its opposite side provided cover for the soldiers when they arrived. Lots of things for them to hide behind and shoot from. Also, it was a direct approach to the village. From that spot, the soldiers would likely advance against them. He followed the stream bank to a fallen tree across the creek that abutted it at almost a right angle. He splashed across and set his foot atop it. "Warriors with rifles can ambush them from here and the creek bank if they try to cross."

The warriors observed where he pointed. "A good plan," one of them said.

Billy paid no heed to the grumbling prophets, displeased by his lack of faith in their incantations. After he ate with his children, he planned to go on a scout to find the American army. Although the Holy Ground possessed an excellent location, he had few warriors to fight and even fewer guns.

CHAPTER FORTY-THREE

Their saddles creaking and their horses' dusty odors mingling with the woods' pleasant scents, Thomas and Doctor Holmes rode at the rear of General Claiborne's columns as they marched out of Fort Claiborne. The soldiers' strides kept cadence with the snappy tune "Over the Hill and Far Away." The frosty weather stung Thomas's cheeks, and his frozen hands clutched his mount's reins.

Thomas imagined Phineas's violin accompanying the army's drummer and two fifers. When this war ended, he'd make his way to Georgia to learn the verdict on his ministry. Doubts lingered. Without Phineas "in his corner," would it be approved?

While visiting Annabelle and the Oglesbys in Mobile he sent his presiding elder letters informing him of Fort Mims, which he had probably already heard about, and Phineas's death. No response had reached him yet, so he figured he'd stay with the army till this awful conflict ended.

Thomas ducked beneath low hanging branches as they pressed deeper into the timber. Problems plagued them on their march into the Creek Nation. Many men were barefoot. Some didn't wear shirts. Not a single person possessed winter clothing, nor blankets. On top of these difficulties, their supplies were limited. No roads. Not even a packhorse path. Scattered coughs and sneezes reverberated through the ranks.

Nevertheless, General Claiborne persuaded his officers to agree to this advance on the Holy Ground and prevailed upon General Flournoy to allow it. Despite their difficulties and the officers' respectful protest, every man expressed eagerness to avenge Fort Mims. Even kill Billy Weatherford, whom everyone knew led the massacre.

Thomas released his horse's reins to smack life back into his stiff fingers. Shafts of sunlight spilling through the timber lit their way. Nevertheless, the sky's golden orb didn't keep him, nor anyone else, warm this day.

"I'm wondering, Doctor, if I oughta go ahead and do it after this madness is over." Thomas spoke once the music ended.

"Do what?" Doctor Holmes placed his horse's reins on his lap. His and Thomas's horse kept pace.

"Get Dempsey and Kana hitched."

"Don't see why not."

"I ain't in full connection with my denomination yet."

"You are licensed to preach, aren't you?"

"Yes. I sure want to go ahead and marry them two. I'm supposed to be in training, on a two-year trial of my ministry, before I can get ordained, but only on condition I pass my training. Phineas, you recollect, was my teacher. If they don't send me out to a circuit of my own 'cause I ain't in full connection—"

"Don't fret, my friend. You've done things quite satisfactorily so far. I'm certain your superiors will receive you into your full connection."

"Much obliged. Needed that encouragement." He so wanted to preside over his friends' wedding. Somewhere on their flanks, Dempsey marched with Gray Eagle's and Pushmataha's warriors.

Eighty miles later, south of a swamp, the army camped on some high ground.

Next day, Thomas prayed for the assembled army before it marched out, Sam Moniac and General Claiborne in the column's van. Thomas, Doctor Holmes, and other soldiers stayed behind to guard the supplies and care for those who'd become sick.

CHAPTER FORTY-FOUR

Billy galloped into Econochaca, sprang off Arrow's saddle, and sprinted to Josiah Francis, seated on a stump whittling a stick. His scouting paid off. He'd spotted the army. He gestured southward. "It's on its way. Three columns, two miles from here."

"You're sure, my brother?" Francis brought the stick he'd been whittling closer to his nose and studied it.

"Yes."

"They saw you?"

"No."

Though Francis resumed whittling, Billy detected the prophet's squirm. He wasn't as calm as he tried to appear. Billy rubbed his nose.

Sheathing his whittling knife, Francis left, his rapid feet "eating earth."

"Where do you think you're going?" Billy demanded in a loud voice.

Francis leapt onto his horse and galloped off. Panicked Creeks scrambled to their mounts and followed, splashing through a swamp.

"You're a fool, Josiah. A coward." Billy, fuming at him and the others who'd fled, darted into his cabin. "Hurry, Supalamy. Get the women and children on the other side of the river. Polly. Charles. Go with her." Polly scurried out the door, Supalamy and William right behind her.

Billy raced among the cabins and wigwams, past sacred fires and people darting out of their dwellings. He shouted in Creek for them to run to the canoes below the bluff and cross over.

Ten prophets, countermanding his orders, kept hot on his heels.

"Stay," one prophet said.

"The White devils won't get here," another prophet said.

"The soldiers will drop dead." A third prophet waved anxiously at those in flight. "Come back. We have magic."

Five women stopped running and faced him.

"No. No." Billy aimed his finger at the river. "Josiah Francis has fled. I'm in charge now. "Cross the river."

"You. Women. Children. Do not leave," a big prophet snapped.

Other women and children, uncertain what to do, stopped beside Billy and the prophet.

Billy bristled. His glower scorched the man whose hot, rapid breaths smacked his face.

"Your brave leader, Josiah Francis, took off like a frightened rabbit." Billy yanked the big prophet nose to nose. "You will carry our women and children to the other side in our canoes, to the safety of the woods." Billy released him, raised his rifle, and touched its muzzle to the prophet's mouth. His stern gaze took in everyone watching as though they were debating what to do. His veins pulsed. "Do what I say. Quick. The soldiers are a short distance away." Billy's roar echoed through the village. "On the other side of the river. Now."

Startled by Billy's rage, the prophets and a few warriors gathered the women and children together and hastened them down the steep bluff.

Billy collected the other warriors around him. "Come with me. Hurry." He led them splashing across Econochaca Creek below the upper part of town. He barked his orders. "You warriors with guns, wait for the enemy behind this tree." He strode to the fallen tree, then pointed to another group of warriors with rifles and took them to the creek bank. "And you men, here. This is where the soldiers will try to advance on our village."

The warriors took their positions behind the fallen tree and the creek bank.

"You men with bows and arrows, come." Billy returned to the other side of the creek and posted them at a spot behind the ambushers hidden along the creek bank, then raced back to the village for Arrow.

Two hours later, with the women and children safely across the Alabama River, war drums rolled from the village and gunfire erupted from the creek. Billy, positioned between his bowmen and ambushers, directed tactics.

Inch by inch, the soldiers advanced. Kneeling behind stumps, shooting from behind trees.

Billy's warriors laid on them a withering fire. Musket balls clipped past Billy's ears, yet unafraid, he stayed astride Arrow. He gave the signal—his upraised hand.

His bowmen nocked their brass-tipped arrows.

"Now." Billy dropped his arm.

His bowmen released their missiles. Whistling in a high arc, the arrows landed way behind the enemy.

The struggling soldiers darted forward, stopped once in a moment to return fire.

"Keep shooting. Keep shooting." Billy trotted Arrow back and forth.

As the soldiers advanced on Billy's lines, Billy understood their intention— a flanking maneuver. The soldiers knelt, aimed their muskets, triggered shots.

Billy's men withdrew, splashing through the creek toward their village. A few warriors fought the soldiers at close quarters.

Galloping Arrow through the timber, Billy passed a dancing and singing prophet who suffered a musket ball in his head. He sped past Creeks who'd thrown aside their guns. If the army captured him, he'd be executed for Fort Mims. Musketry reverberated in his ears. Iron balls hissed around him. Warriors scrambled down the bluff for the canoes. Soldiers swarmed into the village. *Surrounded.*

Two soldiers charged him. He kicked one in the chest. The other one seized his leg to jerk him off his saddle. Billy kicked that attacker away too and galloped Arrow to a hollow amidst a storm of iron balls. He reined his horse to a stop at the edge of a bluff and stared at the river below. A long way. Was it possible, for him and Arrow, to survive such a high jump? Twelve or fifteen feet into the Alabama River? A glance behind him. Soldiers, though out of range, worked their way his direction. Trapped. He glanced back at the river, then again at the soldiers.

Billy stroked his faithful mount's neck. Taking a deep breath, he reined Arrow around and walked him back up the hollow for a short distance to give him a good running start.

Arrow surged forward, hoofs pounding and nose blowing hard. The animal sprang off the bluff and splashed into the river. Billy held tight, the icy waters rushing up his legs and over his head as he sank beneath the surface. When Arrow swam back up, Billy maintained his saddle and musket as the powerful horse swam toward the opposite bank.

Musketry pop-popped and clipped water. Within a minute he reached the other side, out of range. Once ashore, he puffed and heaved to catch his wind. He dismounted and patted Arrow's head. "I'm glad you're a strong, healthy horse, my brave boy."

Arrow snorted and shook his mane.

"Are you wounded?" He removed Arrow's saddle to examine him. Arrow shook his mane again.

"I'm glad you're not." Billy stroked the animal's withers. "Thank you for your courage. You are a good horse. You saved my life." Billy removed Arrow's saturated blanket and twisted it tight to wring out the water. Next, he laid it again on Arrow's back and resaddled him.

He shook his fist at the soldiers watching him from Econochaca, then rode away. He bore no responsibility for the women's and children's deaths at Fort Mims, and he wasn't going to let himself be executed for something he didn't want to happen.

Insults reverberated from across the river, threats to hang him, to shoot him. He was a marked man.

CHAPTER FORTY-FIVE

THURSDAY, MAY 12, 1814
AN ISLAND ON THE ALABAMA RIVER, ALABAMA COUNTRY,
MISSISSIPPI TERRITORY

"**D**on't go, Father." Polly's voice quaked.

Billy willed himself to reassure them. Dirt and mud clung to his daughter's doeskin dress. Her hair's topknot sat askew on her head. "I must go to the fort, Daughter," he said. "It is the only way to get help for you and our people."

"But General Jackson will execute you." Teary rivulets stained Polly's cheeks. "F-For what happened at Fort Mims."

"We don't want you to die," Charles said.

Billy patted his small son's head. "Your father is not afraid."

The chiefs of the Red Stick bands had come and told him that General Jackson ordered them to capture him and bring him to Fort Jackson, a new fort above the head of the Alabama River. If he allowed them to do that, it'd humiliate them. To spare them such embarrassment, he'd turn himself in. To leave his children, to never see them again … He swallowed his regret. They must learn to be brave.

Billy squinted in the sunlight hammering them. Women and children and a few old men, dirty and haggard, milled about the island's scattered bushes with vacant stares. Others hugged their bodies and paced. Two boys sat on the ground playing catch with a pine cone. A girl put on her friend's faded moccasins. Small children clung to their mothers' tattered dresses. Starving babies bawled. Thanks to General Jackson, they were all starving.

What would happen to his people now, since they'd lost the war? Though he didn't fight at the last great battle, Horseshoe Bend, he'd heard about it. His people, about a thousand warriors, fought under Chief Menawa. The Cherokees and Creeks, commanded by his cousin Chief McIntosh, fought alongside the Americans. Jackson's victory broke the back of Menawa's warriors as well as their nation.

What Jackson did to the women and children, burning their crops and cabins and chasing them into the woods and onto this island … Billy's anger flared, a whirling rage, a firestorm savaging him. No woman or child on either side should have suffered in this war. After the way General Jackson had treated the innocents, he'd fight again for his people. He crossed the island to Supalamy and her friends, boiling acorns over a fire. He uttered an oath. *Acorns for food. It should not be.* "I am going to Fort Jackson."

Supalamy scrambled to her feet. "Are you sure it's wise?"

"What choice do I have? Look around you. At our people wasting their lives in idleness because they've lost their homes. And at what you're eating. Acorns. This is no way for our people to live, on an island in the river."

"If General Jackson does not kill you Big Warrior will. He is probably there waiting for you." Supalamy brushed a wayward black tendril behind her ear.

"The chief of Tuckabatchee is of little concern. If the White man plans to execute me, I will let him, but not before I kill Big Warrior if he attacks me." Billy placed his large hand on Supalamy's shoulder. "I must go and surrender and get help for all our people."

"Please be careful, my husband. Especially of Big Warrior."

"Big Warrior better be careful of me." He enveloped her in his powerful arms, kissed her forehead and cheeks, and whispered in her ear. "Be brave, Supalamy. You must be brave."

Nodding slowly, Supalamy broke away.

After he bid his people farewell Billy grabbed his musket from off the ground to kill any game he might encounter on the way. Then he'd load his gun with double shot to kill Big Warrior in case that giant of a chief came at him.

He mounted Arrow. The steed swam to the riverbank. Soon, they took the road to Fort Jackson, a few miles away.

FRIDAY, MAY 13, 1814
FORT JACKSON, ALABAMA COUNTRY, MISSISSIPPI TERRITORY

Soldiers quit their drills and card games when Billy, erect in his saddle and his bearing proud, passed through the fort's entrance. "Where is General Jackson's quarters?" he asked the first man he saw.

Before the soldier responded a neatly dressed man in a brown calico shirt and buckskin trousers pointed at a white wall tent.

"Thank you." Billy rode toward it, feeling the garrison's anger and the fierce stares boring into him.

"Ah. Bill Weatherford. We have got you at last."

Billy twisted in his saddle to encounter the enormous man who'd shouted—Big Warrior, the chief of Tuckabatchee, wielding his tomahawk, who rushed upon him with six long strides.

"Big Warrior, you traitor," Billy growled. "If you give me any insolence, I will blow a ball through your cowardly heart."

"I will kill you first, Bill." Big Warrior raised his tomahawk to throw it.

"Stop it. Both of you." General Jackson, clad in a blue uniform with golden epaulettes, emerged from his tent. He gripped the sword dangling off his hip so tightly his tanned knuckles turned white. His eyes shot daggers at Billy. "How dare you, sir, to ride up to my tent, after having murdered the women and children at Fort Mims."

Billy, his shoulders thrust back, fisted his hands. "General Jackson, I am not afraid of you. I fear no man, for I am a Creek warrior. I have nothing to request in behalf of myself. You can kill me, if you desire. But I come to beg you to send for the women and children of the war party, who are now starving in the woods. Their fields and cribs have been destroyed by your people, who have driven them into the woods without an ear of corn. I hope that you will send out parties who will safely conduct them here in order that they may be fed."

Jackson's glower softening, he folded his arms over his chest. "Continue, Weatherford, if you have more to say."

"I do, General. I do. I am now done fighting. The Red Sticks are nearly all killed." Billy spoke louder to everyone listening. "If I could fight you any longer, I would most heartily do so. Send for the women and children. They never did you any harm. But kill me, if the White people want it done."

Roars from soldiers and militia besieged Billy. Raging demands for his scalp rocketed to the sky.

"Kill him!"

"Hang him!"

"Death to Weatherford!"

"Silence." General Jackson's order quieted the demands for Billy's death. The general lifted his voice. "Any man who would kill as brave a man as this would rob the dead." To Billy, he said, "Sir, if you would alight your horse and join me in my tent, I have a glass of fine brandy we can share."

Billy and the general entered the tent. Billy marveled. Was General Jackson letting him go? No punishment? Stunned, he scratched his head. *No punishment at all.*

CHAPTER FORTY-SIX

One year later, the war with Britain finally ended and Thomas now in full connection with his Methodist Church, he returned to the newly chartered town of Providence to preside over Dempsey and Kana's wedding before he returned to his circuit in Florida. The ceremony was held in a new meetinghouse its citizens had built. The settlement's previous name, King's Brook, was fast forgotten. Zander Oglesby served as its mayor and Dempsey, its marshal. After the joyous ceremony, people resumed their celebration in the Ox Yoke.

Beaming at Thomas, who stood behind the packed crowd, Annabelle climbed up on a stool, her smile so huge and sunny she displayed all her teeth. "It's been a mighty good thing, these two good people getting themselves hitched," she said.

Thomas squirmed. He shared her happiness for the couple. Strange, though, her staring at him, instead of at them, while she speechified.

"And now, friends, my special present for our new marshal and his bride. I'm going to sing them a special song." Annabelle admired Thomas for a forever minute. "It's called, 'Meet Me by Moonlight.'" With her bright countenance fastened on him, she sang.

Oh! Meet me by moonlight alone,
And then I will tell you a tale
Must be told by moonlight alone
In the grove at the end of the vale.
You must promise to come for I said,
I would show the night flowers their Queen.
Nay turn not away Thy sweet head,
This the loveliest ever see.

Thomas started. Did she mean for him to meet her by the moonlight? Alone? He gulped and averted her gaze.

Oh! Meet me by the moonlight alone
Meet me by the moonlight alone.

Gray Eagle, Kana's Aunt Panola, Red Panther, and Chilita tapped their feet in time with the slow, beautiful melody. Applause echoed when the song ended. Zander assisted her down.

Thomas, clearing his throat, wove through the crowd and climbed up on the stool. He took in Dempsey and Kana. Dempsey wore a tailored black suit and bright blue cravat, Kana a blue cotton dress with a red sash tied around her tiny waist. The glowing couple held hands. He dove into a short speech, congratulating Dempsey and Kana for their marriage.

Hands clasped at her waist, Annabelle stood beside him. Too close. *Stop it, Annabelle.* Thomas fidgeted, grasped at fleeting words. "Er, Dempsey and Kana, er, I mean Mister and Mrs. King, the fine citizens of this town took up a collection for your honeymoon trip. They paid your fare to New Orleans." Thomas reached into his pocket and produced a piece of folded paper sealed with wax. "Here it is, my friends."

Jaws slack, Dempsey and Kana looked at him. More applause rocked the tavern.

Back on the floor, he gave it to Dempsey.

"Thank you, my friend Thomas, for all you've done for us." Mist touched Dempsey's eyelashes as he turned to the people. "Thank you, thank you. All of you are our greatest friends."

People clapped and shouted their agreement.

On tiptoes, Kana gave Thomas a light kiss on his cheek. "You will come and visit us anytime, Reverend Murcher." She winked. "I may have a big bowl of scuppernongs for you."

Laughing, Thomas licked his lips. "My dear Lady Grace, as Phineas used to call you, I do love those scuppernongs. I figure Phineas is watching us from Heaven right now and rejoicing for you both."

Over the next hour, people slipped out a few at a time till every person except the Oglesbys, Annabelle, and Thomas remained.

Thomas's fist covered a yawn. "Forgive me. I've a long journey tomorrow. I have meetings scheduled in Florida."

Fiddling with his coat's lapel, Annabelle patted his chest. "You did a good job today, Thomas. I'm proud of you."

Much obliged." He turned toward the staircase. "Er, excuse me." On his way up the stairs, he caught Annabelle out the corner of his eye blowing him a kiss. A deep blush burned his cheeks as he darted into his room.

TUESDAY APRIL 18, 1815
PROVIDENCE, ALABAMA COUNTRY, MISSISSIPPI TERRITORY

Next morning, when Thomas left his room, he'd hoped to leave Annabelle a letter explaining his departure before she arrived at the Ox Yoke. He'd put much figuring into his explaining and sought for the right words to pen his thoughts— warm friendship, a promise to return.

One step into the tavern's dining area, however, he found her seated at a table reading her Bible. A floorboard creaked beneath his feet. This time, she did more than smile at him. She radiated joy. She'd carefully styled her hair. Beaded earrings dangled from her small ears and a colorful beaded necklace circled her neck. Choctaw jewelry. Not exactly dressed for work, was she? The bigger question—why did she wear such things? She'd never worn jewelry before, at least not around him.

"Nice thingamabobs you got on." He touched his ears.

Annabelle toyed with her earrings. "Kana gave them to me." She waited another minute.

Waiting? Great. Now what did she expect? Another compliment? Planning to throw him another kiss? Females. Such riddles. Should he ask her why she smiled at him all the time? Would she figure him strange, or would she get mad? "Oh, Thomas." She dashed to him, halted, adjusted her pinafore. Her eyelashes fluttered. "I'm so glad to see you. It's been a long time."

"Uh." Thomas scratched his chin. "Yesterday was a long time ago."

Annabelle squirmed and giggled. "Too long, I reckon."

"Uh-huh."

Hey, Stupid. She thinks God made you look funny. You're ugly. That's why she's giggling.

Thomas flinched. Where'd he get that thought? "Uh, I need something to drink. A cup of tea suits me fine."

"I'll fetch you some." Annabelle hurried toward the pantry. Turning back, she arched her brows, giggled again before she closed the pantry door behind her.

Here he was, alone in this place with a beautiful woman and when she left, it was as though a dark cavern hollowed out his heart. None of this made sense.

Annabelle returned with the tea and placed it before him. Her sparkling eyes roamed to his own. He stared at her tapered fingers, brought the cup to his lips.

She slid into a chair beside him, so close their elbows touched.

Goosebumps responded, all over his arms. Did he whiff perfume? Rose water? His heart flipped twice. "You, uh …. uh…smell … uh …"

"Smell pretty?" Annabelle's hand closed on his.

"Uh-huh. You smell."

Annabelle burst into laughter. "Mrs. Oglesby brought me some rose water from Mobile."

Thomas, pondering his uneasiness, fell silent. She'd been brave at Fort Mims, never complained when they'd spent days dodging Red Stick camps on the way to Mount Vernon and cared for the Heathrow children as though they were her own. All the makings of a good preacher's wife and a good mother. During the past few evenings he'd asked the Lord to help her find the perfect husband.

It sure isn't you, Stupid.

"You're right. It's not me."

Annabelle drew back. "What on earth are you talking about?"

Thomas shrugged. "I have no idea." He finished his tea and stood. "I'd better get a move on."

"Thomas?"

"Yes?"

Annabelle stood and inched closer. "You are a great man."

"Not that great."

Annabelle leaned into him. Her fingers touched his lips. "Oh yes you are."

Thomas withdrew. "I, uh, I really gotta leave."

"I'll miss you, honey."

"Me too." He hesitated. "Wait a minute. Honey?"

"You know, what bees make."

"I'm not honey."

"I know you're not." Annabelle stamped her foot. "It was a—" She gestured angrily at the door. "Oh, go. Just go on back to Florida." Tears erupted.

Thomas gasped. "What'd I say?"

"Nothing." Her shoulders heaved violently. "Get on to your meetings. To Pensacola, where you said you was heading." She shoved him hard. "I said go, since you're in such an all-fire rush." She pivoted, wailed, and fled into the pantry.

Thomas pursued.

She slammed the pantry door behind her.

He flinched. "I'm sorry, Annabelle. I truly am. What did I say wrong?"

"Nothing. You said nothing. Get out of here."

"Well, whatever my nothing was, I'm sorry." Thomas grabbed his hat off a peg, mounted his horse hitched to a rail outside, and struck out for the Federal Road. That girl addled him. A lot.

Tuesday, April 18, 1815
The Federal Road, Alabama country, Mississippi Territory

For several miles up the Federal Road Thomas's head sagged. His horse, probably sensing his mood, trudged along at a mournful clip-clop. He struggled to make sense of Annabelle's recent behavior. Her sudden tears. Her burst of anger. How was he able to make things right with her when he had no idea what he'd said or done? "Lord, why did You create females so difficult?"

Time and again, he rehearsed their conversation's last exchange. What was it he said? "Nothing," was her reply. All right, he said nothing. So, why did she get upset? Was he supposed to say something that was nothing, or nothing that should be something? Or something out of nothing or nothing out of something? "Doggone it, Annabelle. Talk sense."

The more distance he put between himself and the Ox Yoke the heavier his burden weighed, a load of sand pressing hard against his heart. "Females. All y'all. Y'all confuse my poor brain."

"We do, Reverend Murcher?"

Thomas suddenly noticed the friendly speaker. A young lady, astride a black horse, approached. Her light brown hair was swept back beneath a red bonnet and rippled over her narrow shoulders.

"Peggy Bailey. I didn't see you."

"Of course not. How could you notice anybody, the way you're hanging your head." She and a female companion turned their horses around to ride with him. "I've never seen you so sad."

"You would have had you been in Fort Mims during the massacre. Where are you heading?"

"Providence. To visit Annabelle."

"I just came from there. She's not in her right mind at the moment, so be gentle with her."

"Oh?" Peggy leaned toward him in her saddle. "I don't mean to be a busybody, but Thomas Murcher, I declare. You two were peas in a pod at one time. Has something happened?"

Nodding sadly, Thomas recounted his and Annabelle's recent spat. He ended his story with this: "When I asked her what I said wrong, she told me I said nothing." He looked Peggy straight in the eye. "What does that mean? If I said nothing, why is she so upset about the nothing I said?"

A small smile flickered on Peggy's and her companion's lips.

Peggy slowed her horse, which inched a little ahead of Thomas's. "Let me tell you something, Thomas Murcher. And you listen to me good, you hear?"

"Yes ma'am."

"That girl loves you. Every time we went to Boatyard Lake to bathe and wash clothes, you were all she talked about."

"Me?" Thomas pointed at himself.

"Indeed." Peggy jabbed her finger at him. "You." She glanced at her friend.

"I was at the lake too," her friend said. "You were the sole subject of interest."

"But my birthmark, and—"

"What about it?" Peggy shrugged.

"How can she love a man as ugly as me?"

"Look." Peggy sounded a little stern. "I mean really, really look at me." She pointed at her face. "See all my blemishes? All those freckles gathered around my nose?"

Thomas squinted. The verse from Psalms came to him again: *I will praise thee, for I am fearfully and wonderfully made.* "Never noticed 'em before."

Peggy drew rein. Her friend and Thomas also.

"We're all created in the image of God," Peggy continued. "Of all the people on this earth, you should know that. You are a brave gentleman and have lots of fine qualities. You judge yourself too harshly. Annabelle and I both admire you. Besides, I don't know of anyone at Fort Mims ever commenting about your birthmark, not even those who hated you."

"Really?" Thomas touched his forehead.

Sighing, Peggy scanned him from foot to head. "Now listen to me, Reverend. And you listen good. We girls won't wait on a man forever. You wonder what your nothing is? I'll tell you. Your nothing was supposed to be something in regards to marriage."

"M-Marriage?" Thomas gaped. "T-To m-me?"

"Annabelle wants to marry you," Peggy's friend said. "She more than admires you, sir. She, in fact, loves you."

"Me? P-Propose to her?"

Peggy nodded and chuckled. "Yes. I think that's how it's done. And if you don't go back and apologize to her and make a proposal of marriage, you've lost your chance."

As Peggy and her friend continued to explain the ways of women Annabelle's behavior started to make sense. Annabelle loved him, and he loved her. So, why not accept himself? Why, the Almighty had created him in His image, after all.

He and his two female friends turned their horses back down the Federal Road toward Providence. He'd get on his knees and grovel at Annabelle's feet if he had to.

An hour later, they approached the Ox Yoke. Its door flew open and Annabelle, hiking her dress calf-high, rushed to him. Oblivious to Peggy's and her friend's presence, he jumped from his saddle, dropped to his knees, opened his mouth to ask that fateful "will you marry me" question, but quicker than he could speak, Annabelle pulled him to his feet and threw her arms around him. "Oh, yes, Thomas. I do! I do! I will marry you!"

THE END

HISTORICAL NOTES

On Research

In researching history, historians and historical fiction authors often encounter conflicting information. My subject, the Creek War, provided special challenges. Much of the information conflicts with each other. Complicating this issue, the Indians left no written records.

I am indebted to many sources for my story. I especially want to mention Albert J. Pickett's classic, *History of Alabama, and Incidentally of Georgia and Mississippi, From the Earliest Period*, which was originally published in 1851 (Republished by Birmingham Book & Magazine Co. of Birmingham, AL. Copyright 1878 by Mrs. Sarah S. Pickett), Gregory A. Waselkov's *A Conquering Spirit: Fort Mims and the Red Stick War of 1813-1814* (Tuscaloosa: The University of Alabama Press, 2006), Mike Bunn & Clay Williams's book, *Battle for the Southern Frontier* (Charleston: The History Press, 2008), and Benjamin W. Griffith's work, *McIntosh and Weatherford, Creek Indian Leaders* (London and Tuscaloosa: The University of Alabama Press, 1968).

On Places and Setting

The historical places include Othlewallee, Econochaca (the Holy Ground), Bassetts Creek, Fort Stoddert, Fort Mims, Fort Jackson, Mount Vernon, and Saint Stephens.

During its history, Saint Stephens went through two other name/ spelling changes. Originally, it was a Spanish settlement called Fort San Esteban (1789). In 1795, when the boundary line was drawn between Spanish Florida and the Mississippi Territory at the 31st parallel, the Americans occupied the fort. In 1807, it was renamed St. Stephens and in 1811 it became Saint Stephens. The name changed back to St. Stephens in 1815. I spell it Saint Stephens throughout the book.

Bassetts Creek had a Baptist church as well as a Methodist society, so this is accurate. Other aspects of its description, however, stem from my imagination.

The fictional towns are Maryvale, Foha (and Foha Creek), and King's Brook.

ON COMETS AND EARTHQUAKES

I briefly mentioned a comet and an earthquake. Legend has it that Tecumseh told his listeners at Tuckabatchee that when he returned home, he'd stamp his foot and the earth would shake. He also "prophesied" they'd see a comet to demonstrate his power.

Before he left his Ohio home for the Mississippi Territory to raise an alliance against the Whites, Tecumseh had learned about the comet from British scientists in Canada. In September, it sailed southward through the sky as he entered Upper Creek country. In November, while he headed home, it faded.

Regarding the earthquake, Tecumseh was lucky. This was the New Madrid Earthquake, a series of quakes and aftershocks that lasted three months. Although its epicenter was in Blytheville, Arkansas it's named for New Madrid because that Missouri town had the largest population in the area at the time. Alabama and Georgia felt their tremors. Peggy Dow, the wife of circuit rider Lorenzo Dow, mentioned this earthquake in her memoirs, *Vicissitudes*.

ON SAMUEL MIMS

We know the location of Samuel Mims's home, a site which archaeologists continue to study. Because he settled in the region when it was under Spain's control, he and his family became nominal Catholics since Spain only let Catholics own land. Did Mims play the violin, though? Did his son Joseph play it? I have no idea, but we do know Mims loved parties. We have no portrait of him, nor any of the participants and victims in the massacre except for one—Doctor Osborne's. Therefore, Mims's description as well as the others in my story stems from my imagination.

ON FORT MIMS AND THE MASSACRE

Knowledgeable readers probably noticed that I did not write anything about the more commonly mentioned sand as blocking the East Gates. When I visited the site I found no evidence of sand— only clay and dirt, but mostly clay. It's my opinion that Pickett's mention of sand is a mistake.

For his history, Pickett interviewed Doctor Thomas G. Holmes, Jesse Steadham, and Peter Randon for much of his information. The doctor recorded his memories a few years after the massacre while the details remained fresh in his mind.

I was unable to find Doctor Holmes's religious inclinations. Like most of the region's earliest American settlers, he may have been a nominal Roman Catholic. According to one source, he was born in Silver Bluff, South Carolina in 1780, so it is possible he came to the region after the United States took control of it. Because the good doctor escaped, he was the perfect candidate to befriend Thomas and Phineas. As I portrayed him, based on Waselkov's research, Doctor Holmes was an African métis.

Although Jimmy's name is fictional because we don't know his real name, his character is not. When he was sent to check on cattle the morning of the massacre he fled to Fort Pierce, two miles southeast of Fort Mims.

Henry, too, is historical though his name is fictional.

Hester's name and person is historical, as well as her heroic action after her escape.

Sam Moniac's son, David, became the first minority graduate of West Point. He was later killed in 1836 in the Second Seminole War.

Peggy Bailey's grandson, Dixon Bailey Reed, gave an account of her survival in an interview in 1908, which is repeated in Waselkov's book. As shown in my novel, Peggy and some friends were doing laundry at Boatyard Lake during the massacre. Upon hearing the battle, she and her friends raced two miles to the Alabama River where they spotted a flatboat on its opposite bank. Peggy leapt into the water and swam to it. She brought it to the other women and carried them to the safety of a mill and a small fort garrisoned by eighteen militiamen, fifteen miles south of the lake. Her brother, Dixon, died later of his wounds.

The number of people killed in the massacre is uncertain. Although we do know the names of some who perished, not everyone who perished has been identified. The estimated numbers range as high as five hundred.

On William "Yellow Billy" Weatherford

My research on William Weatherford presented quite a challenge.

First, why did he join the Red Sticks when he was living like White men with whom he was on friendly terms before the war? A few historians believe he willingly joined them. Others say he didn't want to be a part. It is true that before the war he advised the Creeks to stay neutral because he knew they couldn't win. The account of his reason, which I gave in my novel, is but one explanation.

According to Weatherford's third wife, Mary Stiggins, he'd returned from Pensacola and learned that Red Sticks had taken his family to a village. He went there to sneak them out but before he could do it the Red Sticks and the militia had fought at Burnt Corn Creek. The villagers then assumed he'd become their leader. Therefore, he joined them since he didn't see any other option.

According to Weatherford's descendants, he joined them in the hope of minimizing the loss of life. On the eve before the massacre, family legend relates that he told his warriors to spare the women and children. Some historians, however, question this since he was the main architect of the attack.

According to Waselkov, Weatherford had an emotional attachment to the cause. His wife Supalamy and her father had joined the Red Sticks.

Much of the information I used for Weatherford's character comes from Pickett's *History*. In a note, Pickett relates that it was Weatherford himself who told him about his and Arrow's famous leap off the bluff at the Holy Ground.

Although historians have debated Weatherford's leap, the eyewitnesses who were there agreed that some sort of leap took place. The height from which he and Arrow leapt is generally accepted as fifteen feet.

My account of Weatherford's surrender to Andrew Jackson is just one of several versions of this event. It is a fact, however, that Jackson respected Weatherford for his bravery and conduct at his surrender, so the general let him go. Also, Weatherford helped persuade other Creeks to lay down their arms.

After the war Weatherford had to constantly watch his back, fearing someone would kill him for the Fort Mims Massacre. He died in 1824 and is buried in Baldwin County, Alabama.

ON SUPALAMY WEATHERFORD

Some accounts say Supalamy died in childbirth at the Holy Ground on December 25, 1813, whereas another account said she was ill and taken across the river, where she later died.

Susannah Stiggins Sizemore, Weatherford's sister-in-law, said three months after Supalamy and Weatherford's son was born, in 1816, Weatherford left Supalamy to marry Susannah's sister.

ON WILLIAM MCINTOSH

At the outbreak of the Creek War William McIntosh journeyed to the Cherokee Nation in north Alabama where he persuaded them to take up arms against the Red Sticks. He also led his warriors as Jackson's allies at the Battle of Horseshoe Bend.

After the war the Creeks suffered famine and deprivation. McIntosh worked with Indian agent David B. Mitchell to get the supplies and food they needed from the U.S. government. In 1821, he signed a treaty with a new Indian agent, John Crowell, in which McIntosh received one thousand acres of land on Indian Springs and another six hundred forty acres on the Ocmulgee River.

On February 12, 1825, McIntosh and five other chiefs signed another treaty that ceded all Creek land in Georgia to the United States, for which he received $200,000. This angered his people, for he'd committed a capital offense. Creek law forbad the sale of land without the full support of the Creek nation. On April 30, 1825, former Redstick chief Menawa and hundreds of warriors burned down his house and killed him.

ON ANDREW JACKSON

Jackson's victory at Horseshoe Bend launched him to national prominence. He replaced General Thomas Flournoy as commander of the Seventh United States Military District, captured Pensacola from the Spanish, defeated the British at New Orleans in 1815, and fought the Seminoles in Florida. Later, he became President of the United States.

In the Treaty of Fort Jackson, he made both the Red Sticks and those tribal bands who'd fought alongside him cede land to the settlers. As president, he signed the Indian Removal Act (May 28,1830) that forced the Southeast's tribes out of their ancestral homeland. The massacre at Fort Mims is cited as one of the reasons for this Act.

In Alabama today one Creek tribal band remains, descendants of those who'd served as scouts or traders and stayed loyal to the United States Government. They are the Poarch Creek Band, named for Poarch, Alabama where they have a reservation close to the reconstructed Fort Mims.

ACKNOWLEDGEMENTS

I would like to thank the following people who helped me in writing this book. I could not have written it without them.

Shannon Dunlap
Norma Jean Lutz
Terri Miller
Angela Shelton
Patti Shene
Sherry Shindelar
Susan Sloan
Erma Ullrey

www.ingramcontent.com/pod-product-compliance
Lightning Source LLC
Chambersburg PA
CBHW070726280626
47159CB00023B/2800